Sheila read.

REDHALL COU T
CHALDON RD
CATERHAM

This edition, issued in 1963, is for members of The Companion Book Club, Borough Green, Sevenoaks, Kent, from which address particulars of membership may be obtained. The book is issued by arrangement with the original publishers, Wm. Heinemann Ltd.

THE BURNING SHORE

"A blessed companion is a book"—JERROLD

THE
BURNING SHORE

*

ELLESTON TREVOR

THE COMPANION BOOK CLUB
LONDON

The men who shoot and shout a long feather of five from the runway, as the 'Rhoda' pitched and spun, its second shadowed alternately at the construction rows of the twin-roofed airport building. The three Chinese reached the airport of the shed and turned and pointed as the plane began moving. A Shell traffic officer

★ I ★

THE noon plane from Singapore came in low over the jungle, just ahead of the storm that had built and followed it north to the airstrip. The men in the control tower could already see it, five or six miles away and poised, looking motionless from head-on, a thin black splinter floating in the gold light. As fast as the aircraft neared, the storm closed in behind it and the gap of gold light narrowed to a crack across the bruise-blue sky.

The plane had made its call-sign a minute ago to Pasang and now Walsh stood in the heat of the control room and watched it come into the circuit, settling steadily across the coastal fringe of coconut palms and then straightening for its final approach. Walsh took a last look at the landing-area and flicked on the green signal-beam, confirming permission to land. Across the airstrip the Shell crew had not moved. Their faces were lifted to watch the storm. It was almost here, a thick belt of tropical rain driving across the jungle and the sea. There would be no chance of refuelling the S. and P.A. plane before the storm was on them, and so they dragged the tarpaulins over the bowser and began trotting for the airstrip buildings, three thin Chinese figures neat in their clean white overalls, their hands in their pockets and their heads down, their canvas shoes raising dust that in another minute would be mud.

A group of king-vultures feeding on a goat's carcass among the bamboo flew up in a flurry of mad black umbrellas, loud with anger at the planes sudden coming. From a high tree they watched it, their beaks bloodied, their eyes hating the huge size and noise of the bird now drifting over the ground. A parakeet screamed from the mangrove swamp a mile away and a team of gibbon went vaulting to the higher trees and then swung round and peered, suddenly silent, at the landing-area.

9

The machine shivered and ripped a long feather of dust from the runway as the wheels touched and spun; its sound followed, slamming at the corrugated-iron walls of the Nissen hangars and the airstrip building. The three Chinese reached the shelter of the bowser shed and turned and watched as the plane began turning. A Malay traffic-officer was waving his markers urgently, a snatched-up sack already draped over his head.

From the control tower Walsh watched the plane; and from the window of his restaurant Wan Chai watched it, thinking how good it was of the Lord Buddha to provide these travellers with a drenching, so that the humble Wan Chai might in his turn provide them with food while they waited for the storm to pass.

The plane turned and began bouncing clumsily towards the Malay with the markers. From the edge of the jungle and from the distant mangroves and even from the coconut palms three miles away on the coast there suddenly rose a chorus of mixed comment as gibbon, parakeet, grey monkey, hornbill and jungle fowl sounded off in the wake of a leading cry; as suddenly, silence fell. In the streets of Pasang town on the coast it was always possible to know when a plane had arrived even when the monsoon wind obliged it to approach from inland, because the birds and monkeys voiced their excitement without fail.

The Malay paddled his markers desperately; the Dakota braked one wheel and swung in its own length and the cabin door came open the moment the engines were cut; two dark-skinned Tamils thrust the mobile steps into position; and the rain came. The rain came at sprinting-speed across the trees and drew a dark stain as fast-moving as a cloud's shadow over the runway and then hit the aircraft with the sound of a rattle of shot. A kind of noon twilight fell as the sky was blotted out. Voices called, feeble and bird-thin through the deafening beat of the rain on the wings and fuselage; fifty yards away the corrugated-iron hangars had become a giant percussion drum.

The passengers came out of the cabin and lurched half-blinded towards the building, some helping the others

10

along. The Chinese stewardess came last at a thin sloping hobble in her high-heeled shoes and the main doors were banged shut against the deluge.

Inside the stifling customs room questions had to be shouted against the drumming on the roof. Hands were flung out in gestures of innocence, frustration, appeal; pools of water formed on the concrete floor as trousers and saris and rain-stained shantung suiting dripped and sent rivulets to swell the pools where the feet moved and jostled in their once-smart Singapore-styled leather shoes, white buckskin, muddied suede, rope-soles, delicate golden sandals. Nothing —*nothing* to declare—how could there be? To be drenched was to be innocent; to stand here was to suffer grave discomfort and the collapse of dignity, a subjection to wrongful suspicion.

Dry and dispassionate, the two Malay officers sought their paltry treasure: a bottle of whisky, a paper-knife in damascene work, a Hitachi transistor, a Sankyo camera, brooches, watches, lighters, the beautiful toys and baubles, the little-found comforts of the lost generation, great assets anywhere in civilized society but a distinct liability inside a customs shed. The rain hammered the roof, half-drowning the cries of the innocent.

The main doors banged again and the crew came in, Captain Chong and his navigator, brushing and beating at their soaked uniforms as they sought the refuge of the staff offices, remote from the bedlam of the customs room. Copland followed them through, pausing as a Malay official darted at him—"Customs, sir! Must make declarations here please!"

"Airways staff," Copland told him.

"I not know you, sir! You have—"

"It is all O.K., Ismail!" called Captain Chong from the doorway in bazaar-Malay. "Mr Copland, taking over from Mr Walsh." He steered the thin young Englishman into the staff-room.

"Thanks, Captain."

"Not at all." Chong spoke perfect English, the only trace of accent an illusion, if one were looking at his clean white smile and his lean yellow face—a face so lean that like the younger Chiang Kai-Shek's it looked, in uniform, all cap-peak and shoulder-straps. "I'll take you to Mr Walsh."

But Walsh was already halfway down the wide bare stair-case that led to the control room above; he was stodgy-figured and untidy-looking in khaki shirt and slacks.

"Copland?" He peered below the ceiling-well.

"That's right." Hugh Copland didn't think it was much of a greeting; there was no welcome in the tone, only surprise. Half the other man's age, he couldn't quite bring himself to add: "Walsh?" He took off his linen jacket and draped it over a chair-back to drip. "Mr Walsh?"

"Yes. I didn't expect you till tomorrow. What happened?" Walsh came down the rest of the stairs. "Hello, Chong."

"Nothing actually happened," Copland said deliberately. "I got bored with Singapore. But I shan't get in the way." He found a dry packet of cigarettes and lit one. Chong and the navigator were handing over the flight-log to an Indian clerk. The noise of confusion surged and lapped at the door to the customs room.

Walsh fitted his lined defensive-looking face with a bright cold smile—"You're very welcome, of course. A lot on my hands here, y'know—didn't expect you so early. A very good thing. Let's have a drink. Whisky?" He opened a cupboard on the wall.

Copland said he would like a whisky, and stood in his already-steaming shirt and trousers, looking round at the office, Chong, the navigator, the two Hindu clerks, the litter of papers, files, charts and manuals that were heaped on a table against one wall as if swept there by a giant broom. The overhead fan wasn't working, though the air was sticky with heat. The lamps had no shades and the windows were filmed with dirt. The office, like Walsh himself, was untidy.

"Things in a bit of a mess," Walsh told him, "just at the moment. Changes of staff, changes of regulations, too much bloody paper-work by half—they're even changing the language here, now we've pulled out of the Peninsula. If you ask me I think it was a big mistake, just as it was with India.

12

Is India any better off for so-called self-rule? Nor will Malaya be, you'll see." He passed Copland a generous shot of whisky. "Water with it?"

"Thanks, I've seen enough water."

"That was bad luck, of course. Cheers."

Captain Chong signed his trip-report and straightened up from the desk. "We saw an ambush," he told Walsh, "about ten miles south of here on the Pasang-Pintu Besa road. The car was on fire and there were some men running for cover."

Fear came immediately to Walsh's eyes and Copland noticed it. "Why didn't you call us?" he asked Chong.

"I did, of course." The tone of the slight-figured Chinese captain suggested that Walsh was making a very human mistake—but all the same a mistake—in thinking Chong had failed in a matter of routine efficiency. Walsh was already shouting above the din of the rain to one of the Hindu clerks:

"Why didn't you fetch me, Hussain?"

"Sahib was in restaurant!"

"God damn it, do your feet ache?" He was shivering as if in a fever and veins showed dark blue around his temples. He told Copland, "This is the sort of thing you'll find yourself up against!" He turned and went jerking up the flight of stairs to the control tower.

"An ambush," murmured Captain Chong into Copland's ear, "is unusual in this State. We have to report anything like this direct to the Sultan's palace."

"I see. What sort of ambush?"

Chong shrugged elegantly. "A few stray Chinese terrorists thought they'd make a pounce. On the other coast it is much more common."

"But what are they after?"

Chong accepted a cigarette and lit it deftly. "Anything. An important traveller—some minor official or other whose death would give them prestige in Pekin; or simply money, or a camera, or clothing; or a woman." He watched the sad young-looking English face politely, obliquely. "This is your first time in Malaya."

13

"Yes." Copland felt callow and untravelled. "I was in India for a year as a traffic-officer. Karachi." It sounded hollow and brave.

Lee Kwei Chong affected surprise, giving an impression of sudden respect for a man who had been in Karachi. For a whole year. "You have no need to worry, Mr Copland, in any case. In the State of Tamarah there are fewer terrorists than anywhere in the Peninsula, and the Sultan has a picked army of Sakai jungle troops. This ambush will be forgotten as an accidental occurrence, you will find." He inclined his head gently. "I hope you will enjoy your stay here." His navigator was waiting for him by the door, and Chong picked up his brief-case from the report-desk and joined him. Copland was left alone in the middle of the airless room with the two Hindu clerks, the glass of whisky, and the sound of Walsh's voice shouting over a telephone in the control room above. What was *wrong* with Walsh?

A week ago in London the chairman of Straits Airways had given Copland his final briefing and said: "The last two managers we had at Pasang were failures. The first went troppo and the second turned dipso. The third one is there now and you'll be taking over from him personally, so I won't say anything about him. Pasang has got slack. See what you can do about it for us. I think you could do a lot. Call it a mission we're sending you on."

Walsh wasn't a dipsomaniac. Perhaps going troppo, or on the brink, cracking under the subtle slow pressures of the heat, sweat, mosquitoes, white ants and the stink of monkeys —the loneliness of being lost out here on a narrow strip between the jungle and the South China Sea and six thousand miles from real beer and the nip of frost and the chimes across the Thames—the boredom of seeing only brown eyes and brown faces with ancient childish minds and jabbering tongues, of wanting another drink and stopping yourself and then having it just the same, of wanting a woman and shying away from the thought of acrid sweat and pubic hair as black as a sweep's brush and then having her just the same, and, worst of all, enjoying it—the diverse, devilish pressures that find any man prey when he is out of

14

his element and cut off from the mores of his own country and his own kind.

There'd been two failures, and Walsh, the third.

"Call it a mission we're sending you on." It had sounded rather good, rather dramatic. They could call it what they liked; the fact remained that he was out here in Pasang with the noise and the smell of it already driving out the sounds and smells of a week ago: the drum of the double-deckers and the whiff of diesel gas, the crack of a dry twig and fog raw in the park.

The rain drummed on the roof; the room smelled of soaked clothes and Bengal cheroots and betel-juice.

He would have to straighten himself out before he could tackle this "mission". Two years London Airport and a year Karachi, then the end of the world and that awful last scream of hers that had cut out part of his heart as clean as a knife and left him mentally paralysed for days, then the long year in Southampton, the long bleak year of trying to forget, and failing; and now Pasang. And early, a day early, because of Santha.

Santha May Swee, someone he had never met before the flight out to Singapore five days ago; someone whom he might never see again. She had come and gone, a bird darting through the tangled branches of his life. But at this moment the memory of her was the only comfort to him as he stood in the middle of this fetid room, finishing the whisky, aware of the quiet Asian eyes of the two clerks who sat watching him, of the dying hubbub of eastern tongues in the customs room and the harsh frightened bark of Walsh on the telephone above.

He put the empty glass on to a trestle table near him, making a place for it among the pens and ink-wells and littered ashtrays, and in the drumming of the rain on the roof he was able to murmur aloud, like a rueful prayer unhopeful of an answer, "Santha . . . Santha May Swee", to ease him in his desolation.

2

THEY left the airstrip in Walsh's Land-Rover; a hard top had been made for it from petrol drums and angle-iron struts, and the noise was a plague on the ears the whole time the thing was in motion. The Land-Rover, like everything else on the airstrip, was due for a major overhaul.

The storm was beating itself out after an hour's fury and there was an inch of standing water on the runway; the plane in from Singapore, now bound for Kota Bharu northwards up the coast, was climbing through grey haze above the coconut palms and turning across the sea. Walsh and Hugh Copland had seen it away before they left, Walsh starting up the car with a jab of hands and feet and jerking it into gear with the cylinders still dry—"I've got to pick up stores anyway, and we can see a bit of the town so you'll get the hang of it."

Slewing the Land-Rover past the end of the runway and on to the long nearly-straight road that ran through padi-fields and then patches of jungle and mangrove swamp, Walsh spent most of the journey shouting above the rattle of metal, going at the bumps and puddles and ruts at a fierce pace—"It's not much of a dump. You saw it from the air, I expect, and that's the best view of Pasang. The airstrip wasn't put down because it was near the town: the town sprang up because the strip was handy. You know the history I suppose?"

"Some of it." The words were jerked out of Copland as he bounced on the seat; he sat braced with both arms.

"Beginning of the war the R.A.F. put a Hurricane strip down and ran this track to the coast for Navy liaison to bring stores and spares in. Pasang was just a fishing-kampong then. Soon as the Japs came in we cleared out and by the time the little bastards left the place there was no runway to fly from. Then the Sultan patched it up again and parked his own personal plane here. When he died—about '53—his son took over the throne and had those hangars put up. He's no fool, either. The British have pulled out and if anything starts again, Commy China's going to come in quicker even than the Nips did. That's why he's got his aircraft here, five miles from the palace—first-class escape-route to get him out in time. He pays for half the maintenance of the strip and Straits Airways the other half. You met Spencer, in London, I suppose?"

Waiting for the right interval between bumps Copland said "Yes!" in a jerked half-shout. They ran through a tunnel of jungle with the windscreen-wiper clogged with the debris of dropping foliage and mud thrown up from the wheels.

"Well, his old man had the land ceded to him by the State to plant rubber, but the war started before they could even drop a seed. The airstrip was put down instead, and that's why the chairman's got a share in the place today. My God, if I were him I'd sell out and concentrate on the India runs!"

The car went into a sudden slide and he had to fight it out with the wheel. A jungle creeper as thick as an elephant's trunk was caught and ripped by the bare edge of the roof as they bucked straight again over corrugated ridges in the road. A short-barrelled repeater-gun was jerked out of its clips and fell against Copland's shin. He managed to force it back.

"What do you keep this thing for?"

"We're not in rural England, y'know. Last week a tiger came down from the north—took a woman from the fishing-kampong a couple of miles up the coast. The bastard's still in the area and half the Sultan's army are out hunting it. Take my tip and you'll always keep this gun handy. There's more than tiger in this bloody outpost."

Did he mean animals, or men? Perhaps he was scared of both, perhaps of everything. Copland knew nothing about the man; Spencer in London had told him nothing. Had Walsh been sacked or was he quitting? It hardly mattered; in a few days he would be gone.

He was shouting again above the racketing of the car and Copland moved his head closer: "What was that?"

"I said is your wife joining you out here?"

Copland felt the knife go slitting into his bowels as it always did, even now after the last long year of waiting for nothing except the next day and then the next. In England he would have answered, No. But distance had begun to heal him, where time had failed.

"She's dead." New to the admission, he used the simplest and most brutal words, as if the ending of that small world couldn't be put in any more subtle way.

"She's what?" The metalwork clattered around them. They bounced on their bucket-seats.

So it had to be said again. "Dead." Yet there was a kind of relief; it was a purgative word.

"Oh—I'm sorry. Damn' bad luck." He made even more business of keeping the car on the track and for another minute speech wasn't possible. They cleared the last patch of jungle and Copland saw the white shining dome of a Buddhist temple through the haze of the lifting rain. The track improved suddenly and they ran on to dark tarmac. Roofs made a frieze across the horizon, topped by the shaggy green heads of coconut palms beyond the town.

"We'll find you a couple of decent rooms," Walsh said. "I don't recommend my own. Don't think in terms of a hotel; there's only two and one's a brothel and the other's got no electricity."

"Don't you live at the airstrip?"

"My God no!" Copland couldn't see if the eyes looked frightened again, but there was fear in the voice. "Not a damn' soul out there at night."

"Don't we get any night-flying?"

"No. So what's the point?"

"Save rent, wouldn't it?"

Walsh gave a cracked laugh. "You've got a point there, but I'd still sleep in the town at double the price." He drove at a group of chickens and sent them scattering across the bright soggy grass of the roadside. "That's the police-station up there—whitewash all over it." Suddenly they were in a street

18

of rainwashed concrete shop-houses. "Welcome to Pasang..."
The town seemed to have no fringe dwellings; perhaps
they were on the far side, towards the sea. Long wooden signboards with Chinese characters broke up the perspective of
the street. An Indian stood outside a coffee-shop, peering
down the long narrowing channel of signboards and
drenched washing and abandoned rickshas that made an
obstacle race for the Land-Rover. Two women called to
each other from their windows across the street, leaning far
out and pointing along it.

"Where the hell is everybody?" Walsh swerved in and out
the rickshas and barrows, driving past a market-square of
huts and stalls and hanging coloured cloths and rattan cages
with fowls cramped inside them. A small tawny-bodied boy
came darting into the street and ran in front of the car, twisting in his run to look back at it with a delighted grin, perhaps
playing his own game of being chased through the jungle by
a wild buffalo. Walsh kept hooting at him but the boy
wouldn't move until the street ran into a wider way; then
he trotted beside them, pointing and squealing something in
Malay; and suddenly he was on board, clinging to the angle-
iron uprights and chattering at a rate that gave Copland no
chance of sorting out his sketchy knowledge of the tongue.

"What's happened?" he asked Walsh.

"Not sure. Someone been run over, I suppose." Then they
saw the crowd. It was very large and blocked the wide street
completely, from this distance a heaped flower-bed of
colours with white predominating; petals of people broke
from it and were blown as if by the wind to another part of
it where they clung again.

"Someone important," added Walsh. He pulled the car up
at the edge of the crowd, where rickshas were parked at all
angles and massed together in what looked like an outsize
perambulator dump. The crowd was murmuring; whatever
excitement there had been was now dying away. Walsh
began pulling at the people, calling over his shoulder—
"Follow up, or you'll lose the gangway, Copland!"

As they eased through the thick of the people the smell of
over-ripe durian fruit rose on the hot damp air; the season

was on, and this was just after eating-time. Copland was fighting off nausea by the time Walsh had pushed his way to the centre of the crowd. A saloon Ford stood in the road, mud-streaked and with most of the glass shattered, a front tyre in ribbons and blood all over the door.

"In there," Walsh called to him, and pressed through the pack of people half-jamming the doorway of the Rest House. Copland followed. The hallway was easier, and voices more quiet. Two Malay constables were keeping some kind of order and the main throng was halted in the street outside.

"What's happened?"

"Tuan Duppy—in room there, tuan."

"Come on," said Walsh.

In the main room a man was lying on a couch and a brown-armed woman was bathing his bared shoulder; there was the reek of some kind of balm in the airless room. A few men were gathered around the couch.

Walsh told Copland: "Arthur Duffy. Got some rubber here." It didn't seem much of an explanation. The man looked very pale but his eyes were open and he was talking to the men nearest him. Walsh moved round behind the couch and said: "Hello, Duffy. You badly hurt?"

"Oh no." His voice was strong but he spoke slowly; pale blue eyes looked up at Walsh from sandy brows; a ragged moustache was pinned on to the lean lined face like a shred of coconut-husk.

"Hit something?" Walsh asked him.

"No. Something hit me." The woman in the sarong cupped his face and turned it gently so that she could go on with the swabbing. There was a lot of blood soaking into the ripped sleeve and his forearm was caked with it. Suddenly Copland realized. It would be about an hour's run through a storm like that from the stretch of road ten miles from Pasang, south along the coast towards Pintu Besar; with a wounded arm and a burst tyre, half an hour more.

He looked quickly at Walsh and saw that Walsh had also added things up; his face had gone as pale as Duffy's and his voice was rough:

"What hit you, Duffy?"

Before he could answer, a man came across the room from the hall, quietly hurrying with long strides, his presence suddenly in the room, and the room made different by it. Copland always remembered how he had first seen Stratton come into that room. He was tall, gnarled and hairy; he stood over the man on the couch with his large hands hanging loosely as if emptied of something big they had once held.

"They tell me you met with an ambush, Duffy." He looked through the man and beyond him.

"That's right," Duffy said slowly. The woman was cutting away the sleeve of the green bush-shirt; one or two of the Malays watched her; the others watched Stratton.

"Tell me about it." Copland was awed by the fierce nervous energy implicit in Stratton's whole body, despite the low voice, the loose hands, the ease of his stance. He would—thought Copland—have come to question the injured man even if he lay dying. Stratton had to know. It seemed that he was the first of them to have asked; perhaps the others had held back until Duffy could recover; they now moved a step closer; Stratton had taken the initiative and they could all hear the story for themselves.

"They weren't after me," the slow clear voice told them. "It was laid for someone else, two chaps—Europeans—running for shelter in the ditch. I didn't stop."

With no shade of meaning in his tone Stratton simply repeated: "Didn't stop?"

A faint smile moved the moustache. "Would you?"

"Where was this?"

"Five or six miles this side of Pintu. I came round a curve and there was a car on fire, half across the road. When they started shooting I put my foot down and found a gap and took it. You should have seen me go . . . . Tonight I'm going to write a letter to the Ford people. That thing accelerates just as they say. If—"

"Is that all you got—the shoulder?"

"That's all, thank you very kindly."

Stratton stooped from the waist and straightened again in one easy movement, inspecting the wound.

"What sort of shooting? Rapid?"

"That's right."

"How many guns?"

"I didn't stop to count." He turned mild blue eyes on Stratton. "If you're so interested, laddie, it's an hour's drive. You'll know the place, by the burned-out wreck."

"What sort of car was it?"

"Hot."

"Which way was it facing?"

"Broadside-on."

Duffy eased himself on the couch and with his good hand patted the woman's cheek. Her fat bronze face broke into a split-melon smile and she cooed to him in Malay.

"There were two people in the car," Copland said to Stratton. "Men, I think. They were running for cover when I saw them." He found a light-grey penetrating gaze focused between his eyes. For moments Stratton didn't speak. Copland found his stare discomforting.

"You weren't with Duffy?"

"No, I came in on the noon plane and we were low, trying to run in under the storm——"

"Oh, I see."

"This is Copland," Walsh said, "taking over my job."

Stratton seemed not to have heard him.

"Two men, you think. Did you see any of the C.T.s?"

"What are they?"

"Chinese terrorists."

"We only saw the two men. They were running for cover, into the trees. The car was already on fire."

A little Indian was suddenly among them in a rumpled white Palm Beach suit. He put down a bag and greeted the woman before bending over Duffy. The other people began talking among themselves and within a minute there was a full-scale discussion raging in the room. Someone had switched on the overhead fans and the long slow blades stirred the heat. Stratton had simply nodded to Duffy and was loping out of the room. A bigger space was being made around the couch on the plea of the Indian doctor, and the woman now employed herself in fanning the patient with a yellowed copy of Whiteaway's Mail Order Catalogue she had found on the table.

"Let's go," Walsh said to Copland.

Outside the Rest House most of the crowd had been cleared by policemen but a throng still surrounded the Ford, and among the jostling young male Malays and Chinese a brisk competition was in progress to find and point out yet another bullet-hole, another spot of blood. Two lines of holes ran in parallel across the rear quarter of the body; it needed only a boot-lace. Brown hands, yellow hands flickered and pointed; their eyes were bright and wide. The youth of Pasang was filled with excitement; the elders were silent and full of foreboding; it was just as it is when a war comes, anywhere.

Stratton had disappeared. Copland asked: "Who was the tall chap?"

Walsh moved quickly through the thinned crowd, bumping into them when they wouldn't move, impatient with them, angry, as he had been with his staff at the airstrip after Chong's news of the ambush.

"Name's Stratton," he said, impatient with the raw new-boy.

Copland persisted. "What does he do?"

"God knows. Nobody knows. It's the first word I've heard him speak for a month to anyone. A cat that walks on its own."

They went side by side now through the smell of durian fruit. The rain had stopped and a hot white haze covered the sky. Some of the rickshas had gone from the place where the Land-Rover was parked; others were moving slowly up and down the street.

"Taksi, tuan? Taksi?"

Walsh motioned the ricksha boys aside. Most of the life that had become magnetized by the shot-up Ford saloon was now drifting back to business and the street looked normal again. Copland was surprised to see so few Chinese in the town and he put another question to Walsh.

Walsh said: "This is where the Malays live, the east coast. Chinese and British are on the other coast and down south,

23

grubbing the money. After all, they built the bloody place, out of virgin jungle."

The street had begun to steam in the heat and Copland realized his clothes had almost dried on him. They got into the Land-Rover and Walsh jabbed the starter. A fat smiling Malay was setting up his coffee-stall at the edge of the monsoon-gutter outside his little shop, and seeing Copland he bowed and with spread hands wafted his smile through the steaming air—"*Tabek,* tuan!" he called above the beat of the running engine.

Copland gave him a wave of his hand, pleased not only to know the Malay word but also to be greeted by it. All right, the man was only trying to sell him some coffee, but just the same it was a greeting from a native of the place, and it came as a refreshing antidote to Walsh's old-hand cynicism. Copland had found the same thing in Karachi: this personal feeling in him that valued a word from a native—even a beggar—more greatly than a whole flow of speech from a man of his own kind. His existence had been acknowledged by the native of a place so far from home, so that by one small degree his home was here.

The car jerked away from the gutter and the rich scent of the coffee was lost to them. "You'll get plenty of that," said Walsh. "You're new in Pasang. Far as I know you're the eighth European here. Quite an event for the wogs."

"I'm flattered."

"You'll learn."

Copland lit a cigarette, taking trivial pleasure in not offering the packet. "Where are we going now?"

"Find you a couple of rooms. There's a Chinese here who's less of a crook than most, and he owns a house near the bus-terminal. Let me do the bargaining or he'll sting you good 'n' hard."

"It's kind of you, but I'll sleep at the airstrip."

Walsh took his foot off the throttle and turned his head. "Are you serious?"

"There's a room there, isn't there? Store-room or something I can clear out and put a bed in?"

Walsh drove on again through the steaming street, past

24

the Rest House and the group of boys and the bullet-scarred Ford saloon. With harsh contempt in his tone he said: "You'll find all the room you want on the airstrip at night, with only the mosquitoes for company—if you're lucky. Don't say I didn't warn you."

"I won't."

3

FROM the flat roof outside the windows of the control tower
Copland stood and watched the sun go down on his first day
in Pasang. In the afternoon the white haze had cleared from
the sky and now the huge blood-red sphere of the sun
touched the tops of the eighty-foot-high coconut palms in
the west, and from the upper sky the light deepened and the
blue thickened; from the sun the orange light flowed into the
darkening trees of the jungle; and slowly the jungle took fire.
The trees became charred as the fire burned among them
and after a little time only their petrified black ash was left
as a horizon; and half the sun was gone. Minutes later the
day died, and all that remained was rose-pale light where
thin cloud floated along the horizon; and when this last
light faded the jungle was black, and the sky was black; it
was as if the day had never happened.

Awed and unnerved by the sight of so total a death, Copland waited until his eyes accommodated and he could see
the first of the stars; then he went into the control tower and
down the flight of wooden steps.

The airport staff had gone, nearly an hour ago. Unused to
the building, he stumbled into a trestle table before he found
the light-switch. The room looked a little tidier. Perhaps
Walsh had given orders for a quick clean-up to impress the
new manager. Was Walsh leaving Straits Airways, or only
Pasang? Would there be a request for Copland's report on
the state of the airstrip as Walsh had left it? Or had the man
found room among his fears and angers for a little shame?

The place smelled of betel-juice and Indian cheroots;
probably it always would, however tidy it was made. He
went through the customs room and the main hall. Shutters
were banging outside the building and he went into the
cooling night air to find Wan Chai locking up his restaurant,
which was a small low attap-roofed extension of the building.

The cooking-smells drifted through the slats as the Chinese snapped the padlocks and uttered a yip of fright when he saw Copland.

"It's all right, Mr Chai."

"I not see you! It velly dahk!" He expressed relief in a musical titter. "Now you come, Mistah Coplan'—I got cah."

Copland had seen the venerable machine; this afternoon Chai had been trying to start the engine with the crank-handle. It had looked like a struggle to the death with a dragon. Would it start now, he wondered? Mr Chai would be extremely upset if it didn't. He was standing almost on Copland's feet for company with the night close about them.

"Thank you very much, but I live here."

"Live? Heah?"

"Yes."

Wan Chai shook his head rapidly. Mistah Coplan' didn't understand. Here it was impossible to live, at night.

"You come now! It late!" As if to demonstrate the idea by example he took a series of waddling hops in the direction of his mechanical dragon that was lurking somewhere in the dark. His face bobbed palely in the faint light from the main hall windows as he waited.

"No, I'm staying, Mr Chai. To make sure your restaurant is safe all night." That should please him.

"Lestaulant? It safe!"

"That's fine. Goodnight, Mr Chai."

"But you come! In my cah!"

Copland was a bit bored now and he explained that he was in actual residence here (which was rather a lie because he had no idea where he would sleep) and if he accepted this exceedingly kind offer of a lift into the town he would only have to walk all the way back. This was anwered in a very rigmarole way, the gist being that Mr Chai thought he was mad and would surely be dead by dawn. He didn't suggest by what agency, though.

Finally Copland called out: "See you in the morning!" and Chai practically bolted for it, as if a tryst with a ghost were being thrust upon him. After ten minutes of extra-ordinary sounds from the half-dark, the elderly dragon sprang into a kind of fit and went clanking away round the airstrip to leave a delicate shower of incandescent soot falling like fireflies across the gloom. From the jungle came the cries of alarmed birds; then it fell silent again.

For a moment Copland rather wished Mr Chai hadn't gone; then he remembered Walsh—"Don't say I didn't warn you"—and thought: "Damn the man." Walsh had been too long in Pasang, or too long in his own company. The staff here resented him; he had no friends. During the afternoon he had shown Copland the airstrip, its layout and organization; and his contempt for the "wogs" did not escape the Malays and Sikhs, Hindus, half-bloods and Straits-born Chinese who ran the airstrip as best they were able, under a wreck like Walsh.

Despite Copland's experience of Karachi, Spencer had reminded him at the London briefing: "Bear in mind that the British haven't withdrawn from one of their colonies. Malaya never was a colony. Even if there was ever any excuse for a white to treat a native like a dog, there's none now, in the country you're going to work in. Remember that a brown skin is the colour of the king's whose land you live in, and whose laws you are governed by."

Copland had resented the warning but later he had wondered if it hadn't been a slight hint about the man he was replacing: Walsh. It could even be that the Sultan of Tamarah had personally requested his removal from the State.

"That's his personal aircraft," he had told Copland on the tour of inspection this afternoon. "Aladdin's magic carpet for the quick getaway." His side-glance had hoped for Copland's appreciation of the nickname "Aladdin". It was not lost on Copland, who had checked briefly the details of the State whose laws—as the chairman had said—he was governed by. Its ruler was Sir Rahman Hamid Alam Sha ibni Al-Marhum Alaiddin, K.C.M.G., O.B.E., Sultan of Tamarah, a prince in his own right and of his own State, who would one day serve his turn as His Majesty the Yang di-Pertuan Agong, King of Malaya. However little this meant to the foreign subjects of once-great empires it was important to the

Malays; and it could be that the chance overhearing of that nickname "Aladdin" by one of the airstrip staff had led to a palace decision on removing Walsh.

Not that it mattered to Copland. Walsh was leaving here tomorrow, and no tears on either side.

There had been only one formal introduction during the tour; this to a pleasant bunched-up little Malay with a good clean smile and bright eyes and the hint of compressed force in his stance.

"Major Yang ibni Yassim, personal pilot to the Sultan."

"An honour, Mr Copland," Yassim had said in educated Malay. With an awkward but determined flourish Copland had been able to return the compliment in the same language and didn't care what Walsh obviously thought of the gesture. In English it would have sounded a bit too much of a good thing: "This day affords me much pride in having made such high acquaintance, Major Yassim." Walsh had said with his bright shrill laugh:

"The Major speaks perfect English, by the way."

With Yassim were two mechanics, personally responsible for the maintenance of the royal aircraft; the three of them were on duty at all daylight hours, with a relief crew taking over for two days in every ten. The aircraft—a brand-new Bee-76—was kept in a corner of the larger hangar, fenced-off with a light wall of rattan cane within which nobody was allowed to go, except these three men and the airstrip manager.

The rest of the place was in a state of neglect, the fire-tenders were filthy; the crash-tender was undergoing some desultory repair-work with bits strewn about; the guard on the freight transit-shed was a dark-skinned Tamil who squatted outside with his rusty tin of betel-nut and who staggered up when Walsh ordered him to get on his damned feet and fell down again the moment they had passed; and the white paint on the landing-T had peeled off years ago. Walsh, after his first show of conscience about the staff-office being "in a bit of a mess", had made no further effort to excuse himself as he hurried through the main details for his successor:

29

"Apart from our stuff there's a charter freight service calling once a week and the Kuantan-Kota Bahru planes that drop in every morning. Every other day we get the noon plane from Singapore, and that's about all. I suppose Spencer told you this but frankly he's a bit out of touch—hasn't been out here for months."

"How often do we get emergency landings?"

"Now and again. Storm drives them in, or an engine packs up, or some passenger finds the wrong end of a snake that's got on board for the ride—I've shown you the first-aid room."

"Yes." A closet with a stained sink and a cupboard full of once-used bandages.

"You've seen some of the weather for yourself. Nothing I can tell you about it. Just when you think you're going to die of the heat the rain comes and it looks like death by drowning. Prevailing winds are east-south-east and west-north-west. Monsoon blows in December and January, when the aircraft come in over the sea and the beach and the town. Rest of the year they come in over the jungle. Have you checked up on all this already?"

"Spencer gave me a batch of books and maps, and I think I know the set-up."

"I dunno how much you'll learn from books."

They had stood in the white heat-haze outside the main building, watching the faint shape of the Singapore-Bangkok plane crossing the sky from the south. Copland stood now in the starlight, the echoes of Wan Chai's car fading away. From the jungle night-birds called and there were the smaller, more secret sounds of nocturnal life: the stir of a leaf, a threat low in the throat, a squeal of fear almost inaudibly high; the thud of a leap, the struggle and the kill.

Listening here, one could realize that nothing in that vast spread of jungle, swamp and rock was dead. Leaves, falling, turned to rich humus and fed the stems they had grown upon. Mammals, reptiles, birds, insects, in their death fed the living. Listening here, alone with the black massed trees, one could feel that the jungle was on the march, slower than a tide of lava.

Copland had seen three or four Tamils at work all day, hacking and chopping at the jungle's fringe five hundred yards from the runway, clearing the low scrub and pouring poison upon roots too deep for digging, trying to keep back the jungle as seed and shoot and tendril sought the light. They worked at it every day; their life was a struggle with this primitive living thing that had been here a million years before them and would never die as they must.

Given a year, Copland thought uneasily, the jungle would make headway, absorbing the ground and the attap-huts on the airstrip perimeter road; in ten years the whole runway would be devoured, and this building become a skeleton in the green gloom where the sun never penetrated, an outline, an image fading in a dark picture.

He shivered in the cool air and quietly cursed Walsh, who had offered him so bleak a welcome to this place where fears came easily to a lonely mind. But the very need of cursing chastened him: his first night in Pasang, did he want comfort, already? And from a man like Walsh?

He moved into the building and raised his voice—*"Hey, ho, with a hey-nonny"*—but the sound of it was alarming as the echoes sent it back, and he shut up.

Within half an hour he had chosen his apartment in the building, clearing the junk out of a room next to the control tower and stacking it in the passage. Tomorrow the staff would sort it out and store it or burn it, and they'd do the job properly. This place was due for fireworks.

The room had windows facing north and south, across the runway on one side, into the dark of the jungle on the other. There was a tripod hand-basin fed from the tank on the roof and he stripped and washed and got the sleeping-bag from his luggage; then he went down the wooden steps into the staff room to put out the lights.

A brown trickle moved across the concrete floor and coiled near the door that led to the outside of the main hall. Copland watched it. He was wearing a pair of rope-soles. It wasn't a good thing to wander about here at night with bare ankles. He would have to remember these things.

The only kind of stick he could find was a map rolled on

31

a metal rod; he picked it up and went over to the door, watching the little brown coil the whole time. It looked very young; even when you had never seen a certain animal before, so that you didn't know how big it should be when full-grown, you could always recognize the look of in-experience about a young specimen, a tender, green-horn look, very disarming. They didn't have these anywhere near Karachi. All he knew was that it wasn't a krait. If it had been a krait he would have gone for a shot-gun. This was prettier and less murderous-looking—or did a krait look so ugly because you knew there were only two minutes more to live after it bit you?—and it was trying to glide under the door; but there wasn't enough gap. It was barely two feet long, and frightened.

Copland reached over and opened the door, inching it inwards carefully, not to drive the snake against his feet, until it smelled the cool night air and poured itself through the opening as fast as a vanishing-trick. But it had been good to see another living thing, even a small frightened reptile. He opened the door wide and went out to where the black sky sprang with stars, to look up at them for a minute before he turned in, reluctant to climb those steps again to the lonely room and the long hours of the night in which he would try to forget the sight of the car with its shattered glass and the ribboned tyre and the blood, and the frightened face of Walsh, and the smell of fear about the fat Wan Chai as he stood here begging for company on his journey to the town. Fear contaminated and infected.

From somewhere above Copland's listening head there came a dry sound louder than the rest and rising to a rush of air, the kind of anonymous sound that menaces by its name-lessness; he turned his head and tried to place the sound and was shocked by the crashing finale of it. The night was split open by the impact and he was deafened, lurching back and almost falling, his breath choked and the nerve-light flashing across his eyes.

Echoes receded and then the trees cried with the calls of alarm; wings moved heavily across the stars.

Something fell to the ground near the end of the building

and he swore aloud at the banshee wailing of the gibbon in the trees. There was a torch on a table by the door and he went in and got it, and came back to swing the beam of light across the ground, fixing it on a dark shape that lay in a moving pool of liquid. It was the size of a human head and was thick with brown hair. He moved towards it, keeping the beam steady though his hand and whole body were shaking.

It was a coconut, a big ripe fifteen-pounder from one of the eighty-foot palms that stood above the corrugated-iron roof of the building. It had hit the roof and bounced. It lay in its pool of milk, split open like a skull.

The protest from the jungle died away; the silence and the stars remained. He snapped off the torch and went back inside the building. There was some brandy in the cupboard and he drank it straight from the bottle.

★ 4 ★

LYING sleepless because of the brandy—it had been a stupid and feeble thing to do—he listened for the thin nearing whine of the next mosquito and held his hand ready in the dark. His head ached from slapping his own face. An hour ago he had got the torch and searched the whole building, but there wasn't a shred of mosquito-gauze anywhere. There was some Paludrine in the first-aid cupboard, though, and he had swallowed a couple of tablets to guard against a malarial bite.

Twice he had wound his watch, the second time forgetting it was already wound and straining the spring. It mustn't stop; there had to be some measure of this never-ending night. If the watch stopped, everything would stop. Except the jungle.

He thought once of his dead wife and then of Santha May Swee, only to push her dark face out of his mind because it would hurt the dead if it were known he had started to think about the living so soon; and then the morbidity of this repelled him—you could be unfaithful to the dead only by forgetting them, or rather by never remembering them, so he would never be unfaithful to her. After a decent and deliberate interval he let Santha and the scene come back: the half-lit narrow doorway of the caged-bird shop in the street across the square from the Cathay Pacific terminal, the beating sound as the rain fell and bounced and fed the flooding roadway, the roaring of the monsoon drains where debris was jamming up.

"Does it often rain like this?"

"Oh yes."

In Asia the ear is always alert for the accent; it is not enough that one's own tongue is spoken; one wants to know where it was learned, and why. But the timbre of her voice was so interesting that the accent didn't matter; she said the two words in a soft low chime.

34

In the narrow doorway they stood pinned among other people who had run here from the deluge; their faces, white, brown, yellow, caught the glow of the lamps in the street; across the lamps the rain made a bright steel veil.

Pressed against Copland stood a thin dying dreamer from the opium-house two doors down; his breath reeked of *chandu* but nobody could move.

"Have you got far to go?"

She lifted her face to answer him; in broad daylight her skin would be matt bronze, he thought; even in the dark these eyes would glow like this. "No. But anywhere is a long way, tonight."

Birds chittered among the stone and glass, crammed in their wicker cages in the shop, fragments of colour and music convicted of beauty and committed to life imprisonment for the casual pleasure of man.

"If you like I'll see if I can find a taxi." But he hoped she would dissuade him.

"There will be no taxis for a little time." Beautiful, and with a voice that chimed, shouldn't she too be in a wicker cage? "We must wait." Cages were for the patient and she should beware.

He hoped they would have to wait all night, even with the dreadful smell of the *chandu*.

She asked: "You have not been to Singapore before?" How did she know? Because he'd asked her if it often rained like this.

"First time," he said.

"I hope it will not deter you from returning." There was a practised, professional ring to that. Who was she? Not a prostitute.

"I'll come back every time you do," he said, immediately embarrassed by his own schoolboy gallantry. But he had meant it—had meant, anyway, that he'd like to see her again, in any weather.

She had pretended not to have heard; a faint smile was left on her small ivory-brown face so that when he looked at it again it would be pleasing. A professional smile. Not a tart. A dancer? No. Why not? You couldn't tell a dancer

35

when she wasn't dancing, could you? Yes, and she wasn't one.

Flotsam was jerking and drifting down the torrent that was building up from the edge of the square and pouring into the monsoon gutters: paper packets and split timber from boxes, tin cans and a dead rat gleaming and turning over with the wink of sharp teeth, a posy of small torn flowers, melon rinds, a bottle ringing through the hiss of the rain as it bobbed and spun, hitting the stones and ringing out *Abandon Ship?* The street was inches under swirling water; then the rain fell harder and the street danced with it. White light hit the eyes and blinded; a second later in the gloom the street lamps flickered, then held steady; another second and the thunder shook the lamps, the shops, the doorway, and after it had gone there was no more song from the birds in their cages.

"I should face the other way."

"Please?"

"Stand with your back to it."

"To what?"

"The lightning."

The smile became genuine. "I don't mind it. I like being surprised."

"Then this is your night."

In half an hour the sky was clear and the first taxis were ploughing round the square with front wheels in a bow-wave. People flapped towards them from the shelter of the doorways. When the street looked solid again the smoker stepped on to it and glided away with the other-world gait of the somnambulist, back to the opium-house, perhaps not knowing that he had just come from there.

"Good night," the Eurasian girl said to Copland and left the doorway, and he was so interested in watching the way she walked, swiftly and gracefully in low-heeled soundless shoes, that he stood like a fool until it was too late to hurry after her and catch up without making it seem like an actual chase.

He walked for two hours through the gleaming streets, at first angry, later rueful, by midnight merely fed-up. In the morning he remembered her but by the evening had forgotten, and spent a dreadful time with a party of young Dutch sailors in the Happy World, traipsing through the mud whose daytime curdled brown colour was now turned by the glare of the thousand naked bulbs and Chinese lanterns to a carpet of dappled and rutted rainbows, staring at the bright tinsel displays and the acrobats, the shooting-booths, the whirling celluloid aeroplanes, the bright sweating faces with their bright salesmen's smiles, their only message: We have to live, so you have to spend! The only thing that made the evening cheerful was the determined gaiety of the Dutch sailors that never abated; and it was this —Copland realized later—that got him back to his hotel singing drunk, and not suicidal drunk as he would have been had he been left on his own that night.

The next morning was awful but after an emetic and a pint of processed milk he was back on form by the afternoon, and took a bus out to the airport along the coast, where fishermen stood waist-deep in the sea, dragging their nets, never looking up as the great hundred-ton airliners climbed above their heads and floated down from five miles high in the blue. They came in from Seattle and Honolulu, Tokyo, Hong Kong, from London, Cairo, Karachi, Bangkok, from New York, Cape Town, Moscow, Sydney, by Pan-Am, TWA, BOAC, Qantas, Air France and KLM, plying the air-clipper routes and manned by a special race of men who worked aloft and lived aloof above the groundlings, running a gigantic system to ensure that at any given moment a thousand American business-men should be in south-east Asia and a thousand south-east Asians should be in America.

The bus ran through waves of heat. To the north, high over Johore, thunderheads were piled in a brooding sky, but here the sun beat hard on the runways and airport buildings, and the spread wings of the Dakotas and Constellations and Comets and Jet Clippers gleamed and shimmered in the heat; below them bubbled the tar, whole stretches of it swimming in mirage where the light struck the eyes obliquely.

37

Copland stayed an hour, committing to memory what he could of the airport. From here the Straits Airways and Thai Airways and Malayan Airways planes would follow the coast and jungle to Pasang, where he would receive them and send them north. His head began throbbing again and he bought a pair of sunglasses at a kiosk and sat with an iced Coca-Cola to watch the men in their Palm Beach suits with their Parker 51's in rows as bright as medals, the women in their elegant chong-sams and saris and Paris sheaths, all of them impatient to be going, just as they had been impatient to come. The world spun fast; to walk, to sit, to think was a waste of precious time.

The bus took him back to the city by the same route and he sat next to a stewardess in white drill uniform with the letters S. and P.A. in gold on her lapels. They watched the sea turn amethyst as the sun neared the west over the island; the fishermen had gone and the sea was flat and unbroken by any ship.

He watched the reflection of the air hostess in one of the green windows; she sat framed and poised, a portrait in wavering oils as the bus swung and swerved. The little gold-metal initials glinted on her uniform. Singapore and Peninsular Airways. One of their planes had touched down when he had been sitting with the Coca-Cola. Their Bangkok run would take them through Pasang. Perhaps he would see this girl again, sitting in the restaurant at his own airport. He wanted to take a look at her face directly but talked himself out of it; a keen watcher of reflections in bus windows (London was the best place, with fog outside and the lights just coming on), he had long ago learned that it was a mistake to look at the living original of the transparent and phantom image, because it was always a disappointment. The hard expression, the line of worry, the blemish of hurried make-up was never projected on to the glass of the window; the dream-face was always the more beautiful.

He sat watching the beautiful portrait until the bus stopped and left it painted against the front wall of a shop, so that the portrait was signed in red neon: Cheng Yi Sen, Fish Importer. And for a fish importer, some artist, Mr Sen.

"Please excuse me," the girl said.

"Sorry. Is this Raffles Square?"

"Yes."

"Thank you."

They shuffled through the aisle of the bus with most of the other passengers. An old dog can learn new tricks: she was as beautiful as her reflected image. It was the first time it had happened to him, as a keen window-watcher. No hard expression, no line of worry, no make-up except pale rose lipstick perfectly applied. On the hot pavement the little crowd broke up. "You're Singapore and Peninsular, isn't that right?"

She paused, turning. "Yes."

"I expect I'll see you again, if you touch down at Pasang."

"Yes, we do."

She stood very straight but was small; her skin was dull bronze, her eyes black with gold lights in them as she looked up at him against the sun.

"Then—then I'll look forward to it," he said. She gave a quick smile and turned away and he stood on the burning dusty pavement in a cloud of diesel-gas as the bus started off. She walked quickly and awkwardly in her high heels, perhaps unused to them. In sandals, he thought, she would walk gracefully, as the other girl had done when he had stood, just like this, watching from the doorway on the night of the rainstorm.

Suddenly he began running along the pavement, darting on to the roadway and back to dodge the people until he caught her up and planked himself in front of her—"I've only just realized," he said stupidly. "It was you, in the doorway!"

"I am sorry?"

The same soft bell-like voice, now that he listened—or was he, after all, wrong? That night there had been only the glow of the street-lamps and she had been wearing some ordinary Western-style dress whose colour he couldn't even remember; now it was full sunshine and she was in uniform. She was Eurasian, but so were many of the people here. Was she the other one? Would he ever know? Did it matter?

What did matter? He didn't want to lose her now; that was what mattered.

People nudged past them and the street's din roared in their ears, making it difficult to talk. She was waiting patiently and he leaned closer and said: "I met you in a doorway the other night. In the storm. Didn't I?"

She smiled a professional smile, and now he knew; or was determined to know. Not a prostitute, nor a dancer, but with the professional smile of the perfect air hostess, mothering or faintly flirtatious or calmly reassuring according to the needs of the passenger.

"We have so many storms," she said. "There are so many doorways in Singapore."

No headway; and it was a thin enough excuse for chasing after her through Raffles Square. How could he keep her with him, just for this evening? He had lost the knack; for three years there'd been no need to persuade women into assignations, and during the last year no heart for it. Now life was coming back and he must verse himself again in its ways.

His excitement had passed; almost he would have preferred to say goodbye and walk away, as she too would wish; but he was committed and cared enough not to want to look a worse fool. Dutifully he said above the street noise:

"I'm taking over the airport at Pasang in a few days, as manager for Straits Airways. I thought I should look at Singapore first, as I've got a few days' leave. Now I feel a bit lost." Then all the heart went out of him and he just said, "Are you in a hurry? I mean, shall I clear off?" The brutality was deliberate for some reason; perhaps he wanted her to go, and wanted her to know that he wouldn't care a damn if she did.

"I have to go to the terminal," she said, looking at each of his eyes at a time as people do when they're trying to read you better.

"Right, then I won't hold you up." He stood back, full on somebody's foot, and had to swing round and apologize instead of kicking the idiot as he would have liked. It was a tiny ancient Chinese with no hair on his pear-shaped head

40

and a long dismal grey frond of a beard, with eyes as innocent as a child's, shining from dry yellow puckered skin as he looked up at Copland as if at a steeple.

"All light . . . you not know. No hurt." The whole face gathered itself together for the effort of a big smile.

"My feet too big." He was always saying it. They were. He turned back; she hadn't gone. He had hoped she would have seized the chance. She was watching his face and for the first time the smile was real and some of his heart crept back. As if reaching a decision about him, she said:

"If you would like to come to the terminal, we could show you our organization. We enjoy good relations with Straits Airways."

"Do you?" It made the whole thing formal, a business affair, really. So he went along with her into the cool of the tall stone building, disturbed, after so long, to be walking with a girl. It was as if a part of his youth had come back, leaving a gap in his life; and at last he knew exactly how he would have to regard those three happy years. As a gap, and nothing more. The cruel and only epitaph.

That evening he had dinner with Santha May Swee, and all through it he was melancholy, having to force good spirits. The next day he went to the airport to meet her and in the evening they went to a Chinese theatre which bored him dreadfully; but she said she enjoyed it very much, so that was all right. While they were together he couldn't throw off the odd depression that had begun when he had caught her up in Raffles Square. It was something he couldn't understand, so he drank too many whiskies after the theatre and said goodnight to her at the doorway of a shabby apartment-house near Holland Village.

"I have enjoyed meeting you very much," she said, her hand in his. Her slightly formal over-correct English gave some of her phrases an insincerity, or it was just his mood.

"I haven't been very bright company. Sorry."

"But then, you are sad."

The whisky had made him angry with himself. Poor old Copland, poor sad old sod.

"Not in the least," he said, releasing her small fingers. The

41

quick shadow of pain at his brusque denial went flitting across her eyes in the lamplight, and he knew he shouldn't have said that. One couldn't think of everything. Women were so damned sensitive. Her voice was too casual as she said:

"Tomorrow I am on full tour again for two weeks. If—"

"You are? Damn."

"Perhaps we shall meet again in Pasang. I hope so."

"So do I." Now that he'd remembered how to persuade a woman into assignations, how did you say goodbye to her?

She was watching him steadily, studying his face and not just waiting for him to speak again. He decided he didn't care for being studied. Bus windows were the proper place for that.

"Goodnight, Santha."

"Goodnight, Hugh."

And the doorway was empty.

He didn't get drunk that night, because he knew he would drift into it unless he took a hold. When, the next day, he watched the S. and P.A. Dakota take-off and climb across the sea (he hadn't gone to see her off, but had to watch the plane), he wished he could have been given these three days of his life all over again, to cut them and re-shoot like a bit of bad film. Because the past was dead, and he would have to remember the word for it: that it was a gap in life, this side of which he must live as he always had and would always have to.

The next day he packed up and took the noon plane out of Singapore, a day early, because enforced sobriety gave a sharp edge to loneliness and there seemed absolutely nothing to do on the island now that one out of its million and a half inhabitants had gone. There were so many doorways in Singapore, and he knew the most empty of them all.

A mosquito sang, its thin drone nearing. His hand was ready and he waited, cunningly, until the air against his brow was stirred by the minute wings. Still he did not move, nor did the mosquito settle. Its needling song faded, and his

hand relaxed. He must forget them. He'd taken Paludrine.
He must sleep.

Through the propped-open windows the small sounds
crept from the jungle, but he no longer listened. Only once,
before he slept, did he hear an owl's call, a sound that fluted
through the velvet dark, something like the way she had
pronounced his name ... Hee-yoo ... Hee-yoo. ...

★ 5 ★

AN hour after dawn, the heat came. The sun had become invisible, because one could not look at it; but its heat drove down and beat on the body, knuckling into the eyes and bringing sweat out. In the doorway of his little restaurant Wan Chai stood watching the sky with a look of slightly surprised anticipation. Perhaps he was still not used to the fact that from that remote heaven his customers would come. He had greeted Hugh with even greater surprise, certain he must have been whisked away by the spirits of the trees, during the long night.

Being a practical man, however, he had obviously provided against the bare unlikelihood of Mistah Coplan's being still alive in the morning, for a friend of his arrived on a tall and quaintly tinkling bicycle halfway through the morning and brought it to a halt with a noise like a peal of bells.

"I come to help," he announced to Hugh urgently. "I have velly good clean posh looms in town, all leady for you, because I know you want."

"I'm afraid you're wrong about that."

"Nobody stay heah at night, Tuan Coplan'." He shook his thin bone-yellow skull of a head so vigorously that Hugh was surprised to hear no rattle. "Velly bad place. Evil spilits heah. Evelyone tell you. Got two nice clean looms for you." Remembering the phrase he had picked up at the Rest House only yesterday, he brought it out with a gesture. "Apsolutelee chahming place. I show you at sundown."

"Thanks very much, but not today."

"Ho, yes!" He nodded in a series of well-timed jerks, and expressed his complete confidence in Tuan Coplan' by mounting his bicycle with not another word. It went tintinnabulating away over the airstrip.

It occurred to Hugh that there seemed something not quite decent about his choice of quarters, in native eyes.

44

Voting to reside with spirits in the dark hours, he was himself suspect. Last night Wan Chai had been fear-struck, the last man to leave along that patchy jungle track to the town. The rest of the people here had scuttled off before him in the fading light. Whether or not the bicycle-rider wanted to rent him rooms, and Wan Chai to participate as agent, there was a fixed idea about the airstrip; by day the staff worked here; by night it was as deserted as the moon.

And Walsh as frightened as the others. It would be a good thing for Pasang when that man had gone. Hugh was impatient to begin what the chairman had unnervingly called his "mission" here; but until Walsh cleared out he couldn't start giving orders and trying to reorganize the place.

Outside the hangar the Sultan's smart little Bee-76 was being run-up for engine-testing as part of its daily inspection. There had been a rumour that he was flying today, but Walsh couldn't confirm it. "There are always rumours about what Aladdin's going to do next. Bound to be. He's the star turn here. If you ever want to check up, get the palace on the direct line—they never mind a call."

Walsh was more helpful this morning and in better mood. He began watching the sky soon after eleven o'clock, waiting for the aircraft that was putting in here and taking him to Bangkok. He looked less of a wreck in his buff-coloured linen suit and topee, possibly even seeing himself as the rearguard of the British taking reluctant leave of this doomed outpost that would surely come to ruin in the hands of its own people.

His plane touched down on schedule; the low cloud that had been steadily building up during the morning had not yet formed a storm, and conditions were good.

"Well, Copland, this is it. I hope I've given you a fair idea of how to do things."

They stood in the blowing air as the engines were started up; dust whirled against their faces. Hugh said nothing. The man treated him to a last bright laugh—"Must say I admired your guts in sticking out the night here. Of course you won't do it again—"

45

"Have a good trip, Walsh. They're waiting for you."

A trim stewardess stooped in the fuselage doorway. Chinese. Not Santha. The Malay traffic-officer had his paddles ready. Behind him were two police-constables from the palace staff, standing to some sort of attention and watching Walsh, and Hugh wondered if this constituted an official send-off by the State of Tamarah for the Straits Airways airport manager or if they had been sent here to make certain Walsh left the territory.

A group of Tamils and Chinese watched the Englishman board the aircraft, lifting his topee with public gallantry to the air hostess. She pulled the door closed and the traffic-officer raised his paddles in the O.K. signal. Hugh braced himself against the slipstream blast as the machine gunned-up and swung away, bouncing gently along the perimeter track to the runway with a faint brown wedge of dust behind it.

The wings shimmered in the heat and a reflection sparked once from the cabin window and then the plane sank forward from the released brakes under full power and made its run. A minute later the runway was empty except for a haze of dust.

Walsh had said: "Far as I know you're the eighth European in Pasang." Now there were seven.

Hugh stood in the flat white heat letting his eyes water to wash out the grit; when he could see clearly again he looked across the airstrip. It was a gash of dried mud and tarmac set in the steep jungle green and littered with these few tin buildings. Pasang Airport. A staff of twenty-three, himself the only European. Every day some fifty passengers came through and from now on he was responsible for their lives. At Karachi he had been under orders; here he must give them—and think them out first. But if a man like Walsh could run this place . . . It was the only comforting thought.

He turned across the bubbling tar apron and went into the main building. There wasn't another traffic movement for two hours.

"Ismail!" he shouted.

A Hindu bobbed up from behind the customs counter,

46

all whites of eyes. Ismail was in the restaurant, he said.

"What's he doing in the restaurant?"

"Eat, drink, sahib."

"Fetch him out. Tell him I want to see him at once."

He went into the staff office and told the Hindu clerks: "In seven days from today His Highness the Sultan is to make an official state inspection of this aerodrome accompanied by the chiefs of staff of the army and the Deputy Prime Minister. Did you know?"

They did not know. The announcement practically flung them back against the wall as they got off their chairs. This was better than Hugh had hoped. Walsh had dropped at least one word of truth, then: the Sultan was the "star turn" here.

"Of course you will want to see that this office is fit even for the Yang di-Pertuan Agong himself to inspect." He was able to make all this sound reasonable and clearly understood, rapping it out in quite good Hindi learned in Karachi. "If you need items or materials such as soap, brushes, paint and so on that you can't find in the stores, tell me at once and I will order them. Seven days is a short time, don't you agree?"

They agreed strongly and he decided not to overdo things. Going up the wooden steps to the control room he shouted back for Ismail again. It might be an idea to get hold of Wan Chai and tell him that members of the airport staff would in future be allowed inside the restaurant during certain fixed hours for refreshment, and that if Mr Chai did not refuse admission at all other times he would be requested to take his restaurant elsewhere.

In the clammy heat of the control room, Haji Ahmad sat fast asleep in his chair at the radio switchboard, his beautiful full-bearded head tucked comfortably on his chest. Hugh admired him for a moment and then shouted—"*Snake! Snake!*"

Haji Ahmad was awake in the same instant and drawing his feet up on the chair, his black beard swinging this way and that.

"Where, sahib—where?"

"It's gone. Has Flight 6 made its check transmission yet?"

"Not yet, sahib."

"Call him up and ask why not."

The Straits-born Pathan lowered his feet and fiddled with the switchboard panel, playing for time, but Hugh stood there waiting.

"I have forgotten the frequency, sahib."

"You have?" Hugh leaned against the end of the switch-board and spoke in a lower voice, packing it with drama. "Haji Ahmad, there is a storm building up ten miles north of here over the coast and the aircraft will try to fly below it if there is enough time. It might be vital to the safety of all those people on board that the captain remains in contact with Pasang by radio during the next half an hour. I shall hold you personally responsible for any emergency trans-missions sent from that aircraft that request guidance or help."

Ahmad was already finding the frequency. "And in future, if I see you asleep on duty at the switchboard, I shall make a priority report to the Air Transport Safety Board of the State of Tamarah informing them of your flagrant negligence." It was very doubtful if such an authority existed, but this man wouldn't know in any case.

"I understand, sahib." It was said with a dignity just this side of losing face.

"Good. As soon as possible we shall make the fans work again in here and I have ordered an ice-box to be installed in the staff office so that whenever you need a cold drink you can call down for it." He heard someone trudging up the steps and turned to see Ismail's sweat-bright face looming into the room.

"Ismail, have you heard the news?" The clerks would have been certain to tell him on his way up.

"Yes, tuan Coplan'. In seven days there is to be—"

"That's right." He drew the Malay over to the desk by the south window where there was a heap of junk and paper left by Walsh to suggest he had done some work here. "Now listen, Ismail. Who is the assistant manager of this airport?"

Ismail looked puzzled. He had a broad strong head and a

48

mane of lank blue-black hair; his olive-skinned face as unshaven yet almost hairless; his whole appearance was as racially pure as any Malay could be, a descendant of Chinese and Islamic strains, of Hindu, Muslim, Siamese and Arab, with the core somewhere deep inside him of the primitive aboriginal native of this land. Hugh had chosen him after a good deal of observation when he had gone round the place with Walsh yesterday afternoon.

"There is no assistant manager, tuan Coplan'."

Hugh affected great surprise. "But I have never been on an airport that had no assistant manager, Ismail! He is a very important person indeed!"

Ismail looked dismayed about this, but could offer no help. "Whatever will happen, Ismail, in seven days' time when His Highness makes his request to meet the assistant manager of the State Airport?" He waited, despair on his face. Unfortunately Haji Ahmad was now talking to Flight 6 at his switchboard, so that the silence was broken and lost some of its drama; but Ismail seemed to be aware by now that the entire fate of Pasang Airport was sorely jeopardized by the lack of an assistant manager.

"I will tell you what we shall do," Hugh told him heavily. "We shall award you the title of Temporary Acting Assistant Manager as from today, Ismail. After one month I will forward a recommendation to the chairman of the airline that you be granted a permanency and a due increase in salary as assistant manager—if by that time you have proved yourself worthy of the position."

Ismail straightened his headcloth and asked for a repetition of all this; and Hugh obliged him. When the full import of the occasion was brought home to Ismail he stood wiping the sweat from his face and listening to the rest of the business with unblinking attention.

"Your duty will be to make sure that all my orders are carried out immediately and efficiently, Ismail. For the moment I will give you only these. First, we want a man with a coconut-monkey to clear those trees of nuts, above this building."

"I know a man with a good *berok*, tuan! He is——"

"Right. Fetch him along today." It had been bad enough last night, when he was fully awake; if one of those fifteen pounders hit the iron roof in the small hours when he was asleep, his nerves would die the death. "When the trees are cleared and it's safe to work on the roof, I want the name 'Pasang' painted there in white letters as big as the space allows. From the air this place might be a native kampong for all you can make out. Next, find a good electrician and make every fan in the building work properly, or we shall all suffocate." He swung round to see if Haji Ahmad had dozed off again. "It's too hot in here, Ahmad, isn't it?"

"Too hot, sahib, always."

Hugh nodded and told his Temporary Acting Assistant Manager: "I have ordered an ice-box from the town. It will arrive tomorrow if Allah wills. You must install it in the staff office below this room. I have also asked for twenty-five tins of white paint to be delivered here for the letters on the roof and for the big T board, which must be painted as soon as possible. Lastly, the crash-tender and the fire-tender must be got working properly and you must mount a yellow flag on each vehicle not less than one yard square from a pole not less than two yards high. The crash-tender is to be painted bright yellow and the fire-tender bright red. And at all times—at all times, Ismail—when an aircraft is due to land or take-off, the engines of both tenders must be started up and left running with the crews in their seats until the aircraft has completed its manoeuvre. Now I want you to see to all these matters personally and report to me if you meet any difficulty. Finally, at all times when I am absent from this airport, you yourself will be in complete authority here and fully responsible. Understood?"

After half an hour's careful recapitulation he sent Ismail away with orders to take the Land-Rover into the town and fetch the man with the coconut-monkey, at the same time confirming the orders for paint, brushes and the ice-box to be delivered urgently.

"Copland-sahib!"

"Yes, Ahmad?"

"Flight 6 is now landing at Kota Bharu."

50

"Very good, Ahmad." Surely it was the first time that an aircraft had been followed right to the next point of call by the Pasang radio. "There is a new rule that I want you to comply with. Write it down and remember it. Whenever a machine lands here, you will telephone the airport from which it took off and report its safe arrival. Whenever a machine leaves here, you will telephone its destination and report that it is airborne. Remember that I will be asking you at various times during the day what the position is regarding the aircraft we shall be handling, and that I shall expect you to give me all details straight away."

In bad weather it might make for safety; in any case it would keep Ahmad awake the whole time, because a telephone-call to anywhere a hundred miles distant would fully occupy the wits and patience of a saint.

"One more thing, Ahmad. Please obtain, by telephone or by radio to the aircraft—I don't mind which—the passenger-list of each flight arriving. We may have important people on board and we shall be able to receive them with due honours when they land at Pasang."

"I will try, Copland-sahib."

"Thank you, Ahmad. And with the passenger-list, obtain also the names of the crew. Including the stewardess, of course."

6

THE camp-bed, delivered yesterday and now set up between the door and the tripod wash-stand, was a foot too short; and sleep came less easily than ever. By this, the fifth night alone on the airstrip, he had expected to be more used to the night and the loneliness, but he was not.

Dozing, a sound from the jungle sharper than the others stirred a thought, or a memory; and his mind was occupied again. There seemed nothing to set the seal on the waking day and to invite sleep: no last murmured word in the room as there had once been, lying like this in the gloom but not alone. Sometimes, during that last year, he thought he heard her voice again, sleepily asking the same loved question that had become a game with them.

"What shall we call him?"

They'd never considered a "her."

"Andrew."

The silence considered.

"No."

"Why not?"

"I don't know. Suppose it reminds me of liver salts or something."

Weeks later the game developed.

"We must think of something for him, Hugh."

"Caesar Napoleon Alexander Montgomery."

A drowsy giggle. "Felix?"

"Mickey Mouse."

"Poor little thing. We must think seriously, tomorrow."

"Yes. Tomorrow."

Sleep in those days had come gently.

They had thought seriously, and later when the pains had begun they agreed on the matter.

"Peter."

"Peter what?"

"Just Peter."

"Why?"

"I like it. Don't you?"

"Ye-es. Do we know a Peter?"

"No. It's new."

"Can't he have more than one? One isn't much, darling."

"There's two. Peter Copland."

"Sounds nice, yes. Tomorrow we'll write it down, and see how it looks. Shall we, darling?"

"Yes. Sweet dreams. There's nothing to worry about."

"Sweet dreams, Hugh darling."

The silence had settled like still shallow water.

Half-asleep, smiling, "Sweet dreams, Peter Copland . . ."

Peter Copland, a little murderer condemned by his own unknowing crime.

Something in the jungle screamed and he cursed it for dying so noisily. Death should be silent. A scream was the announcement of nothing.

For minutes he slept and then woke to remember the day that was over but refused to give in to night, to sleep.

In four days he didn't seem to have accomplished much, though several changes were only too apparent on the air-strip. Ismail, finding a peaked cap somewhere, had forced it on his broad head to take on the appearance of a tram-driver rather than the temporary acting assistant manager of any-thing; but he himself, anyway, was impressed by it, and had gone scooting round the place doing his level best to justify his important position. The red paint had been delivered speedily, as it was never in short supply; a lucky colour to the Chinese, it was the basis for every commercial signboard in the town. The twenty-five tins of white paint had taken two days to arrive, but already the giant letters covered the entire flat roof of the building: PASAN. There had been a hasty conference to decide whether the still-wet paint should be washed away with petrol, and the complete name PASANG more carefully re-painted, or whether the G could be added in some manner. Paint and petrol being expensive and timber cheap, Ismail had supervised the erection of an extension to the roof, to accommodate the final G.

53

The fire-tender was now a smart yellow, and not red as ordered. But Wan Chai's mechanical dragon was a beautiful red instead of basic rust, which seemed to explain where the paint intended for the fire-vehicle had gone. The flags had been duly mounted on each emergency-tender but they were not aerodrome-yellow as instructed. They were in fact Malayan national flags and the emergency-crews were awfully pleased with them. Their colours being mostly white, red and yellow, Hugh didn't argue; at this time it seemed a good chance to encourage the national pride of this tiny land just now launched on the rough seas of self-rule, and the real purpose of the flags—which was to prevent any aircraft landing on top of the vehicles, not having noticed them—seemed as efficiently served. The overhead fans were turning again in most parts of the main building, after the over-confident Pakistani electrician had first short-circuited the entire system (already delicate) and burnt a hole in a timber ceiling big enough to take a manhole cover. Ismail had also fetched the man with the coconut-monkey as promised, and now the eight lofty palms stood fruitless above the corrugated iron roof. Nobody had blamed either man or monkey when a ripe coconut hurled down at random had gone clean through the skylight in Mr Chai's restaurant and left him standing in the midst of what looked very much like a bomb-outrage. Monkeys, like humans, claimed the right to err.

There was, for Hugh, at least the comfort of knowing that as he lay on the hard camp-bed unable to sleep there would be no sudden clap of doom from the metal roof above him.

The night was cool and he was glad of the sleeping-bag. The mosquitoes troubled him very little, because he had faith in the Paludrine he took each evening. Forearmed, he had reached a decision still of some courage: if a mosquito settled, he would let it drink its fill. Tomorrow Ismail would start shielding the long horizontal windows with fine metal gauze, a means of protection less claustrophobic than the closer confines of a mosquito-net over the bed.

He lay listening to the distant forest sounds and to the whining flight of the insects. Last night there had been a scuttling noise from somewhere inside the building, unmistakably that of rats fighting over the garbage from Wan Chai's restaurant. Traps had been set today, and poison put down in selected places.

This particular sound was so far absent, tonight.

Between sleep and wakefulness he was aware of the small affairs of the jungle night, his nerves now and again touched uneasily by a strange and unidentifiable animal voice, his eyes half-opening against the gloom and then slowly closing, his senses reassured; whatever death had come, it had not come to him.

For a while he slept.

Caesar Napoleon Alexander Montgomery ...

Her skin dark, not fair like the other one. *There are many doorways in Singapore* ... Forgive me ... It's not that I forget you ... Wherever you are don't feel jealous.

Do we know a Peter?

Little murderer, never loved.

But then, you are sad ... Voice so distant, like the voice of the night-owl ... *Hee-yoo* ... *Hee-yoo* ... Calling his name in the gloom, *Hee-yoo* ...

Movement, not sound, woke him. He opened his eyes. The sleep had drugged him but he felt it important that he should question the movement; but whatever had moved was still.

His eyelids were heavy and sore, but he couldn't close them; something prevented him as surely as a spoken order. He was required, by whatever animal mechanism it was that protected the defenceless, to remain wakeful, and now to pay attention to the slight sensation of pressure against his legs. A weight was on them, that had not been there before.

His scalp pricked. There was a scent on the air, the cheap scent of a whore, stale and musty. He had smelt it on the road at night ten miles south of Karachi two years ago, and his driver, working at the dead engine of the car and trying to get it to go again, had stopped work and said softly and urgently—"Cobra, sahib—cobra!"

The scent was in this room.

He mustn't move his legs. On a rough wooden box by the camp-bed—a present from Mr Chai, it had contained tinned milk—there lay his rubber-covered electric torch. Inching

55

his hand across the edge of the bed, he found its shape under his fingers. The sudden glare of the torch might provoke a strike but it had to be risked. He couldn't lie here in the dark and not know what it was on his legs.

Raising his left elbow to lift the edge of the sleeping-bag as a shield, and sighting along the bed an inch above it, he swung the torch slowly, and guessed the aim, and pressed the button. The glare blinded him and he brought his head down below the edge of the bag, his nerves so ready for a strike that his torch-hand seemed to feel it; but there was no strike. When his eyes had accommodated he raised his head little by little with the torch held as still as possible, its beam down the length of the bed.

They stared at each other. All hope of a false alarm was gone. It was a full-grown specimen, reared and with the hood spread, the small head pointed at the torch.

His first thought was irrelevant: he blamed himself for stupidity. Two days ago he had put a padlock on the plywood cupboard in the staff office where Walsh had collected some guns. If anyone wanted a gun, Hugh had told Ismail, they must ask him for it, and he would unlock the cupboard. In any emergency—a terrorist or tiger in the area—a good kick would split open the plywood door and the guns could be grabbed without waiting for a key or permission.

So the nearest gun was on the floor below this one. If he ever reached there he wouldn't need a gun. He would need the anti-venene from the first-aid room, and half a bottle of whisky.

There was no kind of weapon in this room, not even a knife, but he couldn't move anyway to fetch anything. The snake was a five-footer, half coiled and half-reared. From where it stood it could strike at his throat with ease. He braced his right elbow; the torch mustn't move.

The snake was dull gold in the glare of the torch, still and silent and beautiful, three feet from his face. It must have come to the building to take a rat and now sought the nearest warmth. How large was that brain, in that shining bullet-shaped head with the unwinking black-bead eyes? Too small for understanding; useless to hope to convey the simple message: curl up and sleep, share my warmth, I won't harm you if you don't harm me.

But for its light weight on his legs, only just felt through the padded sleeping-bag, Hugh would have thought it was a brass ornament put there for a joke, so still was it. The silence held the serpent and the man in a strange intimacy; even the jungle beyond the windows seemed to have grown quiet, so that the night could watch this one small world of light in the deeps of the greater dark.

If the cobra struck, he would probably cry out in fear and shock and revulsion just as other animals had cried out in the trees over there; man was pure beast when he had no weapon and must face nature on its own terms. Why hadn't the snake struck at the torch the instant he had switched it on? Because the light had blinded it. Why didn't it strike now, at any passing second? Because there was no threat, no movement, no sound. The snake stood like a spring, cocked and checked by the most sensitive mechanism: instinct. The man had only to move his hand suddenly to feel the fangs go in and the poison squeeze.

Movement was taking place: the hood was shrinking very gradually; in the tiny brain the alarm was dying. The light was perhaps hypnotic, or its faint warmth pleasing, a miniature sun for basking in.

How long would the battery last? Longer than his nerves would stand this strain or his muscles keep his right arm steady. It was already tiring. Beyond the curved gold snake its shadow stood against the wall from floor to ceiling; and now the shadow was swaying gently, the movement of the snake or torch or both exaggerated by projection. It was impossible to tell whether the snake swayed, bemused by the substitute sun, or the torch swayed a millimetre this way and that, so moving the shadow on the wall, or both swayed, the snake dancing to the silent rhythm of the light. But the hood was nearly closed. There was to be a reprieve.

Hugh judged the time at midnight or later: four or five hours to dawn. His nerves would last him another ten minutes at this pitch; already he was prey to the danger in his own subconscious that was bidding him consider—just

57

consider—the idea of hurling the torch at a venture so that the strain should end and the business go one way or the other. To throw the torch he must first draw it back and the fangs would bury in his wrist before he could complete the action.

He mustn't chance this. Anti-venene didn't always work. This could be death come for him, to sit with him for a little while in the pit of night, gold and beautiful and sure, and unimpatient. He must do what he could to arrange that if the snake struck, it would be by his own accident.

The sweat that was crawling from his temples had begun gathering, rivulets forming and trickling to his chin. His eyes were worried by sweat building up in their corners and they were already stinging. His whole face itched the worse because there was no hope of wiping the sweat away. His arm had gone almost numb; a few more minutes in this rigid position and he would lose its use. In his breathing there came the urge to shout, or laugh, as the nerves demanded release. His eyelids burned, for he blinked as slowly and infrequently as he could; the cobra was by now fully used to the light and might detect the bright of the man's eyes as they opened and closed, and turn its attention there. As the matador who fixes the mind of the bull on the cloth lure instead of the man's body, he must hold the cobra with the torch.

Suddenly alarmed he opened his eyes with an effort. They had closed and he realized this. They had been shut for some seconds. The light gleaming on the small gold head was hypnotizing him, just as the torch hypnotized the cobra. This was a dreadful joke—for the two of them to fall asleep in each other's company, a third force—the light—their master.

Cramp was coming into his legs and he longed to move them—to stretch his legs and ease the appalling strain in his right arm and scratch at his face and grind the exquisite torture of the sweat away with bunched knuckles, and go to the basin and bathe his face and slake the dried-up walnut-shell of his mouth with cool water. Even to take one deep breath . . . to shut his eyes and sleep unharmed . . . to be allowed to know some future beyond the veil of these shadows that hemmed him in with the gold and slender death-thing caught with him in the spell of the light. . . .

Whatever action he was to take, it had to be now, before his mind played tricks or the torch dropped from his numbed hand and provoked the strike from the dark. The human animal was too enfeebled by the way of life his over-developed brain had devised for him; unless that brain could cut and outwit, sharper than claw and fang, he was defenceless against this primitive creature that, limbless, could only crawl, yet could remain still, and silent, and prepared, untroubled by the creep of sweat, the grip of cramp, the fatigue of muscle, the loss of nerve. Unhampered by any emotion or the pressures of reasoning, instinctively designed to react with the speed of a whip, it was controlled by a simple equation: any moving thing that threatened it must be struck at in the instant. It was the incarnation of a discipline.

Watching the great curved shadow on the wall he began straightening his right arm by millimetres, moving the torch —the bright lure—farther from his body. As he moved it he turned his wrist by infinite degrees to lower the beam of light and, with it, the snake's head.

Slight though his movement was, it was detected. Against the wall the shadow of the hood was spreading again.

A mosquito had settled on one of his eyelids and was sucking the blood after anaesthetizing the skin. After a while it lifted groggily and its faint sound stretched across the silence like a thread. The whole of his face itched as the sweat crept; tears had run from the corner of one eye to leave a track of stiff dry salt on the skin. The other eye now began watering. The strain of focusing on the small head for minutes at a time—the strain of simply looking at his enemy—was going to beat him, because this enemy could stare all night and never tire.

The saliva had thickened in his mouth and each time he swallowed it was an effort, and audible: once, the snake's head had swung sideways to look for the sound and he had just let his red eyes close: but there was no strike. He almost wished there had been. He was ready now: let the thing strike, bury the fangs and squeeze, and then glide away, to let him free of the sleeping-bag so that he could go down and make a cross-cut and pack the cystals in, and make the injection, and start on the whisky, and wait, and wait, to know the findings of the jungle law that ruled him now. But while his will faltered and the room shrank and expanded every time he blinked, half-blinded now by strain alone, his arm and hand continued automatically to defend his body by keeping to the plan his brain had devised. The torch was lowering, tilting; the beam slanted at a greater angle; and the small gold head was an inch above the coils, the hood retracted.

The thing wasn't asleep. It was part-hypnotized, part-basking in the glare and warmth of the light. Almost, it looked harmless, a gleaming coil of scales, beautiful as a crown, lifeless, never to move again.

If he were going to get away with it, he had to try now. The head had sunk to touch the highest coil and lie upon it. He drew a long slow breath and then dragged at the torch with a numbed arm and brought the edge of the bag up as a shield while the hiss of anger sounded and the snake attacked at whip-speed, head and fangs hitting the padded bag and hitting again before he could draw up his legs and kick upwards, his sob of fear loud in the stifling heat of the bag as he kicked again and heard the dry scuttering of the thing hitting the floor with the sound of a necklace thrown there.

The torch was still on and he flung back the edge of the bag and swept the beam across the floor. The snake was near the open window on the north side, the jungle side, and when he struggled out of the sleeping-bag and lurched towards the door it reared again full-hooded; but he knew it was on the defence now and would wait.

His breath rasped in the stillness as he stood looking at the cobra, safe from it, for all its deadly attitude. Then he opened the door, the sharp rattle of the handle bringing a hiss of challenge. Backing through the doorway, keeping the thing fixed in the beam of light, he felt the cold concrete of the passage under his bare feet, and pulled the door shut, and went shambling down the stairs and out into the open air, and gave himself up to the violent relief of the vomiting.

* 7 *

"I HAVE been expecting you, Mistah Copland."

Sandalwood was sweet in the air: a joss-stick was burning in the inside room through the rattan screen.

"Why?" Hugh asked suspiciously.

"Because I knew it was an expeliment." The sallow-yellow face made a grimace half-smile and half-sadness: experiments were laudable but not always successful. Thus were Hugh's five lonely nights at the airstrip dismissed. "The looms ah twenty-five dollahs a month, with five hundled dollahs tea-money."

"Too much."

"But you have not seen the looms, Mistah Copland!"

"I means it's more than I want to pay, even for a palace."

"Yes," nodded Mr Loo, "I undahstand. Let us go to see the looms now." He seemed very good at dismissing the inconvenient. Hugh finished the cold flower-smelling tea and put the bowl down carefully on the lacquered table. Both looked priceless. Perhaps, if the two rooms were furnished in this fashion, and there were hot water . . .

Swaying along in the ricksha beside Mr Loo it suddenly occurred to him that he was among people again. It had been a mistake to sleep out there on the airstrip. He had done it to annoy that fool Walsh, really. If Walsh had said reasonably: "Well, you can kip down there if you like, of course, but you'll find it a bit uncomfortable," he would probably have answered: "Perhaps you're right. I'll find somewhere in the town." Even without the cobra he wouldn't have stuck it more than another few nights, because of the loneliness. In the daytime a man could work by himself or with a hundred others, it made no difference; it was in the evening that he needed company.

Besides, the airstrip had been deserted by humans for years in the hours of darkness and one might just as well bed down in the thick of the jungle; creatures were used to roaming about the building by night, unmolested by man. It was a wonder there hadn't been a tiger in his bed.

Now there were people around him in the hot glow of the evening, and as the ricksha went trundling past them they saw Mr Loo and saluted him with gestures according to their status. He seemed to be quite important in the town, and Hugh took comfort in the knowledge that if for five hundred dollars plus twenty-five a month he was being taken for a ride in this ricksha, then it was by a big-shot.

Passing the Rest House and then the coffee-shop where the proprietor had given him that big hello the day he had arrived in Pasang, he almost fell out of the ricksha trying to see if the man were in his doorway. Someone waved.

"Already you have many friends here," smiled Mr Loo, his ivory hand ready to grab at him in case he looked like pitching out.

"Oh, one or two."

"You will have many more, Mistah Copland, before the moon is new."

Such was the reward of being seen beside this important personage even for a few minutes through the streets. Or did it follow that if you have five hundred dollars to blow on the tumble-down shack to which they were obviously being taken at such a rate, you would surround yourself with many friends? He was getting as cynical as Walsh. Mr Loo meant that the people of Pasang were warm of heart.

The Tamil ricksha-boy went swerving between other rickshas and bamboo hand-barrows and groups of children who broke up and fluttered and leapt as the rickshas charged at them in a mutually-enjoyable game halfway between last-across and a bullfight. The close air was shrill with voices, bells and gongs and the piping of some instrument where a beggar played, and from open windows came the stony clatter of mah-jongg pieces where the merchants sat at their game.

A voice was suddenly raised higher than any other in the tone used for stopping a runaway horse, and the ricksha gave a backward tilt as the Tamil forced it to a standstill. A hairy brown torso appeared from the jostling people and the face above it said: "Hello, Copland! If you can, eat with me tonight, say around an hour from now—all right?"

"All right." The answer was an automatic reflex. "Where do I—"

"Anyone knows!"

And they were off again, weaving through the streets at top speed.

"Who was that, Mr Loo?"

"That was Joe, Mistah Copland."

"Who is he?"

"He is Joe." A gentle smile of apology spread the creases across the yellow face, the skin crumpling like paper. "It is all we know."

The ricksha lurched so badly across a monsoon-gutter that they had to grip the sides, and Hugh said no more.

"There is my house," announced Mr Loo, and they stopped at the entrance to a small leaf-filled courtyard between a rattan-shop and a Chinese restaurant whose proprietor was already trying to usher them across the ledge of pavement and inside. Mr Loo declined the invitation in a volley of crackling Cantonese, taking his client up a flight of stairs and showing him the rooms, one of which overlooked the courtyard. The other had one small gauze-covered window facing what seemed to be a blank blue-washed wall. Going closer to it, Hugh realized it was the sea.

The room was quiet and smelled of cedarwood, and the heat of the day was still in it; a stray beam of the sun's last light touched a patch of the peeling wall, where an insect beat and droned at the plaster. He looked round in the lowering light at a bamboo bed and chair. A camphor-wood chest with one drawer missing; a table riddled with worm-holes and on it a faded copy of the *Straits Times*; a kind of sea-chest with dragons painted on it, red on black; there was nothing more.

"I'll take the rooms, Mr Loo."

"It is five hundled dollahs tea-money, and the lent is—"

"You told me."

A hell of a price, with the worm-holes and the gap in the

64

camphor-wood chest and the peeling plaster walls; but they were all small things compared with the deep and abiding knowledge already in him like a kind of warmth, that here was home.

Before dark he drove back to the airstrip in the Land-Rover and collected his gear, taking a good look into every room before going in. Haji Ahmad had left the transmitter switched on and one of the fans was still turning in the customs room. Rats were already in for the feasting behind the walls of Wan Chai's restaurant. There were quite a few vacancies here on the staff: a monkey to keep the coconuts cleared, a cat for the rats, a mongoose for the cobras. One good half-wild cat might do two jobs; the snakes wouldn't come here for the rats if they were cleared out first.

Standing in the silence of the staff office he was glad not to be sleeping here tonight. The loneliness of the place was deepened by smells; if no one had ever been here it wouldn't seem so lonely, but men had been here and had now gone, deserting it, leaving it to the night and the jungle as a crew would leave a sinking ship to the devouring sea. Their smells lingered, of Bengal cheroots and betel-juice. It was difficult to believe they would come here again tomorrow and the day after. One could more easily believe that nobody would ever come here again.

He went outside and checked the doors and the shutters of the restaurant. Going across to the hangars in the pale milk light of a hazy moon he stopped now and then to listen, to decide on a sound and place it: a rat, an owl's call from the jungle mists. The rank undergrowth soured the air.

His footsteps were sharp-sounding along the concrete walkway and the huge hangar doors echoed them. Once, he stopped suddenly, cunningly, to ensure the last echo died. It had seemed certain there were other footsteps following his. Now there was silence. By now he should be used to the place at night, yet his nerves were uneasy and his imagination over-active. He longed for the streets of the town, for human company that he could see and talk with.

Something ran across his shoe and he kicked automatically, switching on the torch too late to see what it was. This was the jungle, here; the metal and concrete and glass meant nothing in the dark hours; the jungle moved in and held sway from sundown to dawn. He switched off the torch and turned back along the cement walkway that was still slippery from the afternoon's deluge and aftermath of mud. A shape was set against the background of the hangar doors, three or four feet high; he hadn't noticed it before. It was too narrow for a trolley-acc unit. He went to within a dozen yards of it, and stopped. In the pale light no detail showed; but the shape was of a man, seated, or kneeling. There was no sound.

It couldn't be a man, seated or kneeling. Nobody ever came to the airstrip at night. Yet, there seemed a head, and the angle of shoulders to the shadowy thing. He walked towards it, impatient with his own nerves. In the town it would be bright and noisy, and he wouldn't be alone, and there was his couple of shabby rooms, his home.

When he saw the face he jabbed his thumb on the torch-button and the face sprang from shadow into substance, its eyes narrowed in the light. The head was turbaned and the face bearded. The man was on his haunches, Hindu-fashion. He made no movement; an owl, disturbed in this way, would remain as still and would stare back like this.

On a long breath Hugh said in Hindi: "Who are you?"

"Subayya Jhabvala, sahib,"

"What are you doing here."

"I guard His Highness's air-machine, sahib."

The man's hands were folded in his robe; there might, or might not, be a weapon in them.

Hugh lowered the torch a little so that the man should be relieved of the glare, but focused the beam on his robe where the hands were hidden.

"It is safe. The big doors are locked."

"I guard the doors, sahib."

"On whose orders?"

"I am in the personal service of His Highness, such is the bounty of Allah."

"Then you have credentials."

One of the brown hands emerged from the robe with such

66

swift ease that Hugh would have had no chance if it had held a revolver. A small bone disc lay innocently on the palm and he took it. In the centre of a ring of Romanized Malay words was the etched seal of the Sultan, similar to the rubber-stamp seals on most of the official forms in the staff office. From the few words he could understand, their purport was to the effect that any person molesting the bearer would be taken before the Sultan, whose personal servant the bearer was.

He passed back the disc. "Do you station yourself in this place every night, Subayya Jhabvala?"

"I do, sahib."

"Why did you not challenge me before I approached so close?"

"I had knowledge of your noble identity, Copland-sahib."

"No one informed me that a guard was placed here. As manager of the airport I should have been informed, do you not agree?"

"I agree, sahib."

"If I am to administer this airport properly, I must be acquainted with all facts concerning it. Is that not so?"

"It is so, Copland-sahib."

If the man had been here during the last five nights he'd never seen him. "I am very angry, Subayya Jhabvala."

"The sahib's wrath diminishes me."

The dark lined face remained calm. It was the face of an undiminishable spirit.

"I think it is not your blame. I will report this to the Palace at once. The fault lies there, with the men of papers, whose duty it was to inform me."

A grave nod accepted the exoneration. Hugh brought the torch lower and stepped back. It crossed his mind to warn the man that there were cobras in this deserted place at night; he then realized his stupidity. The Hindu probably had one for a pet.

"Allah be with thee," he said.

"And by thy side, sahib."

Climbing into the Land-Rover, Hugh sent it bouncing

67

along the swamp-and-jungle track to the town with his anger mounting. There was no need of a guard on the airstrip—the hangars were securely locked and no one would ever come here, even to steal or sabotage, in the dark. If the Sultan felt there should be a guard placed near his personal aircraft he should have told the new manager; there was nothing in the maintenance regulations of the airport about it. He would write a letter to the Sultan tonight.

The hazy glow of the town lights calmed him a little. As it had been with Walsh, fear had begot anger. The sight of the shadowy human shape and then the seeming leap of the face in the torchlight had rattled him; afterwards there had been the embarrassment of realizing that while he had spent five bitterly lonely and uncomfortable nights out there on sleep-watch, there had been someone else doing the job much better and wide awake. Further: the man might even have taken him for a marauder and sent a knife at him from the dark.

Children were still playing in the streets; they seemed never to go home or to school. The mah-jongg games were now being played along the pavements, and a silent group of old men stood round a board in the little courtyard of Mr Loo's house watching the four who played. None of them looked up when Hugh passed them with his baggage. Three women—two young Malays and their waddling mother—came jostling down the stairs and he waited for them; their twittering speech was cut short as they saw him in the light of the high iron lamp above the door, but as soon as he offered a "good evening" in impeccable Malay they answered in a little pleased chorus and went trotting and swinging through the courtyard with giggling backward glances. Did they live here too?

Standing to watch for a minute the butterfly figures of the three women, and the men absorbed by the clicking of the ivory pieces, he wondered how he had managed to stick it out for five whole nights at the airstrip.

He turned into the shadowed doorway and tackled the stairs with the baggage, one case at a time because they were so narrow. In his room he dumped them and eased the straps,

68

thinking: how does one write to a sultan, in righteous anger?

Joe might know. It was nearly two hours since that odd invitation had been called to him from the crowded street, as casually as a card skimmed at random through the air. Now among people, it would be good to talk with one of them in his own language. Where did Joe live? "Anyone knows!" Joe had said with careless conceit.

Bathing his face in cool water and changing his shirt he went down to the courtyard and into the smell of coffee and salt fish and drains and the fragrant cassia tree whose special smell was already to him the smell of home. In the street he asked the first young Malay he saw—"Can you tell me where Joe lives?"

The boy nodded quickly. "Come—I will take you, tuan!"

So it was true. From anywhere in the Peninsula you could just write on the envelope: Joe, Pasang.

He followed the boy through the street and the lingering warmth of the day. High over the sea to the east the haze was thinning around the moon, and stars were showing. From the sea a warm wind blew across the beach and coast road to swirl among the streets of the town. His own figure became part of the pattern of colour in the narrow kaleidoscope of the street, and he realized this, mentally standing still by the cross-roads where the fortune-teller had her mat and table, and seeing himself from a distance, going his way among the crowd, no longer a stranger.

He lived here now and the smell of the cassia tree was the smell of home; he hurried with the dark-skinned boy who was taking him to the house of his host for the evening; and with the touch of the salt wind on his face and the feel of the warm stones under his feet he outstripped the loneliness at last. He belonged, like Joe, to Pasang.

8

FROM the windows on the left side the passengers could see the storm that had broken inland over the jungle. Cunim had built up to close on thirty thousand feet during the heat of the morning and now, in mid-afternoon, the rainstorm made a grey-black smudge against the jungle. From this distance the great mass of water looked motionless.

Pasang lay fifteen miles ahead to the north. The S. and P.A. Dakota was not routed to land there, but the pilot had already brought the aircraft down to six thousand feet, because a minute ago the starboard engine had cut again and for the third time, its steady drone fractionally interrupted.

The stewardess made her way along the aisle, taking her time, her gold-brown beautifully-groomed hands touching the seat-squabs, her cool smile instantly reassuring.

"Are we in trouble?" one of the Australians asked. He sat hunched in his seat, huge hands on his lap, his grizzled head tilted up at her. He did this trip, Singapore-Bangkok, a hundred times a year and he had seen too many cool smiles to be taken in by them. They were very good to see, but not when there was a missing motor. You couldn't fix a fuel-pipe airlock or a sooty rotor with a smile.

"It is nothing serious, Mr Broadlea." She knew all their names.

"When you've asked the skipper, just let me know what he says, there's a good kid."

She passed on, pausing to bend over a child and wrinkle her small nose at it, telling it something in crisp smiling Chinese while the Australian abstractedly admired the stooped line of her body in the white drill uniform and forgot, for a moment, the three interruptions in the engine's drone.

Captain Chong and the navigator were in their seats when

she slid back the cabin door and slipped through the narrow opening, giving them a big smile with her profile in sight of the passengers before she closed the door. Chong looked up at her, his face bland.

"We will be going in to Pasang," he said.

"Shall I tell them?"

"Yes. Not the slightest cause for alarm." He watched the weather ahead, throttling back another notch. The forward window was half blue, half green, and now the horizon lifted as the machine settled, and the green rose against the window while on the port side the purple cone of Gunong Tahan's peak began towering, its dark solidity afloat in the jungle mist.

"Fasten seat-belts, Captain Chong?"

"Not till the signal. Normal landing procedure."

She went back to the passengers. The navigator began calling up Pasang tower from ten miles out. The throttles were eased another notch and the machine settled. There had been no sound of a miss in either engine for nearly four minutes.

"What's he say, girlie?"

"There's nothing seriously wrong, Mr Broadlea. We are landing at Pasang."

"That doesn't add up, does it?"

"I am sure it does, sir, to an experienced traveller like yourself. Excuse me, please." She reached the aft locker and made sure that all movable gear was secured for landing. Captain Chong's voice came over the speaker, in Chinese:

"In a few minutes we shall be landing at Pasang. I am sorry to interrupt our schedule but as I expect you may have noticed there is a very slight fault in one motor. It should not take long to rectify. Will you please now fasten your seat-belts and put out cigarettes as usual. Thank you."

He repeated in English. The green warning-panel lit up. Again the machine settled, and everything became heavy-seeming. The sound died. All seemed still, as if the aircraft had come to a gentle halt in the air, becalmed, until the sea and beach and swamp filled the oval windows and a line of palm trees went rushing past like a soft green flock of ostriches. On the left the town was suddenly below, a tumbled pattern of white and brown cleft with the cracks of the streets. Gaudy birds flew up from the mangrove swamps and wheeled away from the plane's invisible path.

Vibration began, trembling in the seats, the floor, the roof. A child whimpered. Then the trembling eased and the long cabin tilted and suddenly the surface of the earth was touched, and lost, and touched again as the balance was found and the tail-wheel shared the weight. The brakes came on.

Chong and his navigator were surprised to see a crowd of people on the concrete apron as the machine swung in to the marker. The crash- and fire-tenders were swerving in from each side and a green flare went sizzling up from the control-tower roof, minutes late but most impressive. Ismail met them as they climbed out of the machine but before he could speak to them he had to turn and shout orders to the fire-crew who were dragging at the extinguisher-hoses and setting up the valves—"No! Back now! Everything all right —no fire!"

Captain Chong stood looking slightly bewildered, his brief-case dangling. "What is the panic, Ismail?"

"We were making sure! You called up about the engine-trouble!"

The crash-tender went swerving back to the sheds and left a wash of dust across the little group of passengers on their way to the building.

"Where is Mister Copland?" asked Chong.

"Not here!"

"I see." He had suspected it. This was the Temporary Acting Assistant Manager's own personal response to the crisis. Another green flare went up and the passengers halted and gazed skywards in admiration.

"No more!" yelled Ismail to the figure on the control-tower roof. "Haji Ahmad! All finish now!" By the answering gestures it seemed that the mortar had jammed, and the last flare had been more or less accidental.

Chong told the two mechanics: "The starboard motor cut slightly three times in ten minutes at cruising speed, altitude nine thousand, and we had fluctuating boost. Everything normal otherwise."

"Were the passengers frightened?" Ismail wanted to know. He had been reading up the airline general manual as a self-imposed duty. "At all times," it had informed him, "the comfort, safety and well-being of the passengers must be the paramount consideration of flight-crews and airport staff."

"I don't think many of them would even have noticed the trouble, Ismail. We were all quite happy." He was looking at the sky to the south; the tall thunderheads they had seen over the ocean when they had taken-off from Singapore were now towering and darkening in a yellow sky and had moved in towards the Peninsula. The air was already oppressive.

"How long will you need?" Ismail called urgently to the mechanics.

"How can we know that?" They flung up their hands. The airstrip had been a much quieter place before Ismail's promotion; there was a spider's web across the mah-jongg board this morning in the workshop.

Chong said to Ismail: "If they can't fix the trouble within the next hour we shan't be taking off again before tomorrow morning."

"But the passengers! They will be—"

"Show them the sky, Ismail." He tucked his brief-case under his arm and went into the building. The customs room was like a hen-house with a fox in it, as usual.

Will you have your passports, landing-cards and health-certificates ready please?

But we are going to Bangkok! We do not wish to be here! Our tickets do not say Pasang! When shall we ever get to Bangkok where our wives and husbands and children and all our friends are awaiting us?

They surged and revolved in the heat of the echoing room, castaways of the air, while from the doorway of his restaurant Wan Chai watched them with a shining hospitable smile.

There were bowls of small Chinese oranges on the black carved table, but they sat with tea as they talked. Mr Chai was honoured to have as his guest a captain of the airline; Captain Chong was most honoured in all the restaurant, for its proprietor was his host.

"Will Mr Copland prove troublesome, do you think, elder brother?"

Wan Chai appealed with his eyes to the cold charred joss-stick for an answer. "We will need to take more care, Lee Kwei, than we did with Mr Walsh."

"Then we will take more care."

"When will you visit my brother at the plantation?"

"Tonight." Chong leaned his elegant elbows on the edge of the table, a cigarette in his long ivory fingers just touching his lips. "If he wishes."

"He is very uneasy, Lee Kwei. He trusts no one."

"To live, one has to trust."

"But to transgress, there is a price on trust. What is the trouble with the aeroplane?"

Lee Kwei Chong gazed a few inches above the hairless skull of his host. "The trouble with the aeroplane, elder brother, is that it was due in Bangkok this evening, whereas I am due at Loy Lin Chai's plantation, in Pasang."

"But the mechanics will find nothing wrong with the machine."

"It always takes much longer to find nothing than to find something. The storm will be here before they give up their search."

Wan Chai seemed as uneasy as his brother of the plantation. It had been the war that had made him as old as this so quickly. When Lee Kwei Chong had first seen this man, stumbling down the rocky foothill of Gunong Tahan with his dead son in his arms and his wife following crouched and swaying in grief and the riddling patter of bullets in the air from the Japanese patrol among the scrub, Wan Chai had been twenty-five years old. Now he looked sixty, seventeen years later, and he had given two of his sons and a brother to the cause of war, each time trying to protect them and readier than they to die. This was his tragedy; that he still lived.

Of the three secret societies in the Chinese community of

74

Pasang, one had only four members: Wan Chai, his brother Loy Lin Chai, Cheng Loo of the house in Jalan Burong where Copland was living, and Lee Kwei Chong himself. They were all that had been left, in 1945, of the anti-Japanese guerilla force operating in Tamarah during the occupation. The bond that had been between them then was between them still; it had been their word. But the times had not been easy since the war for men to keep faith in sworn things; the Communist terrorists had infested the jungle clearings the moment the Japanese had left. In Pasang itself there were families with a son or brother living inland, a member of the secret army that awaited orders from Pekin.

Trust had less value now. One learned to conceal even trivial transgression.

Wan Chai sat talking with Lee Kwei Chong in the silk-screened alcove of his private room, worried by the need to gain dishonestly in life, consoled only by the certainty that he would be worried more by loss.

Chong left him with a word of reassurance. "If your brother is willing for the merchant to see the prospects, the merchant can be shown. If your brother is not willing, no one will speak. We shall risk nothing."

Wan Chai lit the charred end of the joss-stick. "He who goes often into the forest must one day meet a tiger." A curl of smoke moved upwards from the sandalwood, grey and aromatic. "I have one package for you, Lee Kwei. Two katis and a half."

Chong nodded. "I smelt it when I came in. We should soak the wrapping in strong cheap perfume. Give it to me just before take-off in the morning."

"Where will it be going?"

"To Bangkok, then to Hong Kong by the next plane."

"Do you trust the one in Bangkok?"

Chong smiled. "I trust all men, elder brother, and all men trust me."

9

FROM the verandah they could see men tapping the rubber. The trees ran in neat ranks, the only order in an area of swamp and jungle scrub. In the far distance towards the town there floated a wash of virgin green where the young rice grew.

Driving in along the track from the main Burong Road, Hugh had seen the Ford saloon standing outside one of the attap-roofed outhouses; the front tyre was renewed and the shattered windscreen replaced, but the bullet-scars were still there.

It was Joe who had told him he should call on the Duffys.

"You should call in on everybody," Joe had said. "Even Thorne."

"Who is Thorne?"

"We-ell, you just go see him. He won't like it, but afterwards he'll be glad."

Joe lived in the top of a well-built Malay house at the other end of Jalan Burong, alone but for the wah-wah monkey. They were rather alike, Joe and his monkey, except that the man's eyes were brilliant blue and full of some philosophy he had found and was going to keep to himself, not from avarice but a sense of privacy, and the monkey's eyes were bottle-brown and luminous with a light of innocence even at moments of rich mischief, such as when he had carefully dropped a lump of Joe's modelling clay into a full cup of coffee from ceiling height.

Joe's main room was crowded with examples of his work, attempts at the Asiatic style that didn't quite deceive. With Hugh he shared a confection of his own preparation, a curry with salt-fish strips, banana-shoots and a delicate pink fungus served on a huge green tanya-leaf for a plate, "to save the washing-up. As a special guest you're lucky. Next time you eat here it'll be with chopsticks. I can give you a complete breakdown on my own time-and-motion analysis of just how much longer it takes to wash a three-pronged fork than one chopstick." Later, when they were drinking pitch-black coffee and keeping one eye on the rafter where the wah-wah was perched with something ready to bomb-aim with, Joe said: "At least you've met Stratton. That's a start."

"I said a couple of words to him, that's all. What's his background?"

"Blank. You met Duffy, too. What about Smith?"

"No. Who is he?"

"We don't know very much about him. Right now he's in Singapore, they tell me. But see the Duffys anyway." He cut deep into his melon with an ivory paper-knife. "Then there's Thorne's wife. Lovely kid. When you meet Mrs Thorne you want to meet Mr Thorne too, same time. I mean, keep it nice and social, everybody happy."

"I don't quite—"

"Can't really advise you on this letter you aim to send to the *istana*. Duffy's the man to put you right, though. See him. He got up from his bamboo stool and wandered away to the window with the tanya-leaf crockery, looking, from behind, like a native of the place with his sarong and leather-brown shoulders. He dropped the leaves out of the window and wandered back. "I have some chickens right below. Are you interested in anthropology, I mean in a homely kind of way?"

"In a homely way I'm interested in most things."

Leaving the house before midnight and walking right down the deserted Jalan Burong to Mr Loo's house, Hugh remembered it had been the only question Joe had asked about him—the reference to anthropology. Though he had talked most of the time, the subject was always the same: Pasang. "Every man has his true element, it doesn't matter where he was born. This is mine. I guess I was late finding it but I'm making up fast."

Joe was somewhere about forty, Hugh judged. Despite his immediate invitation on seeing him in the ricksha, and his lengthy description of the town, he had a reserve about him that was like an extra skin. The only man he had suggested anything bad about was Smith. Clearly he liked the Duffys. Clearly he thought that Hugh as a newcomer should go the rounds leaving his card; that was partly why he had, this afternoon, driven out here to the rubber estate after supervising the last aircraft movement of the day at four o'clock. He also wanted to put his mind at rest about the letter he had sent by bearer to the palace. From this distance it was beginning to read rather terse, and for all he knew the Sultan of Tamarah might simply order his deportation on the next plane out.

"I can't tell you," Duffy said as they sat on the long verandah, "what his reaction would be. We don't see very much of him. The Resident's been gone, of course, nearly three years. He would have handled it right. Comyns-Edge —did you ever meet him?"

"No. This is the first—"

"A wonderful man. Everyone still talks about him in the town. Keep Elspeth off the subject; she burns incense to that man's idol." Elspeth, a clear-eyed buxom woman with the whole history of the place in her heart, was still within earshot mending a mosquito-net in the room they had taken tea in. There had been sponge fingers and Crawford's Regency biscuits and a silver teapot, the whole ceremony straight out of Tunbridge Wells, with the thermometer on the wall at a rising hundred and seven degrees and the weight of the air as burdensome as a heavy coat.

"Mr Comyns-Edge was the most human, the most intelligent, the most wise and altogether the greatest man I ever met," Elspeth's bland tones reached them through the verandah doors. "Except for Arthur."

Arthur Duffy turned his pale blue eyes on Hugh. "Tell me if you can hear me all right. This pedestal's some little height."

"Loud and clear, Mr Duffy." He wanted to ask a good many questions but hesitated to disturb the deep spell of tranquillity here. Duffy had worked as usual through the last five days with his arm in a sling, and was still pale under the ginger freckles. It must have occurred to him many times during those days that all this had nearly ended for

78

him. At this moment he seemed lost in the insect-drone that served for silence, but said suddenly: "Elspeth and I hope you'll like it here in Pasang. Don't take any notice of the atmosphere; it'll pass off when the people have forgotten the ambush."

"I didn't notice any atmosphere. Are they worried?"

"Uneasy. We hear news from the other coast and up north near the border, but this was the first time things came close."

"How significant was the ambush, Mr Duffy?"

"Well, we don't know. As far as the Peninsula goes, this is in the front line of the Communist battle in Asia. If it all blows up in Laos or anywhere else, nothing can save us. At any time Pekin can order a real marshalling of jungle forces here and they won't stop at ambushing. I think this was just an isolated incident, not a planned attack on a particular person, like Gurney up near the Cameron Highlands. This bit of coast is different and we don't get much trouble. The people here are worried as much by the tiger as the ambush and they won't breathe easy till it's shot."

"They told me it had gone."

"Sometimes people say what they hope, laddie. He'll be around here for a while unless they can shift him. He's a lone male, working to a pattern of his own. The nearest female is fifteen miles away, north, but she might call him up there if we're lucky. Yesterday he took three rubber tappers—not mine—on the other side of the ridge. As soon as this arm's got some feeling back in it I'm joining up with the jungle-police for a couple of days. We're short of a rug in the dining-room."

Elspeth's voice was hardly lifted but it carried authority: "You'll buy one in Singapore the next time you go there, Arthur."

"They're too expensive! You always say it's the most wonderful thing in the world to live off the land."

"But not to die on it. Offer Mr Copland a drink, please."

"I must be going," said Hugh.

"Stay for a s'tenggah." He shouted for the house-boy. "As soon as you can, we hope you'll join us here for a meal in the evening. When the sun gets low, and you sit just here where we are now, you can see the shadows of those rubber trees start playing tricks—you know those advertisement panels you see everywhere in Singapore, like shutters—"

"They seem to move as you walk past?"

"That's right." He looked up at the house-boy who was in the doorway. "S'tenggahs, Iakob. Lime-juice for Mem." He leaned towards Hugh, gazing across to the columns of his thousand rubber trees. "That's what happens, then, with the sundown light. As each shadow of a tree falls on the tree behind, it goes dark; then the shadow falls between the two behind, and they're light again. When dusk comes, the whole plantation seems to vanish, then come back, and disappear again." He eased himself in the chair to comfort his arm. "I hope it never does."

They sat with their whisky and Elspeth came out to join them. The sun was reaching down to the peak of the great mountain and in the heat even desultory talking became an effort, as they listened to the incessant lifting and falling of the insect-drone. For a few minutes they thought the lower cello-note was made by a dragonfly somewhere above their heads; then Duffy said:

"There's an aircraft. Hear it?"

Hugh got up, and the sudden effort brought sweat running down his sides. "Yes." He stared at the sky eastwards and in a moment saw the plane coming in low across the sea and the town. "Can I use your phone?"

"Iakob! Show visitor-tuan telephone now please!"

Hugh followed the boy through the long Western-furnished room and after a lot of crackling and buzzing was through to the airstrip. "Haji Ahmad, what is that aircraft?"

"It has trouble, sahib, with an engine, but not grave. We are all prepared and Assistant Manager Ismail is making the precautions. I will send green flare now. The book says that in event of aircraft making emergency landing—"

"What trouble, Ahmad? What did they radio?"

"Slight trouble in starboard engine, sahib, request permission to land. I will now send—"

"What machine is it? Straits Airways?"

"No, sahib. If I do not soon send—"

"Listen, Ahmad, when you have seen the aircraft in, speak again to me. I will not leave the telephone—understand?"

"Understand, sahib."

Hugh put the receiver on to the table and went to the open window, watching the machine turn out of the circuit and begin its final approach, black against the saffron sky.

Duffy called to him—"Everything all right, laddie?"

"Yes, thanks."

Watching the plane settle and drift across the fringe of mangroves four miles away north and east he felt a sudden affection for Haji Ahmad and Assistant Manager Ismail, who were obviously well on their toes. Despite their will to co-operate with him after that first stirring-up, he would never have let them bring an aircraft in on their own until the new routine had become a habit with them. Now they were doing it in an emergency, however slight.

The dark shape floated for another half-minute above the mangroves and then sank from sight. He went back to the telephone and waited for Ahmad, but when he put the receiver to his ear he could hear the line had been closed by the exchange. It wasn't worth asking for a reconnection. He went out to the verandah. "I'm sorry about that."

"Walsh wouldn't have bothered."

Hugh finished his whisky. There was no further sound of the aircraft; she was down.

"If you'll forgive me, I'll get over there. Like most people with small authority, I'm over-zealous."

They watched in surprise the green flare that curved suddenly above the mangroves.

"Bit late, isn't it?" asked Duffy.

"I haven't got the monopoly of over-zealousness."

He said goodbye to Elspeth. She said with a smile as real as a queen-mother's: "I know your stay in Pasang will be a very happy one." To Duffy she said: "Now do mind that arm, Arthur. It's septic weather."

He nodded at this obviously habitual injunction and went down to the Land-Rover with Hugh. "I see you don't carry a gun, by the way. Why's that?"

81

Hugh started the engine. "To be quite honest, it's because Walsh advised me to."

"You can pay high for a prejudice, laddie. The next time you come here I want to see your gun, and if you don't have it with you, you can bloody well go and fetch it." He gave Hugh a grip of his good hand and waved him away.

The yellow light shone into the trees on each side of the track, and before Hugh had gone a hundred yards it was tinged with green and he turned to look north. It was a second flare. Putting his foot down he judged that if he could reach the airstrip within fifteen minutes there was a chance of saving about half his stock of them.

He had not seen the crew and passengers at the airstrip, because a pothole in Duffy's track had sent him into soft ground—driving too fast, he had delayed himself. Now he followed them into the town. Nobody seemed to be about; there was no hubbub of voices and mah-jongg, no radios squawking from the wide-opened shutters.

The mueddin was calling the sunset prayer. Tonight it was not obligatory—because it was not Friday—for the faithful to go to the mosque; even so, many would have been willing, if it weren't for the colour of that sky. They might reach the mosque without a drenching, but it looked certain they would never get home again dry. It was a dilemma. Allah might resent the implication that his praises were worthy of being sung only in dry weather; on the other hand he in his great wisdom should realize that even the best believer would find it hard to sing at all if he were dying of pneumonia. They stood in quiet groups, watching the sky. The wail of the mueddin ran through the narrow streets, lost as a soul in a strange place.

Some boys were on the ground where Hugh parked the Land-Rover, solemnly playing main-choki, looking up and grinning a greeting to him by name, pleasing him. Copland of Pasang. Care of Joe of Pasang. Following Duffy's advice, he had picked up a revolver at the airstrip, but left it in the car; he was damned if he was going to tout it round with him on his hip. Even Walsh hadn't gone that far.

"I have come to make sure my passengers are comfortable." he told the Malay manager of the Rest House.

"But they are in luxury, tuan Coplan'!"

"Ah yes, that is so." The Rest House smelt of haunting old church smells: dry rot and the work of woodworm; but it wasn't, at least, a brothel, and it had electricity. "But they may not have overnight things, you see, and we would like to help them."

"You will find them in the restaurant." He couldn't bring himself even to name the restaurant, of which there were a dozen in this street alone. Any guest at the Rest House who did not wish to eat the sumptuous fare provided could, if he chose, visit some less luxurious establishment, which should rightly be nameless.

"I expect they wish to see the town, Mr Sahgal. It is an opportunity for them."

He went back through the hall and stood for a moment listening to the voice of the mueddin. It wasn't a good voice, being pitched too high and forced; but its purpose was to carry the words and not to grace them, which would be most presumptuous.

One of the half-naked boys looked up from the main-choki board and saw Hugh standing in the doorway of the Rest House.

"Big storm come, tuan!" He clapped brown hands across black head and cried—"Ai-ya!"

"May come, may not." Hugh looked along the cleft of sky between the buildings; the yellow was darkening but the great thunderheads had sailed inland. With any luck Pasang would be on the fringe of the storm. The stranded passengers would at least have this much fortune.

Somewhere in the Rest House a piano had begun playing and he went back through the hall to listen, for it was a French tune, something that Edith Piaf had sung last year. Thinking it might be one of the passengers who was not hungry or who had stayed here to enjoy the solitude, he traced the sound and opened the door of the bar. It wasn't a passenger, but the stewardess of the aircraft, her dark hands drifting across the keyboard, Santha May Swee.

THEY went to a restaurant right at the other end of the main street, Jalan Burong, because three of the passengers were Europeans and Mr Broadlea, now pleased with the enforced break in their journey, was trying to organize an all-night party with the drinks on him. It was almost a shame to disappoint him.

The restaurant was in the building next to Joe's house and the people eating there were nearly all Chinese and less noisy than Malays. When they had sat down Hugh said:

"I wrote to you, when I arrived in Pasang." The little bowls of sauce began coming on to the table like rain-puddles forming. "Did you ever get the letter?"

"Yes. I was going to answer it."

"I didn't know if you would," he said. "It was only an apology, really, for being so gloomy in Singapore."

"You were sad, not gloomy. You don't seem sad any more."

"No. Tonight I'm on top of the world. Tonight, it's you who seem sad."

"I was worried about the passengers."

He accepted the lie. The shark's-fin soup arrived with flourishes, the patron himself helping the boy. There was more noise from the kitchen than in the restaurant, though fifteen or twenty people were here. He wondered if they would see Joe from next door.

Able sometimes and for long moments to study her face in the glow from the Chinese lantern above them, he came more easily to realize how very beautiful she was, the small face sculpted from bronze, a serenity lying upon it as if all quick childish thoughts had been stilled and only their innocence left.

"Why were you playing that tune, Santha?"

"I like it. It reminds me of a time when my father took me to his country for a month, in the autumn when there was wood-smoke in the air. I remember the smell most of all."

"You are French?" He knew so little about her.

"My father was French, my mother Indian." She smiled, shy of any suggestion she might have given of sorrow. "But I was brought up with a Chinese family."

"You're so young, to have lost your parents."

"After the war, many young people grew up like me."

Becoming unable to look away from her face, he said: "Your parents must have been wonderful people."

"I think so. My mother was the daughter of a Singhalese minister, an adviser to the throne. I don't really know what my father did; he was in the Resistance during the war and it was the last anyone heard of him. When I was seven years old my mother died, and there was nobody to care for me so my amah's family adopted me in Singapore. That is why I call myself by their name, Swee, as a courtesy to them, because they have looked upon me as their own daughter." She looked up and saw him watching her. "My life has been full of wonderful people."

"Now you are sad."

"Yes, but that is foolish of me. There is something that I have to do, of my own free will, and there are things about it that will be—annoying"—he knew she hadn't quite found the word she wanted—"but if you decide to do something you cannot be sad about it, or you would not do it. That's right, isn't it, Hugh?"

"Not a bit right, no. We spend most of the time deciding to do things that are liable to 'annoy' us, but we choose the lesser of evils. If you don't do this thing, you'll be unhappier still."

"Yes, I think so."

There was an emerald bracelet on her wrist; he concentrated on it instead of staring at her wonderful sad little face.

"Were you really going to answer my letter, Santha?"

It had been composed even more carefully than the one to H.R.H. the Sultan of Tamarah. He had been waiting for the answer to his letter more anxiously than he had admitted to himself. Now it would never come.

"No," she said. He found the little characteristic appealing: she would lie once, then tell the truth without the least embarrassment. She had said she was not sad, but that she had been worried about the passengers; then she had told the truth. She had told him she had been going to answer his letter; now she confessed the lie.

"Why not?" he asked, and she smiled up at him, at his indignation.

"There are many reasons for not answering a letter."

"No good ones. I might have pined away."

"I did not think so."

"Well, I'm extremely glad you had engine-trouble and I hope it'll occur regularly. If necessary I shall ask Captain Chong to fake it by switching the ignition on and off."

"Do not be cross, Hugh."

"How is the shark's-fin?"

"Very good. He is a Cantonese, the cook here."

A game had started in the far corner where the lanterns floated like small moons across the rattan walls; the ivory pieces clacked and shuffled; it was already a sound that Hugh associated with Pasang; many other sounds here were also heard in Karachi, but not the movement of mah-jongg bricks.

"Would you ever come here to see me, Santha, even if the engines didn't break down?"

For a time she looked away and watched the other people; he was left to admire her face now in profile, and the moment began coming when he would want very much to kiss it for a long time, somewhere outside in the dark. It wouldn't, of course, be possible. This wasn't Clapham Common.

"Yes," she said without turning back to look at him.

The patron was bobbing in front of them and they sat without talking while the bowls circled between them in the deft hands of the conjurors: noodles and the chopped meat of tiny suckling-pigs, huge prawns in batter and sweet-and-sour, and hot rice-wine.

"Does it all look well done, Miss Santha May Swee?"

"It looks perfect."

"No, I mean does it really? You're an expert, I'm not."

"Yes, really." She gave a compliment to the patron and his boy and they retired delighted.

From tomorrow, Hugh decided, he would start learning her language, or at least, this one of her several languages. He said: "Because I want you to enjoy this evening. Unless there is more engine-trouble you won't come to see me again."

"No." She looked crestfallen until she heard his quiet laugh. "What amuses you?"

"The thought that I must never take any notice of your first answer to a question. Always the second. Why don't you want to see me again?"

She looked very serious, meeting his eyes steadily but with an effort. "I shall want to, Hugh." Her pronunciation of his name, like the soft owl's cry—Hee-yoo—and the chime her voice made of it was undermining his resistance; and he had to take a grip on his senses.

"But you won't come, all the same?"

"No. You are not just—ordinary—to me."

"You find me extraordinary?"

"I am serious."

"I'm sorry." He put his hand across the table between the mounds of exquisitely-cooked delicacies for which he had lost all appetite. "What am I, then, to you, if not 'just ordinary'?"

Now she looked away and his thoughts, which were passing his mouth gently across the dark wing of her eyebrow, were disturbed. The tips of her fingers touched his hand.

"There is someone I have to marry," she said.

"Me." But it had taken some getting out.

She said nothing, but drew both her hands down on to her lap. He said: "Are you hungry, Miss Santha May Swee?"

"No."

"Nor am I. But we should make a better gesture than this, don't you think?"

"For politeness."

"Yes. We won't talk any more. Not about that, anyway."

Silently they set about a demonstration of deep enjoyment as they finicked with their chopsticks, she expertly, he

87

with many slips; whether or not the patron was deceived they did not know; it was the best they could do for him. After five minutes of the torture Hugh leaned across to her; for all he knew, the patron might speak English or at least follow it.

"Beautiful Santha, will you please say in your best Chinese to our smiling and noble host that since one of his guests at this table has just fallen violently in love with the other and lost all appetite for food, it will be no reflection upon his cooking if we both leave?"

She was trying to smile and he wondered if it was not the thing in China to veil a real feeling with facetiousness, or if she knew him well enough to understand that he was serious.

"I will say that to take more of his hospitality would be to disgrace ourselves in the eyes of Providence."

"All right, tell him that."

Night had come when they walked to the end of the street and across the coast road that ran from Singapore to the Thailand border. Here in the small town where fishermen were still important members of the community the coast road did not look as if it linked great places; sand had blown over it during the day from the beach, and there was no traffic. Since the news of the ambush had appeared in the *Straits Times* four days ago the traffic had been less along this stretch.

Half the night-sky was black to the west where the storm had gathered. To the east over the faint pale sea the stars trembled.

Above their heads stood the dark clouds of the coconut palms and they walked side by side between the slender trunks, the sand under their feet. Their hands were not even touching.

"What is that?" she asked.

"A gunboat." They stood looking at the black shape on the water half a mile out. "They're trying to catch any Communist landings. She came in two days ago."

"I wish there were not always war, Hugh."

"It's a habit that men forgot to lose when they learned

to speak." Perhaps, though, it was easy to say that when you'd never been in a war, except as a boy of ten and an evacuee at that; all he remembered personally of the war was the wonderful greenness of Wales. He had never been committed to anything bigger than his own small world, and sometimes felt the lack of a dimension in his life, a time of suffering that so many others had longed to be spared.

How much had she known and loved the daughter of the Singhalese minister, adviser to the throne, and the son of Gaul who had resisted to the death? Did she think of them still as her mother and father, or just as "wonderful people"? He wanted to know everything about her life, but already felt he had encroached too much.

"I shall be in Singapore," he said, "a week today."

"Yes?"

Somewhere in one of the fishermen's houses that were built right on the beach, raised on stilts against the danger of flooding when the surf reached high, a man or perhaps a woman was playing a one-stringed instrument, picking a meaningless unrhythmic series of notes from it, as if it was not being played by hands but had been left forgotten somewhere outside the house for the leaves and the wind to touch. There were no voices from the houses; everything alive, man and animal, waited for the storm, afraid that a single word or cry might bring down that tower of wrath that stood in the west sky.

"So when I'm in Singapore," he said, "I'll come to see you. Shall I?"

"No." She held his arm. He knew it was true, first time, that he mustn't see her; she kept the endearing little trick of the polite lie for ordinary conversation.

Then if he mustn't see her again—if this were to be the last time—he could risk offending her; a stranger's memory was short. He asked: "Because you are to marry?"

"Yes."

"But you may change your mind about him. You said you 'have' to marry."

He was certain it wasn't the time-honoured reason. She was a virgin; and he knew this just as he had known that

89

the little brown trickling snake had been a young one, not fully grown.

She took her hand from his sleeve and stood looking at the flat still pallor of the sea; all he could see of her face was the glimmer of her eye among the soft shadows of cheek and brow. He cupped her small face gently, his fingers moulding to its shape, the very skin of his hand sensible of beauty under its touch.

"Miss Santha May Swee . . ." even a whisper seemed too loud on the hot and brooding air . . . "I wasn't just looking for companionship when we met in that doorway. Singapore hasn't got to be lonely for a man who needs someone to talk to. But from then on I didn't want to talk to anyone except you. I still don't." She had turned her face at the gentle insistence of his hand and was looking up at him as she listened, and now he could see the whole faint pool of the pale sea reflected in her eyes and thought that all he would ever want to see in them was the reflection of his own face, that had always bored him with its daily sameness. "Whatever love is, it's in me now, whether it's a big need or just the fear of a big loss, the losing of something beautiful that I might hope to keep all my life. You can call it possession or fascination if you want to, but all I know is that it's just the ordinary common-or-garden kind of falling in love that suddenly makes a new place of the whole world—"

"You must—"

"I haven't got very long, you see. There's only tonight, and no chance to show you what I mean without having to put it in poor words like this, because you won't come here to see me again and if you won't let me go to see you, then I shan't try. For all I know, you love this other person and I'm too late; so anything I can do about it has got to be done now. And I wouldn't say any of this if you hadn't told me two things: that there's someone you 'have' to marry, and that it makes you sad."

She had put her hand against his and was keeping it pressed to her face as if helping him to shield it, just as someone alone and very troubled will shield the face with a hand to keep away the fears while thought tries to deal

90

with them. In her eyes the sea was darkening, and a tremble came into the air from the west; high above their heads the dry leaves shuddered and a great whisper ran the length of the fringe of palms.

"It is too late, Hugh—"

"Not till morning. I don't ask anything except that you'll let me see you again."

"It would take so long to tell you—"

"We've the whole of the night—"

A flash cut through the black sky and the long strip of the beach was set flickering, the sand so bright that the shadows of the palm trees were etched in a clear-cut frieze. When the thunder reached them she gave a little gasp and buried her face into his hand, her body shivering as he held it. The cries of birds piped thinly through the dark in the sound of alarm; already the second flash came and the sea turned silver.

In the fisherman's unseen house the notes of music had stopped, and in a moment the thunder rolled roaring across the town.

"We must go," he said. There was no shelter here.

"Yes." She lifted her face from his hand and he kissed her without ever thinking that he should not; and she made no movement either of approach or retreat; but it was not simply acceptance; perhaps she was stilled by surprise. To him it seemed the deepest intimacy he had ever known, just to stand here with her against him and no one near, his mouth resting on hers. Her tears were on his cheek when he straightened from her.

"I love you," he said, and she let the sobbing begin out loud because it was too much to withhold; and though he tried to give her peace by taking her hands and kissing them she broke away from him and he had to run after her and catch her up, finding her hand and helping her as she stumbled through the sand where the onshore wind had driven shallow dunes between the columns of the palms.

The smell of rain was coming into the air from the far side of the town but none was falling in the streets, as yet. All the shutters were slammed tightly across the windows

91

for fear of the lightning; a group of ricksha-pullers stood near the crossing where the fortune-teller still sat with her mat and little table, her Chinese ivory-yellow face as old and fragile as the miniatures her people make with their delicate knives, exquisitely fine. She called to them, but the harsher voices of the ricksha boys were calling too; one of them had a jinrikisha with the hood raised, a vehicle for lovers or money-lenders and their debtors to ride in from place to secret place; here were lovers and the boy tilted his jinrikisha towards them and wheeled it across their path as if it were a trap to catch them with—

"Taksi, tuan! Taksi!"

"Taksi—taksi! Storm come, tuan!"

"Rain come very bad now—must take taksi, tuan!"

They broke and wheeled their flimsy carriages and tried to trap the two people as if they were food, which indirectly they were; but Hugh had stopped and was looking down at the old woman, who was crying thinly to him—"It will not rain, sin-shang, it will not rain. Stay with me and I will tell you all—and you, heavenly daughter—"

"No!" Santha's fingers were digging into his arm and she struggled to bring him away; her face in the light of the street was lost and agonized and she was trying to find a way through the rickshas that now surrounded them; lightning flared, freezing and blenching the street and the figures of the boys and their shouting faces in the instant before they flinched in its awful brilliance. "*Aeii-ya!*"

"No harm, no harm!" the old sing-song voice intoned. "Your future—all your future—"

"Please, Hugh—"

"Come on, then!" He swung the nearest ricksha aside and pulled her through the gap as the thunder came, hammering down from the black dark and beating through the street; and the lamps went out, everywhere.

"Hee-yoo—"

"It's all right." He put an arm round her and they hurried past doorways. "Power-station's hit, that's all." They made their way through the shadowed intervals between the few kerosene lamps that hung in doorways, their flames oily and

92

squat in the heavy air, their glow feeble but enough to give a guide and keep back total dark.

She had stopped sobbing but her voice was shaky—"Where are we going?"

"Home." Though without hope, he said it for both of them.

BARS of light and shadow fell across her face and small perched body; she sat on the bamboo stool as if it were not there, as if she were poised in the air by mystic means. He thought he had never seen anything alive so still. They drank their tea from the little bowls Mr Loo had left for his use.

The electricity was still dead, and he had pumped up the Kitson lamp and set it going; its light was harsh, so he had put it on the floor behind a bamboo slatted screen to break the glare. For the first time initiated to the tea ceremony in which she was long versed, he found it calming. Squatting like this, cupping the delicate porcelain bowls, sipping the fragrant smoke-tasting tea and watching her stillness he was in a measure bespelled; even the long crackling peals of thunder seemed remote from the quiet room, though the mosquito-gauze of the window was set drumming by the vibration.

She had said nothing more about herself, though he had tried to learn more of her life and of the things that were troubling her; instead she had made him tell her as much as he wanted to—which was very little—about himself. He had felt it was important for her to know one thing, and had forced himself to the mention of it—the Peter who had come into his life for those few dreadful minutes, Peter, the name of a scream.

"We'd been very happy," he said.

Slowly she had opened her eyes, after keeping them tightly shut for minutes like a child trying to shut out a noise that frightened it.

"Poor Hugh."

"Well, for three years I'd been rich. I suppose it sometimes happens that there's just one degree of consolation for the one that's left. Nobody's perfect; she wasn't perfect, thank heaven, but our life together was." The tea in the bowl had

94

got cold; he sipped it without tasting. Behind the bamboo screen the lamp hissed steadily. "I wanted you to know."

After staring at him for a while she said: "You are older than I thought."

"I see what you mean. No, not older. Only by the three years, and the gap."

"What is the gap?"

"In my case something that comes between life stopping and life starting again."

The window-gauze went ashen and her face leapt to one-sided clarity during the instant of the lightning. This time the thunder followed almost immediately, racketing down as if the sky were breaking up like so much pack-ice and clattering into the streets.

In the flash he had seen the thin emerald bracelet glow suddenly on her wrist. He could never afford to give her anything like that. How much could she be seduced by beautiful gifts? If at all, he'd lost points already.

"Did you think you'd see me when you landed here, Miss Santha May Swee?"

"Yes."

"Did you hope you would?"

"A man mustn't ask questions like that."

"This one must. This one's time is short."

She reached out her hand to touch him. "I don't like to hear you say that—"

"I don't like it either, but it's true."

After the next thunderclap the rain began dropping; it made a sound almost never heard in England: the first drops were so large that they might have been acorns hitting the roof—*tok*—*tok*—*tok-tok*—*tok*—*tok-tok-tok*—and then it turned into a staccato roll on the drums. It sounded like anything but rain: rain as heavy as this would surely brain you if you went outside.

"It is late, Hugh."

"Yes." He'd been willing her not to say it, not to call an end to the young night so soon. Tomorrow would begin when she left here. The time was up. "I'll take you"—he had nearly said "home"—"to the Rest House."

Standing, she turned into a magical creature, a ringed faun strayed here from a fable, the bars of light and shadow striping the white uniform and the dark wing of her hair.

"Why are you staring, Hugh?"

He turned away. "I couldn't see you properly. The light's odd, because of the screen. Come on, or you'll get soaked." The thunder seemed to beat with small rapid fists; there had been no flash. A voice shouted his name.

He went through the other room and opened the door to the landing. Joe stood there in a robe and sandals.

"I know it's late, but I need a hand—"

"Trouble, Joe?"

"Uh-huh, sort of." Joe saw Santha coming through the room. "Hello there, Miss Swee!" He looked at Hugh and away again, perfectly explicit: he wouldn't have come if he'd known she was here.

"I was just going to take her to the Rest House, Joe—"

"I'm sorry, I—"

"Has something happened?" she asked. The beating of the rain played tricks with their voices.

"Not a thing. I just came here to talk to Hugh." He gave a heavy grin. His shoulders were dark with rain and his grey-streaked monk's-cut hair glinted in the hard light of the pressure-lamp. "You have a flashlight?" he murmured.

They went down the narrow stairs, Hugh first, pointing the beam of the torch downwards and behind him. The courtyard was a dense grey curtain of water and before they had climbed into the Land-Rover their clothes were dark with it.

Outside the Rest House Hugh said: "I'll be a minute, all right, Joe?"

"Take your time," he said with a jumpy smile.

When they were in the hall of the building she asked: "What has happened? Did he tell you?"

"No." They stood close together in the wan light of an oil lamp; a house-boy was coming. Her small wet hand was in his, trembling for no reason he could think of. Normally she didn't mind storms—"I like being surprised," she had told him in the doorway in Singapore. One thing he knew about

96

her, this one small thing; and he could say to anyone, as if he knew her well: "Santha? Oh, she doesn't mind storms." A small enough keepsake.

"Thank you for such a very pleasant evening, Hugh." The measured little tune of Asian manners, while her eyes looked at him with worry in them. He held her hand between his own and kissed it and against its wet gold skin said:

"I love you." He waited until the boy came with the light and then went back to the street. Joe said as soon as he was in the car—

"Look, are you sure you were—"

"Yes. What's happened?" The downpour on the tin roof of the car was deafening and they had to shout.

"It's that guy Thorne—"

"Who?"

"Tom Thorne. He's in Yat Kee's place and I can't get him out single-handed."

"Where is the place?" He started the engine.

"First right from here and a half-mile down Jalan Lebar." They jerked away and he went on shouting dutifully above the din—"I guess I shouldn't have come for you but there wasn't anybody who—"

"I'm glad you did. I'm really very glad." He switched on the headlamps and turned the whole street silver.

When the car stopped, Joe clambered down and pulled his robe more tightly around him. "That doorway," he called in the hammering rain. Hugh followed him and nearly walked into the woman who was pressed against the wall; she was a young Malay, her sarong and coatee drenched and her black hair pouring from her head in lank ribbons.

"Kamala," Joe said, "what are you doing here?"

"I come to help—"

"Go back home."

"No, I stay—"

"Listen, you just—"

"I stay, Joe."

"Then get in the car, huh?"

She nodded and slipped into the screen of rain.

A passage led to three shallow stairs where a lantern burned; the opium-smell was strong. Two or three Chinese had heard Joe's voice and were huddled on the low landing, their faces dismayed.

"You not bling police—"

"No, friend of mine. He still in there, Mr Kee?"

"Oh yes!" He beckoned them along to the higher passage where the cubicles were. "He more quiet, now!"

The light was very low; in one or two of the cubicles a face floated among the shadows, but most of those clients who had stayed were grouped by the curtain of the cubicle at the far end. Kee murmured to Joe: "Tly to give him pipe, to make calm, but no good."

"We'll be as quick as we can, Mr Kee." He was sorry for the Chinese, whose house was for those who wished for dreams and silence at the end of the day, or quiet words with a friend over a pipe. Thorne had come here drunk, a bull in a china-shop. To Mr Kee and his friends this was the extreme of all unseemliness and they were very distressed.

Joe said to Hugh: "Whatever I say, follow my lead. I know him pretty well."

The group fell away to let them pass through into the end cubicle. Something snapped under Hugh's foot; he believed it was a pipe. Thorne was naked to the waist and wore no shoes. He was crouched on the bed, just as he had been when Joe had tried to take him home and had then left to fetch help. If it could be avoided he wouldn't start anything strong-arm; it would add ugliness to unpleasantness. There were one or two people here who could very easily apply their knowledge of *kung-fu* and knock the man cold; but Yat Kee had forbidden it, because Thorne was a client and even now a guest in his house.

"Joe! I thought you'd deserted your poor old friend!" Thorne wasn't very obviously drunk, perhaps not even very drunk; that was the trouble. The alcohol had aggravated whatever black-souled mood he was in, giving it power. Hugh looked at him and even in the poor light recognized him. "Who is this, Joe?"

"Copland. He—"

"Oh yes. The gauleiter at the airstrip—they told me."

"This is Tom Thorne," Joe said with touching formality, and Hugh offered his hand, following Joe's lead and observing the niceties; but Thorne didn't see it; he sat hunched across his knees, with long pinched-looking eyes staring out of a wedge-shaped face at nothing.

"I was telling them all about guilt, Joe, and all about innocence, and life, and death—you know how it all goes—a bastard in every bed and no hope for the wicked—"

"We're going along to your place now, Tom. Kamala's waiting outside in the car—"

"*Christ!* Who thought of the word—guilty? Wha's it mean to anyone, Joe?"

The Chinese drew back, looking away, not at one another, distressed, appealing to the Europeans to deal with this man of their kind.

"I'll tell you what it means, Tom. I have a whole lot of ideas on that. You give us a drink at your place and we'll make a real wing-ding of the evening, eh?"

Hugh couldn't look away from the crumpled sharp-boned face of Thorne. Did Joe know who he was, his real name? But he might be wrong; the light was feeble.

Joe slowly sat down on the bed and slid his hands into the sleeves of his robe, and began talking to Thorne as quietly as he could against the sounds of the diminishing storm. The voices of the Chinese occasionally lifted along the passage, to Hugh unintelligible, word-figments in a dream, the rattle of dry leaves where no wind was. Their sound and the scent of the drug was trying to coax him from reality; even Joe's monotone was soporific.

Why had Joe come to him for help? Joe must have a lot of friends here among the natives; he dressed as they did, ate as they did, and spoke their language; the soil of the place was on his feet, its clear noons lingering in the tan of his skin. It must be because there was still an unbridgeable gap: he was still and would always be an Occidental. Thorne was the same; therefore this business had to be confined and contained inside the European community of Pasang; and the Malays and Chinese and Indians would for their part pretend not to have noticed anything wrong. Strange tongues were no impediment to such a code; everyone understood. Was Hugh, then, the only European able to help? He counted the others. Walsh gone, Stratton who "walked by himself", Duffy too far away at the rubber estate with his loved and loving wife, Smith—a man to stay away from, according to Joe. There were no more here. When Walsh had gone he had left seven Europeans in Pasang. At this moment three of them were in Yat Kee's opium-house at midnight, one of them drunk. What would Mr Comyns-Edge, the Great White Resident, have said to this?

Joe was still talking, his low voice mesmeric; perhaps that was his object: to lull Thorne and send the brute in him to sleep. Hugh looked again at the wedgy clown's-face in the glow of the lantern; it had the narrowed eyes and the blue lips of the habitual smoker.

". . . Besides," Joe murmured, "if we don't drive that poor kid home she'll be frozen. You thought of that, Tom?"

"There isn' anyone who knows . . . knows . . ."

It was hopeless. Hugh asked quietly: "Joe, shall I drive her home and come back?"

"Guess not."

"Who is she?"

"His wife."

That Malay girl? She was a child. And sitting out there in soaked clothes in the open-sided car she was risking pneumonia. "Can't she at least come into the house, Joe?" He was never unfeeling towards women, but on this night with Santha only a street away he believed there to be nothing so precious in all creation.

"Guess not," Joe said again. "It's forbidden. We'll go, now. He's had enough time."

The shadows of the Chinese moved on the wall as they crept to watch and went away, to return and share the curious game of patience; they hadn't witnessed this before among the Western people of the Peninsula; but then Mr Joe had been slowly shedding many of his Western traits in the last two years here, and it was said of him among the people of Pasang that he had "come home" to this place.

"So now we go, Tom. Take it easy, though—folks are enjoying their smoke." He got up from the bed and Hugh noticed that even after half an hour of sitting still his movement was flexible and plastic, as if he'd been relaxing, and not devoting all his nervous tension to the task of shifting Thorne.

"We want a drink, Joe. Don't we want a drink?" His voice rose to a shout—"Hey, Mister Kee! Der-rinks on th' house, you hear me? We all—"

Joe cut him across the face with the back of his hand and said—"Okay, Hugh? Rough as we have to make it—but quiet, you get it?" Thorne was rocking on the bed with his arms and legs unfolding and his head trying to shake away the dizziness brought by the shock of the slap.

"Damn you, Joe—you think—"

"C'mon now. We blow." He dodged the swing of Thorne's arm and grabbed it, lugging him off the low bamboo bed while Thorne struggled and summoned breath enough to shout again.

"You bastard! Lea' me—" but Joe clicked his jaw shut with a light blow under the throat and as Thorne dragged his arm free Hugh got the other one and put a twist on it to bring his body more upright and clear of the bed. The Chinese voices rose suddenly in the shadows, birdy and alarmed. The sweat on Thorne's bare skin made it difficult to hold him and though he was not strong he was enraged.

"Get his feet, Hugh-boy—now." Joe turned his back on Thorne and swung an arm round his throat, reaching down and putting the grip on, and when he pitched backwards Hugh caught his feet and locked them with one arm above and one below, catching his own wrist as a safety-link because they were trying to kick.

"It's okay, Mr Kee, we're going now. No noise, see?"

The Chinese made way for them as they carried Thorne along the passage; he was quiet because Joe had the throat-lock on, but his struggling made it difficult to walk straight and a patch of plaster was ripped from the wall and fluttered whitely about their feet in the gloom.

Outside the rain had stopped and the few street-lamps

were shining again; the air was sweet after the musty opium smell of the house.

"I'll take him," Joe said. "You drive." He held Thorne upright as his bare feet hit the ground and told him in a low voice: "Behave, huh? Kamala's here in the car."

Hugh saw that she was asleep on the back seat, her legs drawn up and her wet hair falling across her shoulder; she had tired of waiting and must be very chilled; he decided for the first time that Thorne was a swine as well as a fool. He started the engine and waited until Joe got the man into the back, answering the girl as she woke and uttered a frightened question. "Everything's fine, baby—soon be home now."

"Where is it, Joe?"

"Back down the other way and through the square—I'll keep you right as we go."

The streets were deserted but for a few pariah-dogs and an unknown face peering from a window; the wheels of the car slid along gutters and sent a thin wash of mud against the white-painted walls; above their heads the tin roof drummed, and what Thorne was saying could not be heard properly.

It was a Malay house, timber-built and with a roof of attap-leaves, not far from the rain-darkened wastes of the beach where moonlight now shone, making milk of the sea.

They dropped Thorne on to the bed with his bare muddied feet overhanging the end; and the girl began bathing the mud from them with a cloth and bowl, watching his face all the time. Either he was asleep or a final sly blow from Joe in the car had cost him his consciousness; he looked restful, his face eased as if by the peace of death.

"Is he all right, Joe?" Hugh asked.

"He's fine. We'll leave him now."

"What about if he—"

"He won't." He stooped over the girl and placed his hands on each side of her raised face in a movement like a blessing. He kissed the top of her head. "Soon as you can, you better dry all that lovely seaweed, baby." She wanted to rise and thank him but was too absorbed in her task. Thorne's feet were now clean and somehow less wholesome-looking than before. Joe spoke to her in Malay and straightened up, pulling his robe tight and joining Hugh in the doorway.

In the light of the oil-lamp the girl looked a little less young, less childlike, crouched at the foot of the bed in her sarong and green-gold baju, their bright colours alive in the light as if a small rainbow had fallen here in the middle of the room. She had turned back to watch her husband again, and on her face was adoration.

12

WATCHING the lizards, Hugh lay stiffly and unrested on the bamboo bed that was a foot too short for him; he had slept perhaps a couple of hours after coming home from Joe's place. What time that had been he didn't remember; somewhere between midnight and this dawn.

"They found that man in the sea," Joe had told him. They had brewed coffee and drunk it scalding hot and soot-black and Joe had lent him one of his robes to put on while his clothes dripped over a chair. Joe seemed to have dozens of these robes: the passage between the two rooms looked like the cloakroom of an Arabian baths.

Hugh had been worried that Thorne might break out again and distress his wife, perhaps even hurt her physically, but Joe said: "He'll be okay now, with her there. You know the way they lead a bull out with a steer, quiet as can be? It's like that with him and Kamala."

"Why couldn't she have come into Yat Kee's place, to fetch him home?"

"Forbidden." Joe sat cross-legged on the floor, where there were mats strewn about, grass dyed with betel-juice and white lime. This room wasn't crowded with his work like the other one; by day, it must be the coolest room in the town, Hugh thought; the only way to make cool was to make space, and there was nothing here to trap the heat of noon: a grass screen, the few mats, a single Meranti redwood table, a stool or two. The only ornament was the tall bust of a woman—a Hindu, perhaps a priestess—in the corner facing the window where she would catch the light best; it was probably Joe's work, the piece of which he was most proud, or least critical.

"It was her father who found Thorne floating in the sea, some two years back. Kamala was just a kid then, fifteen. They dragged him out and sent for the magician, who'd done some artificial-respiration drill with the Marines when they were here in '45—that's what made him the local magician. No kidding, he breathed back the soul of the *orang inggris* right there on the beach like they'd seen him do with other men. Then Kamala's family—fourteen of them—took Tom Thorne into their house and he made a fifteenth for a couple of weeks while they got him on his feet again. He couldn't speak a word of Malay or Chinese or any damn language except that clipped kind of sawn-off professional-man's English of his, so they had me round there to see him now and then. He wasn't grateful for what they'd done. You never get much thanks out of a suicide *manqué*. It needled me—I mean I could see his point of view but *their* point of view was that they'd saved his life and got him back into the great big wonderful world he'd almost lost. The only suicides here go on living—find 'em down in Yat Kee's or dead drunk and loaded with rice-hooch. You'd never find any of these boys walking out into that water meaning to stay there, even the poorest. Before they went under they'd grab a fish and bring it right back and eat it and live another day. Anyway I got Tom round to making some kind of show he was grateful to them before he quit their house. I think he learned a lot from them—you know, their simple wisdom and their kindness and that—and for him that was his fish, and he's still living on it. So that's how Tom Thorne came to Pasang—out of the sea."

Joe held his bowl of coffee cupped in his square knuckly hands, gazing at the priestess in the corner. The room was so quiet that they could hear the bark of a jungle-dog miles away in the moonlight, even through the shutters.

"Do you know who Thorne is, Joe?"

"Huh?"

"Do you know who Thorne is?"

"Guess I don't." He didn't ask; Hugh had known he wouldn't. "I know what he used to be, though. You like some more coffee, boy?"

"I'll need some sleep before morning."

"You don't have to worry." He took the bowl and rinsed out the thick black mud of the grounds. "This stuff's partly chala-nut an' partly chicory—I get it from Singapore. The amount of coffee there is wouldn't keep a night-watchman awake." He refilled the bowl from the jug and gave one of his rare and rather mischievous smiles. "Guess it's what you'd call an acquired taste, huh? You just leave it if it's too rough."

"I like it."

"Heats you up better than rum, an' no kicks. Some while after this," he said, settling on the grass mat again, "we had one hell of a storm here—really. You know it scared me? The thunder was about normal, just sounded like the whole town caving in, but brother, the rain! You couldn't see over the streets in full daylight. Hell, it was like sheet-steel come alive an' it fell by the molten ton out of a sky black as midnight—there was mud standing two foot high on the street where the rain hit it up from the ground and the sound was frightening because you could hear it rising all the time an' you got to thinking it wouldn't ever stop till the whole damn' sky fell out. Made you think of the Flood and say your prayers. In a war," he said, staring at Hugh with his blue eyes wide, "even in a bad raid, a really bad one, somehow you know—least I always did—that there's only man behind it, a weak monkey with limited means and just as mortal as you are; but when Ma Nature decides she'll play it rough you know there's no limit you could ever begin to imagine—I mean if the planet got to spin off-centre and fly apart you wouldn't see any difference in the sky, would you, just one point of light go out in a billion billion—and hell, it's happening all of the time, no? Standing and hearing that storm, you thought of things like that—you were part of something that had started and had no limit, the whole sky was going to fall down an' you were underneath it along with the ants."

He reached for the jug and filled his bowl again. "An experience like that knocks the arrogance out of a man, which is a good thing. Next day things were in a mess, naturally—boats knocked around and a lot of roofs caved in. They had to shift the sick-cases out of the medical post—you couldn't call it a hospital, it was before they built the hospital we've got now—and the town looked like Venice,

106

you needed gondolas in the streets instead of rickshas. That was the day our cute little Kamala chose to go sick, sudden. She was very bad, half-dead with pain, an' the magician no help—all he'd learned was artificial-respiration and how to pull a tooth with a lanyard—but he had the drugs, and Tom Thorne did the rest, right there on the spot because we couldn't move her and the medical post was evacuated anyway. I was there too. He used my razor—"

"Your what?"

"Razor—I have a good old-fashioned Sweeny Todd model, just right for getting down to a burst appendix which is what she had. Even used my nylon fishing-line to sew her up again. You ever seen an abdominal done?"

"No."

"I didn't shave for a week after—got to look like Hemingway. Every time I lathered up and got set, all I could see in the glass was that beautiful smooth brown belly . . . it was like watching a slow ritual killing, you know? An' the thing about Tom was this: he'd never said a word about being a doctor, and he's never said a word since. I guess—and this is just my personal opinion, could be wrong—I guess the whole town could've gone down with cholera, any time, and he wouldn't have shown his hand; but that family had saved his life even if they didn't know he was through with it anyway. The only squeak I ever had out of Tom was that he was in some parachute regiment way back; I imagine in the medical corps too. So when you ask me if I know who Tom Thorne is, sure, I know who he is. But you meant 'was', and that's all I know—a surgeon."

In his tone there was the definite intimation that it was all he wanted to know. There were reasons, there must be, why a man should try to drown himself and his past in the sea, and then, having failed, in alcohol and opium; they would be good reasons, and therefore bad causes; and Joe liked to know the good about people and forget the rest.

"Yes," Hugh said. "He was a surgeon."

"Don't remind him about that, huh? He doesn't want to remember. After he did that job on Kamala, the poor kid was a side-show for weeks—the relatives of relatives came

107

from miles away to look at the scar. From that time they began calling him Tuan Doktor, but the way he glared at them gave them the idea it was some kind of insult they were offering, and they stopped. They came to ask me about it: wasn't it right they should call such a man 'Doktor' when he had shown them how mighty he was in the sacred art? I dodged it by saying that in the West if a man claimed any title then it was correct to call him by that title, but when he made no claim to it himself, it would be a false title, however many people used it; and a false title was a kind of insult, sure. They seemed to get this okay and then a few days after they came back to me and said well, couldn't they call him Jesus? They'd heard about this man Jesus, and they felt Tom Thorne just about rated the title. I became his public relations officer, because he couldn't cope with the kudos. That time, he went on a jag lasting two months almost— drank a bottle of Scotch a day an' nearly smashed himself up on the coast road; he kept telling me he'd come to this place for privacy, so he'd been a god-damn' fool to fix the kid and get himself famous—he didn't know it would happen; I guess it was a deliberate jag he went on, to show the town just how bad a man he really was. Didn't work out, though. They think a drunk is a sick man, so they saw him first as hero and then as martyr to his own evils; but they stopped calling him Tuan Doktor and pretty well left him alone, didn't even ask him to go admire the shrine they built for him up on the ridge there: 'To Tuan Thorne, Saviour of the Sorely Afflicted, Bringer of Life to the Dying, Lord of the Knife, come ye who seek comfort to this sacred place.' You ever had your razor mentioned in dispatches, boy?"

He stood up with the ease of movement that Hugh had noticed before, and took the coffee-bowls through the curved archway into the kitchen, talking over his shoulder: "Guess nobody ever thought he'd marry the kid, though. Us good Christian whites had introduced the colour-bar an' shown them how it worked, so prettily; it surprised them when Tom crossed the line." He came back from rinsing the bowls, and Hugh got up.

"What made him marry her, Joe?"

"Well, from the time she was on her feet again after the operation she just didn't leave him. Saw to his rooms and all his clothes—cooked, cleaned, mended, tended, ministered to him, in brief became his wife. So he married her, because he is a very high-principled man, somewhere right down there at the roots of all that caved-in wreckage, I kid you not."

Pulling on his half-dried shirt and slacks (because he was too recently out from England to go through the town in Joe's robe even with the streets deserted) Hugh said: "She's a very beautiful girl, Kamala."

"He'd've married her if she'd been ugly."

"He's lucky, then."

"Sure. Tom Thorne is a very lucky guy."

Joe had walked with him along Jalan Burong to the courtyard where the cassia tree stood in moonlight, sparkling in the light of the high iron lamp, its green fronds weeping under the weight of water-drops.

For a moment, before getting out of bed, he looked at the room and tried to picture her sitting there opposite the bamboo screen as she had been a few hours ago; but the room looked different by the day's light and even with the sun's first warmth on the wall there was a coldness here, and so he got up and began washing vigorously, the action helping to keep thought at a distance. It had been a very stupid thing to do last night, to let himself fall at last in love again, because it would take him a long time to pull out. After suffering the big loss he had let only a year pass before inviting another.

Wan Chai was at the airstrip early, even before the manager arrived. He had sprayed the package with cheap and very fierce perfume, as Lee Kwei Chong had advised. It would be better when the refining-machinery was installed at the plantation; there would be no more smell and no more danger.

They started the aircraft soon after the manager came; he was out there now on the drying concrete apron, standing as still and tall as a heron, listening to the engines as they warmed. Wan Chai had reached an opinion of the new manager: he was a kindly youth but would have no mercy upon a transgressor; no matter that he had been offered the freedom of this restaurant, with all hospitality gratis and with the compliments of its proprietor, during the hours of duty here; Mr Copland had politely declined, and the offer would mean nothing if the day came when the way of the transgressor was revealed. There would be no mercy, for the English held that there could be no mercy greater than that contained in justice, whatever the findings of the magistrates.

Mr Chai stood in his doorway and watched the tall youth and wished himself rid of the package, which in any case had the smell of a cage of concubines.

Captain Chong arrived on the airport bus with the rest of the crew and the passengers; he greeted Chai but gave no hint that he was ready to receive the package; he was more interested in the sound of the engines that filled the whole building with their roaring. Nearly all the airstrip staff were now here, and Major Yassim and his two engineers also stood watching the aircraft. Chong went into the forward cabin and tested the engines personally.

The sun had cleared the highest of the palms along the shore and the shadows were shrinking; the heat began pressing against the face and bringing sweat out, and already the mud was steaming along the perimeter road. The manager had put on his sunglasses.

"How are they, Captain Chong?"

"Without a fault, Mr Copland." They walked together into the building, where Chong signed his clearance sheet.

"The mechanics told me they couldn't find anything wrong," said Hugh. "They're mystified."

"It sometimes happens, as you know." Chong found his brief-case and the zip bag from the cubby-holes.

"I was talking to Mr Sahgal at the Rest House yesterday evening. He rather suspects our bit of engine-trouble—did he tell you?"

Chong faced him seriously, politely. "That is so? I had no idea he understood mechanical things." His very blandness dismissed Mr Sahgal's suspicions.

110

"He's full of the idea of sabotage."

"Ah, yes? Sabotage by whom?"

"The C.T.s naturally."

"I understand." A slight smile moved the immaculate face.

"I wanted to know what you felt, Captain, yourself. Do you think there's anything in it? Has it ever been suspected before, in the case of a forced landing?"

"By Mr Sahgal, perhaps."

"No one else? You see, I want to take any precautions necessary; it wouldn't be difficult to mount guards while aircraft are being turned round."

"We have had the ambush, along the coast road. We have learned of an attempt on the Sultan's life a couple of months ago. A foreman rubber-tapper was found with a Japanese bullet in his unfortunate body earlier this year—as you know, some of the C.T.s are armed with guns looted from the retreating Japanese forces. But these are isolated instances of their activities, and to my own knowledge we've never suspected sabotaging of aircraft on this aerodrome during the last four years. I think Mr Sahgal might be reflecting the quite exaggerated apprehension sometimes felt in the town. I would rather suspect a drop of free oil on one of the contact-breaker points or water in a jet. A good mechanic could very easily remove the traces of such a cause without knowing it, during his examination. Anyway I'm quite happy to take off, with your permission."

"Fair enough. Don't imagine I'm looking for trouble where there isn't any, but I wanted your opinion."

"I'm much complimented that you value it, Mr Copland."

He touched the wide cap-peak in an easy salute and Hugh watched him go. Where did this young airline captain get his confidence? He smelled of it, dressed in it, used it for soap, polished his shoes with it. You could feel safe in an aircraft with a man like that. But on the ground? There was something just a fraction smooth.

Lee Kwei Chong stopped for a moment to talk to the mechanics who had come back to the building. Then he passed on, to say goodbye to his friend Wan Chai.

The passengers were going across the apron, their heads

111

already covered against the sun's heat, their sandals and shoes already raising a little dust where the mud had dried and was crumbling to powder. The stewardess led them, smiling to the Australian, Mr Broadlea.

"What has he been saying, Lee Kwei?" asked Mr Chai.

"He talked about sabotage, Elder Brother. Sahgal at the Rest House has been spreading alarm as usual."

"I am uneasy about Mr Copland, Lee Kwei. I think he is too good a man, too conscientious."

"I prefer good men. You know where you are with them. With a bad man—he might do anything, unpredictably." Chong was pleased with the new manager at Pasang. Walsh had been much too dangerous, because too co-operative; he had been a man to turn on you without warning. Better a strong rod for an enemy than a weak stick for a friend. And Copland had more courage than Walsh. There was no man in Pasang—except for Duffy—who would have slept here at the airstrip at night. The terrorists had known he was here alone and one of their trackers had sent a cobra in for him —the news had reached the tappers, who had told Loy Lin, who had told him about it last night; but it had been a failure, and Copland was still alive. Lee Kwei was very pleased; good men were few.

"My brother too is uneasy," said Wan Chai. "He speaks wisely, I think. We do not know this merchant, who—"

"I vouch for him, Elder Brother."

"But you are young—"

"I would vouch for you. Am I too young for that?"

He was becoming impatient with this talk of "uneasiness". Last night, before the storm had broken, he had talked to Loy Lin Chai at his small plantation; and everything had seemed so propitious; the crop had looked beautiful in the light from the house, a meadow of rich dark blossom through which they had waded waist-deep along the little pathways; in another month the big flat petals would be dropping and the pods would remain for the gathering, a harvest of green to be turned to gold from market to market along the airways of the world. More than a thousand dollars for the two-and-a-half-kati package, paid in Hong Kong; in America, after refining and processing, seven hundred thousand U.S. dollars for the finished product. If Loy Lin Chai did his own processing, here on his own land . . .

But they could talk of nothing save their "uneasiness".

"I did not like the storm, Lee Kwei, last night."

"It is over now."

"But it beat the petals."

"It did not damage the pods."

"I did not like the signs in the sky. It was bad joss."

Lee Kwei smiled carefully. "I am ready to go, Elder Brother." And what he knew would happen now happened; for as soon as the package was in his zip bag, with no stranger's eye the wiser, Wan Chai became more cheerful.

"I will speak to my brother again," he said. "I will tell him you vouch for your merchant as you would vouch for me. You are young but you are wise, I concede it."

"I have always been so, Elder Brother, within the aura of your wisdom." He walked with care across the concrete apron, making it seem that his zip bag weighed very little; in his hand it swung as light as his heart.

The passengers were in the aircraft and the two Tamils were pulling the steps away. The stewardess appeared again for a moment, her white drill uniform framed in the dark doorway; then the door swung shut.

In the control room Haji Ahmad sat poised at the switchboard, fully alert; the air was sticky with the rising heat but at least it was churned and changed by the overhead fans that were now working.

"I am waiting to inform Bangkok of the departure, sahib." He had heard the manager coming up the stairs.

"Very good, Ahmad." Since the lecture, the now proficient Pathan not only carried out every rule by the book but also informed the manager that he was doing it. For Hugh it was a little wearying but otherwise satisfactory.

He stood by the windows with the signal lamp, watching the scene below. He had wanted to go across to the aircraft and say goodbye again, but like renewed thanks twice-told goodbyes were embarrassing and exposed too much of the heart.

They had spoken only for a minute in the staff office, with the clerks there watching them. She didn't look tired this morning, not, anyway, as tired as he felt; perhaps she had slept longer than he. Driving to the airstrip alone, he had tried even after this short time to forget Santha's face, to pretend that last night had been no more than a casual indulgent interlude in his daily life: he had taken a girl out to dinner and in the heat of the dusk on the lonely sands had afterwards thought he was in love with her. Now it was morning, and she had been any girl, a pretty one, his companion for a few hours, nothing attempted, nothing to regret.

When she had stepped down from the airport bus he had seen her from a distance and already knew it was too early for pretence: that was Santha, over there, and the distance meant nothing because he could see every gold fleck of her eyes and all that was in them when she had talked with him in the light and shadow of his room last night; she wasn't any girl, but Santha May Swee, found and lost within a few days and now leaving him.

What would have happened if Joe hadn't come? Nothing; she had been going anyway and he'd been resolved not to ask her to stay. Nothing would have changed. All Joe had done was to give him something else and very different to think about instead of trying to sleep, or walking alone along the empty streets and making the kind of wild plans that always seemed so promising and reasonable in the small hours of a sleepless night.

Nothing could have changed this; not the storm nor Joe's sudden coming nor the dismal business of Thorne. So be it.

All she had said to him in the staff office was:

"I will write to you."

"I don't expect you will."

"Oh yes. I will." So she meant it, had said it twice.

"I'd rather you didn't," he said. A letter coming plumb in the middle of a forgetting-campaign wouldn't make it any easier, and he didn't want to see it in writing, even—or especially—in her writing, that there was no future for them. She'd told him that, without even saying it, when she had pulled him away from the old fortune-teller with the delicate ivory dying face among the crowd of ricksha-boys.

"I would like to write to you," she said, her eyes intent on his face. He knew he must look tired and a little sour despite the effort of putting on a front.

"You know my address," he smiled lopsidely. "I shall be delighted to have a letter." He looked at his watch and said as gently as he could manage: "Time for take-off. Happy landings, Miss Santha May Swee."

They could hear the passengers trooping out of the building. The aircraft had been run up a third time and all was well.

She had gone out to shepherd the passengers, walking a little awkwardly in her high heels as she had done in Raffles Square. Two things he knew about Miss Swee; she didn't mind storms, and she could never manage high heels awfully well.

"Sahib?"

"Yes, Ahmad?"

"Bangkok reports clear weather."

"You sent the report to Captain Chong?"

"Of course, sahib."

From the window Hugh could see the cunim beginning to build up over the sea; it would be hours before the storm arrived, if they were to have one today. Birds flew, wheeling over the mangroves towards the town. On the ground below the control tower the three Shell men stood neatly beside their bowser, one of them waving to someone on board the S. and P.A. plane—a passenger, or Chong or the stewardess. Ismail, with his Temporary Acting Assistant Manager's peaked cap on his head, was urging the crash and fire crews to start up their tenders; the gaudy Federation flags hung motionless from the poles above the vehicles.

The Malay was waiting with his markers, positioned in sight of the aircraft's forward cabin. The engines started up and a ragged plume of smoke fluttered back from them as the oil burned clear from the cylinders. The sound came drumming against the hangars.

Hugh raised the lamp and flashed the green. The marker

began his small and rather graceful dance, swinging the plane away and then standing to attention, giving the captain a magnificent salute according to Assistant Manager Ismail's instructions and taken straight from the book.

"I am about to telephone Bangkok, sahib, reporting the departure."

"Good, Haji Ahmad." They both knew that the flight would probably arrive in Bangkok long before any telephone-call could go through.

The machine reached the beginning of the runway and swung into line; the wings had become a shimmer of silver in the sun's glare and heat flowed in a haze above them.

He raised the signal-lamp again and gave Chong the green, wishing he had asked Haji Ahmad to do it, just this once.

* 13 *

THE Manager of Pasang Airport was driven at a smart pace
to the Sultan's Palace in a six-seater Humber army staff car
with two uniformed outriders as escort. The road was no
better than the one from the airport to the town in the other
direction, but the Malay Regiment sergeant drove with dash
and his passengers marvelled at the silence of the vehicle as
its soft springs took the shock of rut and pothole; and he
made another mental note for his Assistant Manager: their
neglected Land-Rover must run like this the moment they
could spare it for overhaul.

The road was struck through virgin jungle almost directly
inland, tunnelling through green gloom where the sunlight
never penetrated save where the massive and buttressed
trees thinned out to a clearing; most of the route was hacked
out of timber and vine and creeper as thickly interlaced as a
spider's web with a hole torn through by the road; rattan
and thorny thickets armed with murderous rotan barbs
made a wall on either side: along this path one could drive
at forty miles an hour but if one had to strike off on foot at
right-angles, ten yards would take a day and break a parang-
blade.

The second and final version of Hugh's letter had read:

H.R.H. the Sultan of Tamarah,
The Istana,
Pasang.

I have the honour of bringing to the notice of Your Royal
Highness that I was recently surprised to find a guard
mounted near the hangars of the airport without my
knowledge. His credentials appeared in order; but in view
of the general anxiety in this area concerning sporadic
terrorist activities and the ease with which they can be
disguised, I feel that as manager of the airport I should be

offered some official notification as to the extent and form of this guard-duty on the premises I have the privilege of commanding.

Perhaps Your Royal Highness would consider the issuing of some form of roster naming the guard and his reliefs, so that from time to time I can make a check and ensure that all is in order during the night hours.

Your Royal Highness' Obedient Servant,
H. B. Copland.

Long before the reply had come by special bearer, soon after the S. and P.A. had taken off this morning for Bangkok, he had regretted almost every word of his upstart request. The new broom had seen fit to sweep a bit too clean; it wasn't a bad fault but it would probably let him in for some embarrassment. He hadn't expected an abrupt summons to the palace during the precious hours of a working-day. The order—it could hardly be called a civilized letter—had been signed by a dignity styled The Secretary at Court.

The Manager,
Pasang Airport,
Pasang,
Tamarah State.
It has pleased the Sultan to have received your communication, the subject of which will be referred to in a personal interview. The privilege of Audience is arranged for eleven of the forenoon of this day. You will please present this paper to the undersigned on arrival at the Istana.

Col. Abdul bin Putra, D.K.,
The Secretary at Court.

There being no intimation as to what dress was to be worn, he had put on a clean bush-shirt and found a spare pilot's cap in the office that fitted him well—it was probably Chong's, and with any luck the small gold letters S.P.A. would escape the notice of the Governing Director of Straits Airways during the interview. A little of Hugh's previous indignation had returned; for all the Sultan knew, there might be three or four machines to be turned round at the airstrip at this hour, with panic-stations for everyone.

The staff car slid through hollows of mud where the road plunged deep beneath the jungle trees and the sun could never dry it.

From the cool shades of the jungle they ran suddenly into the heat and the glare of open ground. Through a partially-seen confusion of gates and sentries Hugh saw the *istana* for the first time; it reared as grandiose as a wedding-cake against the emerald trees, triple-domed and terraced and hollowed out with arabesque arches and windows. A peacock passed in long slow flight across the white facade.

Nobody seemed to be about, not even the Secretary at Court; it was a rather overworked-looking little man in a white robe and headcloth who led the visitor through a series of marble corridors and left him in the middle of a Persian rug as long as a cricket-pitch. It was just before eleven o'clock by Hugh's watch, and despite the absurd lavishness of the decor and his sense of a purposeless mission he stood a little awed. In the huge silence of this room he was for these few minutes alone and abandoned, a choirboy in a cathedral. The remote and towering walls with their alcoves and silk hangings exuded a spell for him and he was aware of a fate at work; from the moment he had glimpsed a shadow in human form against the hangar doors that night his destiny had altered course and led him here, with the hands of his watch marking the appointed hour. He resisted an impulse to hold it to his ear, half-believing it had stopped.

Movement was stirring, somewhere. The size of the room was such that he had to swing round twice before he could trace it. Gold curtains had parted at the far end and two robed servants held them back. He would not have been surprised to hear a sudden fanfare of trumpets; but the only sound was the irregular footstep of the Sultan as he limped across the marble stones and on to the carpet, a small man in an English-tailored linen suit with a glint of gold on his fingers.

"Mr Copland, it was nice of you to come." He offered a brown hand with friendly ease. "Let's go along there, shall we? This room has the oddest echoes, perhaps you noticed."

"Along there" was an alcove reached by three black marble steps, and he had a little difficulty with them as he led the way. "Please sit down." There were two chairs, each the size of a small throne and of inlaid rosewood, set at angles facing the open doors on to the terrace; beyond the balustrade swam a vista of greensward calm as a summer sea, where the peacock—or another—was now serenely sailing, gaudy as a ship dressed overall.

"Mr. Copland, I mustn't waste your time—I know how keen you are to be always on the spot when we receive aircraft. I wouldn't have interrupted your work at all if this weren't a matter of some importance." He looked round and spoke to one of the servants in rapid and pure Malay, and Hugh realized the limitations of learning the tongue from Ismail. Watching the Sultan's intense and rather chubby face he was again reminded of Ismail, who looked very like him; both had a broad and well-set head and lambent, curious eyes. How far, anyway, was Ismail from the throne, in a territory so small and ruled by a dynasty whose every prince had served a hundred wives? Simple mathematics could surely prove there wasn't a family in the State without this one man's blood among its sons. In fact the Sultan himself was less of his own soil than the lowliest of his subjects; the walls of Stowe and the halls of Oxford were better known to him than the untidy little town that sprawled between shore and jungle within thirty minutes' drive from the *istana*. Probably he had little interest in Pasang; he had been reared an exile in England, France and along the motor-racing circuits of the world until his crash in the Monaco Grand Prix had left him with a limp and a warning.

The servant slid away, barefooted; the other remained.

"In your letter," the English voice came precisely from the Asian face, "you say you encountered a guard at the airport. You meant one man, not more?"

"Yes, sir."

"Do you know his name?"

"Subayya Jhabvala."

Sir Rahman beckoned the other servant. "Have the Hindu

Subayya Jhabvala brought here immediately." He looked at Hugh again—"You speak Hindi, Mr Copland?"

"Basically, sir."

"Please tell me what happened when you spoke to this man who purported to be a guard."

"Purported—?"

"But didn't you suspect?"

"Well yes, but afterwards . . ." He gave a detailed picture of his meeting with Jhabvala.

"And is this the man?"

Hugh studied the face of the Hindu the servant had fetched; he had already learned to ignore, visually, the beard and turban that made one Indian resemble another.

"This is the man, sir."

He tried to follow the fast interrogation that began at once; Jhabvala's Malay was halting, but apparently it wouldn't be the thing for the Sultan to use any language but his own and English, the recognized second tongue of the Peninsula.

"You were found on the airport by the tuan manager. You told him you were guarding the royal aircraft."

"Yes, Highness."

"You had no such orders."

"No, Highness."

"Explain."

"I learned that the official guards had decided to absent themselves from the place of wickedness and evil, being in fear of it by night. I drew upon my unworthy person the un-deserved honour of standing guard in their place, Highness."

"Why didn't you report their negligence?"

"When I am freed of all sin and am without fault, Highness, I shall be qualified to reveal the misdeed of others."

For about a minute the Sultan gazed at the man, who stood with lowered eyes, perfectly still; then: "Subayya Jhabvala, I understand your loyalty not only to me but to these traitors, but you will for your part understand that what they have done is punishable by death. There will be a court-martial as soon as possible and you will be called as

121

witness. During the next few days you will be able to think over all the details of this affair and make sure that the evidence you will give will be true and unconfused. Go now, Subayya Jhabvala."

The Hindu intoned, rather beautifully, the required speech of leave-taking. One did not quit the presence of the Sultan without high compliments and humbling protestations. The last words echoed from the niches and encrustations of the great arched ceiling; then soundlessly the man went away.

Sir Rahman had the face of an outraged cherub. "How did you come to find this man standing guard, Mr Copland?"

"I was checking up all round, as usual, sir."

"As usual? How many nights did you make your check, before discovering Jhabvala?"

"Four, sir—"

"And there was no guard?"

"No, sir—"

"You would have seen one, for certain, of course?"

"If he was anywhere on my security beat, yes. That includes the outside of every building at the front—facing the runway—and inside most of them. The hangar is locked and barred at night, of course."

"The official guard was mounted in front of the hangar." With a chill in his precise voice he added: "That was the order. So there seems to have been a period of at least four nights when there was in fact no guard whatsoever."

Unable to contain his anger without movement he stood up and paced across the floor of the alcove, motioning with an impatient hand as Hugh made to get up—"No, please remain at ease. You will already know the situation here in Tamarah. The times are anxious for us all, throughout Malaya. There are grounds for anticipating a mass invasion such as we've already seen in the north along the Indian-Chinese frontier and in Tibet, Quemoy, Laos and a dozen smaller isolated territories. You have heard the phrase that puts this situation in brief: if Laos becomes another Korea, the fighting could engulf the whole of south-east Asia. Here in Tamarah we can do nothing except keep our defences manned and our fingers crossed. Meanwhile there are two theories to account for the rise in Chinese Terrorist activity in my State; either it has been chosen by Pekin for an early target of some larger campaign—as it is economically the least important in the Federation and the weakest, militarily —or the leader of the Chinese Communists in this area is taking it on himself to stir up trouble and earn himself recognition in Pekin. I hold the second theory. There has been looting and killing in the coastal kampongs as well as in the interior for some months which few people hear about; there has been the ambush along the coast road south; and some time ago there was an attempt on my life that was traced directly to a terrorist group encamped in the jungle between here and Pintu Besar."

He stood looking across the sunlit lawn.

"We're all very glad it failed, sir."

"Thank you, Mr Copland. I hope they'll fail the next time as well. I'm not ready yet. But the affair served its purpose; taken together with the other signs of trouble, it induced the Federal Government to send us a gunboat for coast patrol— we had earlier reports of arms and personnel being brought in by night with small boats, and that should now cease."

He came back and sat in the chair with his stiff leg out straight. "I have orders to keep away from the windows . . . and that makes me very angry. This is my home."

He was lost in thought for a moment and Hugh watched him obliquely as he sat staring out at the lawn and the white wall beyond, as Arthur Duffy had stared at his beloved rubber-trees, hoping they would never vanish except by a trick of the light.

"So it's important that we have a constant guard at the airport by night to stop any attempt at sabotaging my air-craft; that would be a very simple way of dispatching me and earning laurels for the Communist leader in this area. I mentioned this plan to Mr Walsh a few weeks before you replaced him, and he was thoroughly in agreement. I imagine you feel the same."

"But of course."

"I'll see you have full details of these guard duties. If at any time you observe any negligence you will please inform me at once on the direct telephone. There's still a great deal of superstition here among the ordinary people—in the Orient it dies hard—but I never thought it could break discipline within my army."

"Possibly, sir, there's a scare-campaign directed at the airport—"

"That's quite certain, and it's succeeding." He got up again, restlessly. "From this date, it will fail, I give you my word. I appreciate your co-operation and shall know I can rely on you, Mr Copland."

Hugh stood up and was reminded of how small the Sultan was. Small, angry, and rather helpless, an unimportant princeling in a white palace lost in a green land whose peace could at any time be shattered by the rattle of a shot and the shouts of the invader, just as it had been twenty years ago when this ruler was a boy at school in England.

"When we have more time I would like to hear about the changes you've made at the airport. Major Yassim is very impressed. When you return please ask him to begin an immediate and exhaustive inspection of my aircraft, including a flight-test. I'll confirm the order in writing. Tell him to look for evidence of sabotage. This afternoon I am flying to Kuala Lumpur and it might be safer to take a seat on a regular flight."

"There's one leaving at three o'clock, sir. Shall I—"

"Please. But no formality, Mr Copland. The fewer people who know, the safer."

In the evening Hugh was depressed. In the clammy heat of his rooms he washed and put on dry sweat-free clothes, explaining to himself: Santha had gone, and already he was dreading the letter he knew she would write; he wouldn't open it, but would burn it unread. The audience with the Sultan had also depressed him: there was a man with nothing to anticipate but the seizure by violence of all he possessed, including his life. And there had been the sudden discovery about Walsh and his reasons for quitting his job here; it had been already obvious but the certainty left a taste in the mouth. Frightened, he had run.

Today one of the Tamils hacking at the jungle's edge had kicked over a stone and been bitten by a scorpion; he was now at the hospital in a severe fever because he had run like mad for the airstrip buildings and pumped his blood round at top speed, spreading the venom before they could give him an injection. During the afternoon, Hugh had smelt opium very distinctly in the airport building but couldn't trace the source; Mr Chai had looked astonished when questioned, increasing suspicion. If he had simply shrugged and said a friend had made him a small present, nothing would have been untoward; among the Chinese the stuff was as common as cigars in a Western club. It was depressing to realize that Chai couldn't be trusted and might at any time involve the airline in a public inquiry.

But these were small troubles as far as Hugh was personally affected. It had been the sight of the S. and P.A. machine taking off that had chilled the heat of the day: the long slow run and then the lift of wings, the refusal to watch the aircraft once it was airborne and then the last-minute breaking of his will as he had gone to the north windows of the control room and seen how small its shape was in the sky and how uncertain, already, its identity, and hers.

As he washed, the chichaks came flickering in from their hole in the roof, to begin squabbling for the first of the flies across the ceiling.

The note came slipping under the door when he was facing in that direction; otherwise he wouldn't have found it until later. There was no knock. He disliked this sly means of delivering a message, and opened the door without picking it up. Colours floated down the narrow staircase.

"Who is that?" he called sharply in Malay.

The woman stopped and looked up at him in the pale light that came from the lamp outside. He went down the stairs.

"Mrs Thorne," he said, and with an effort and for the sake of courtesy: "This is a pleasure."

She didn't answer; he could hear her breath coming

quickly, perhaps after the climb and the hurrying down
again. Her large eyes were in shadow; the light from the
courtyard made an aureole for her night-black hair.

"I haven't read your message," he said in English. "Won't
you come up?" He pressed himself against the wall in the
narrow space but she didn't move, so he went up the stairs in
front of her. "I'll lead the way." It surprised him a little that
she followed. In the light of the room he saw that her face
was shy and confused; it hadn't been a sly delivery, then, but
a timid one. He tore open the envelope.

> Be glad if you would care to have a meal with us some
> time this week. A reply to the Rest House would do.
> Thomas Thorne.

Kamala stood near the door watching him intently, her
child's face calm, her hands hanging gracefully against the
sides of her sarong, her body quite still.

"This is very kind," he said. "I'll be delighted to come
along."

"I tell Tom." She pronounced it "Torm."

"He's well, I hope?"

"Oh yes. Always well." Warmth came to her leaf-shaped
eyes even when she spoke of him. She moved a hand towards
the door. "Now I go, please."

"If you won't take something—"

"Oh no. Thank you." Her smile came suddenly and was
beautiful. He went down the stairs with her and in the
shadowed hallway asked:

"Shall I send a note to the Rest House?"

"Oh no. When you come, please?"

"Would tomorrow be all right?"

"Tomorrow. I tell Tom." Her musky perfume was in the
air, sharper than the smell of the cassia tree outside. Suddenly
she touched him and whispered into his face—"Tomorrow,
do not say of the night when he is sick, or will be anger."

He asked her to say it in Malay, as it seemed urgent. He
wasn't to mention the matter of last night when they had
fetched Thorne out of the opium-house.

"I understand," he said. When she took her light hot

fingers from his arm they seemed to leave a patch of cold on his bare skin by contrast; he watched her flit through the courtyard and into the street, a flash of kingfisher blue as the lamplight flowed across her. Her scent lingered, and he wished she hadn't come, and hoped she would not come again.

14

THE shutters had been left wide open and the window-space was a sheen of silver where the moonlight fell on the sea; the native-style house was within fifty yards of the sands and a warm wind blew, sometimes plucking at the flame of the oil-lamp. Thorne kept a fly-swat handy, though his rather vicious swipes were becoming haphazard now; after the meal he had drunk steadily for an hour, and was shivering as the alcohol cooled him.

In the silences mosquitoes hummed; from the distance they could hear the short high bark of jungle-dogs; it re-minded Hugh of Joe's house, across the street from this one.

He had tried to analyse the note that Kamala had put under the door; it had a deliberately casual style—*Be glad if you would care*—without the personal pronoun, as if Thorne had shied from normal formality. *Some time this week* . . . In other words there was no immediate hurry, but this week set a limit: for some reason Thorne wanted to see him. What reason? There had been no hint of it during the meal. Kamala had cooked for them what Hugh imagined must be *haute cuisine* in this region, with a dozen dishes of great delicacy, mostly fish; the wine was French, not like the too-heavy hot rice-wine he had tried before. Thorne drank a bottle during the meal and then turned to whisky; Kamala drank nothing.

Hugh watched her sometimes in the long mirror that was fixed flat to the wall; she had put on her green and gold baju over the top of the sarong, and wore a Kelantan gold comb in her hair; she looked towards him often and always frankly, and her glances would have seemed inviting if her child's face were less innocent. Whether Thorne was aware of her interest in their guest—whether he was aware even of her own presence—there was no telling; for the most part he gazed at the bowls on the table, sometimes shooting a look at Hugh as if suddenly remembering him.

"Smith is back," he said in one of his brusque bursts of speech. "Did you know?"

"Yes, I met him when he came through the airport." A thin man with thin hair and thin lips, and something untrustable about the grey eyes, in which there was also some kind of feverish excitement; they were the eyes of a man who had stalked game for a long time and was now bringing the gun up slowly and carefully.

"The town smelt cleaner without him." He watched the wedge-shaped face of Thorne with its blued lips. This room had the taint of opium in it but there were no signs of a pipe. Did this bright-eyed child make his pipes for him in the lonely evenings? If so it was the only ceremony they shared; he was aloof to her quiet adoration. "And what did friend Smith have to tell you, at the airport?"

"Nothing very much. He was kind enough to ask me if I was settling down in the job."

"And are you?"

"I like this place, and the——"

"Why don't you drink, man?" He watched the girl pour whisky for him from the now half-empty bottle, but said nothing to her, swinging his head back to look at Hugh. "It keeps the dark away, didn't you know?"

"That's why I don't. Not whisky, anyway. You can't hold the night off for ever——"

"So you've tried it! People don't often fail."

"If there's some wine . . ." He was annoyed with himself for admitting even this much of his life; there hadn't been more than a dozen drinking-bouts anyway, in the first few months after it had happened; the last one was in Singapore with the rollicking Dutchmen; there wouldn't be any more, now, not even for Santha.

"Wine, then!" But Kamala was already pouring it for him, smiling down at him, her warm thigh resting for a moment against his elbow. Her kind of innocence, he knew now, was dangerous.

"They say you're a lonely man, Copland—that true?"

"I live alone; it's not the same thing——"

"You're a liar. No offence. But I'm older than you. A thousand years older, and no better for it, except that I know more about living and dying than you do. You know," he said, leaning across the table while the girl took the dishes away, "the most difficult thing about life is you have to live it with other people. There's only one worse strain and that's living without them. I've tried both. In the end——" He reached for the tumbler and held it cupped, irritated at having begun something he didn't want to finish. "In the end, there's always an end. Like everything else, it's the waiting—take Smith. There's a man with an end in view. Man with an objective."

"What does he do?" Smith didn't interest him very much but this man did; he wanted to know Thorne's reason for bringing him here, and to talk was the only way.

"Waits." His head began swinging to some kind of rhythm as if he were trying to throw off thoughts even as they came to him; nothing was supportable any more. "Like we all wait. What's an objective, after all, m'm? Man builds a bridge. Good. But t'isn't an objective, you see, it was just something to do while he waited. Like I built——" he sat back in his chair as Kamala glided across him with her bare tawny arms moving the last of the things from the table, an apology murmured in Malay.

What did Thorne build? It wasn't to be known. It was something else he had started to say—to reveal—and regretted; the girl's interruption saved him this time. He raised his head suddenly and looked at Hugh.

"You recognized me, didn't you, last night? M'm?"

"I thought I did."

"You still sure?"

"Yes, as sure as one can ever be. Faces are deceptive."

"Where d'you see me before? In the papers? Or were you there with the morbid mob, thirsting for blood?"

"I wasn't in the country, but I saw some papers. I was stationed at Karachi airport when you went through, soon afterwards. Someone said—'You know who that is?' "

Thorne's hand hit the table with a crash that rocked the tumbler and brought a gasp of fear from Kamala who was in the doorway—"*That name's never been heard here.*" His voice was painfully quiet; the few words were being choked out of him as he put himself to the enormous effort of keeping control. "I'll thank you to remember my name. Thorne. Thomas Thorne."

How had it gone? *Tuan Thorne, Saviour of the Sorely Afflicted, Bringer of Life to the Dying, Lord of the Knife.* Something like that.

Still frightened—perhaps more frightened by the awful hushed voice than the explosion of his hand on the table— Kamala moved with a scuff of bare feet across the resinous floor and stood beside him, adding to the whisky in his glass. He never knew she was there. She looked across at Hugh, bewilderment widening her eyes; the meaning of what had been said, and the cause of the outburst, were unknown to her.

Hugh smiled to her and said: "It's all right, Kamala."

"No. All terrible now."

"Not a bit. It was a sort of mistake, that's all. Don't worry."

They were talking as if Thorne weren't in the room; he had isolated himself. His face had crumpled and his eyes were at this moment immeasurably more bewildered than the girl's; she was afraid only of an angry man, of his anger that she didn't understand; but he was lost, utterly cut off from all known things and landmarks, and was looking out from the shell of his soul for the comfort of any man's hand; and Hugh pitied him for the first time. How did Thorne manage to live, without help? It could only be Kamala who kept him sane, saving his life a dozen times a day, every time she looked at him or touched him. It had been completely mistaken to think he was unaware of her; she was all he had, and therefore he looked at her with no more interest than was aroused by the sight of his own right hand; and she was content; adoration asked nothing but the mere existence of the idol, be it wholly clay.

Hugh had to look away from the collapsed lost face; if this had been the face he had seen last night, perched on the crouched body of the man in the opium-house, he would never have recognized it. The one in the newspapers had been expressionless, half-shielded with a hand or a brief-case or trapped defenceless in the flash of some unsuspected camera; at Karachi this face had been recognizable even from the flat images below the headlines; even in the opium-house all this time later it had been the same face; but not now.

"I must be going," Hugh said, and finished the wine in his glass; but he knew it wouldn't be so easy. Thorne's hands were sliding across the table, flat and white in the light of the oil-lamp; they had never felt the warmth of the sun; in this burning land these hands and this face were kept hidden from the world outside.

"What are you going to do, Copland?"

"How d'you mean?"

"Who are you going to tell?"

"Oh. It's nothing to do with me don't lose any sleep over that." He got up and smiled to Kamala. She wasn't looking afraid now. "That was a very beautiful meal," he told her in Malay. "You must be famous in the town, for such cooking."

In her own tongue she said courteously: "I shall be famous only for your praise." But the compliment had pleased her, probably because it was rare in this house.

Thorne didn't realise his guest was leaving; the spirit had built up in his bloodstream to the point when it overcame him. Hugh was surprised it hadn't happened sooner. If he tried to shake the man's hand it would probably lead to an embarrassment in front of Kamala.

"Goodnight, Thorne. And thank you."

Prompted by earlier training to make a show, Thorne tried to raise his head; his eyes saw nothing; they were simply wounds sunk into his face. "Kam'la will see you out," he whispered. " 'Pologize."

She gestured to the few springs of jasmine he had brought when he had come. "Kind to bring," she said, and waited for him in the doorway; and suddenly it was the formality that broke his heart—her careful preparation of a delightful and complicated meal which none of them had really tasted because of Thorne's mood; his pathetic effort to apologize in the onset of his stupor; and now her thanks for the flowers.

"Don't leave him, Kamala. I know the way out."

"I show." She walked in front of him through the shadowed passage, dropping her gold-green baju on to a wicker chair as she passed, to wait for him near the door, turning to watch him coming, an expression in her eyes he hadn't seen before. He took her hand.

"There's nothing to worry about," he said gently. He didn't know how much of the conversation had made sense to her—she understood more English than she spoke, and Thorne had said: "That name's never been heard here." Did she know what name? He had also asked: "Who are you going to tell?" Did she know what there was to be told?

"I not worry," she said in the tone of a child who knows there is a present for it; and he didn't understand until she loosened the top of her sarong with a casual movement and stood against him with the light of the lamp falling across her shoulders and bared breasts and the slow lifting of her arms as she held his face in her hands. "Kiss now," she whispered. "Kiss now . . . now . . ."

He spoke softly to her in Malay; probably Thorne was now unconscious with his poor head at peace on the table, but that wasn't certain; probably he understood Malay, but there was a chance that he didn't, and wouldn't know what they were saying, if he were listening through that open doorway.

"No, Kamala. No kiss—"

"Kiss now . . ."

"You must think," he said, "think." His hands were on her shoulders so that she couldn't move nearer but she arched her hips against him. She began speaking quickly in her own tongue, softly and insistently, saying that Tom would not know and that he would not care, for the opium had weakened him and he no longer thought of these things nor wanted them from her or any woman; and Hugh felt pity again for the man who had lost so much and now even this.

"I am hungry," she moaned softly, "I am so hungry, for it is a year now, more than a year, so for me you must kiss now—"

133

"Listen, child, and understand. I have just eaten in this house; I am his guest here until I go——"

"Then I forgive, as Allah will forgive." She strained closer to him so that he had to use his advantage and press her away until her back was against the wall.

"You are very beautiful," he said, "and I would seize the chance, as would any man, if I could." It might help her a little at least to know that there was only a moral impediment to this. "It is not possible, and I shall be sad on my way home." He could only hope that his Malay was good enough to convey his meaning; he should have told her in English, though that would have been awkward enough.

"Just kiss," she said, ignoring every word; and for a moment he thought of "just kissing" her and freeing himself; but the heat of her body reached him even at arm's length and her eyes were half-closed as her thoughts leapt ahead of reality. Had she, he wondered, asked this of many men during the tormenting year of nights, or was she afraid of a chance word afterwards, that would send Thorne into a dangerous rage? Perhaps she had decided that the young Englishman was readier than most men, being lonely, and also more likely to keep things to himself.

"Chium, sukakan . . . chium . . ."

He took one hand from her shoulder and found the door and opened it before she could stop him.

"Sweet little Kamala, men are so unkind to you."

She was sobbing and trying to draw up the top of her sarong to cover her breasts, and he waited until she had managed it before he pulled the door open wide and stepped into the moonlit street, walking quickly away, hearing the door click shut, trying not to think of her standing there alone and feverish and unloved.

His footsteps echoed between the walls. How many houses along this street were as desolate as that one? Not any; there couldn't be.

He was inside the courtyard, where the high iron lamp cast shadows across the stones, before he realized it would be

134

impossible to sleep; the evening had left him soured and deeply disturbed.

He turned back into the street. It wasn't yet midnight; voices sounded through the slats of shutters; one or two rickshas were still bobbing beneath the lamps and the restaurant next door was still open. He thought of seeing Joe and talking to him; Joe would know everything about that wretched house and in his philosophical way might rid him of some of his depression. Had she ever asked Joe? She must have. What had he done about it? Anything? It wouldn't be a good thing to talk to Joe tonight.

He had already eaten; the smell from the restaurant sickened him. The Duffys would be in bed. If he wrote to Santha he would say too much and anyway it would set him back badly in his private campaign to forget her.

The Land-Rover stood on the waste-land at the street's end; he got in and started the engine, waiting for a minute while it warmed. A small half-naked boy from nowhere was suddenly clinging to the windscreen and grinning with all his charm—Tuan give him ride now! Hugh told him that if he didn't get off as quick as a shot duck he would take him to his father and see that the entire wrath of Allah would descend upon him for seven days and seven nights. The boy sprang off, laughing delightedly at the flow of rocky Malay.

He backed the car and swung it inland along Jalan Burong, speeding up when the street opened out to the wider mud-track and the houses and lamps were left behind. He would go to the airstrip and see what the new sentries looked like, and if there was none there he would telephone the *istana* and report it and get the whole regiment court-martialled. There had to be something to finish off this miserable day, even if it meant routing an army.

In the wash of light the scrub thickened and became jungle; before he had gone a mile he had to stop and scrape a solid film of insects from the windscreen.

Another mile and he stopped again, this time to clear the glass of the headlamps; their beams had been gradually yellowing behind the scum of crushed insects. As he started off the tin top took up its rattling again. There would be no stealth about this unofficial inspection of the airstrip guard; this din could be heard for miles. The headlamp beams prodded their way through the massed green foliage, dipping and swinging as the car hit the bumps.

The broken tree had fallen just beyond a curve in the track and he almost hit it. His foot stamped on the brake and the wheels locked, but the car slid twenty yards through the ruts before it halted. He sat with the engine running and the lights full on, thinking before moving. The tree wasn't much thicker than a man's leg but its bushy leaves made it look more of an obstacle. The leaves were fresh; the tree hadn't stood there dying for months at the roadside, to topple at last and lie like this. In full life a wind had blown it down.

It wouldn't do. Ready as he was to make light of the rumours and fears that plagued the town it would be stupid to call them groundless. One must size things up for oneself. This tree blocking the track was alive and in full sap, and there hadn't been a wind for weeks. For nearly three miles the car had raised a din loud enough to be heard even from the airstrip to the town. He had stopped twice to clear the insects, taking his time.

They couldn't possibly have known he was coming, because he had started off in this direction on the spur of the moment; but they would have had time enough to hack this sapling and bring it down, once the sound of the Land-Rover and the track of its lights had sent the news ahead.

Duffy's Ford had looked a real mess, with the bullet-holes as straight as eyelets in a shoe, and the blood down the side of the door.

Moving his shoulder as little as he could, he reached down to get the gun out of its makeshift holster under the dash-board, and felt only the empty strap, and remembered leaving the gun in his rooms ready for cleaning when he found the time. Straightening up, he studied the bushy leaves, easing the accelerator down a fraction to close the cut-out and brighten the lights a degree. There was no movement anywhere.

If he used the darkness as a defence by switching the lights off, and got out of the car, and walked to the tree, and tried to move it, they would pick him off with one burst. If he got out and tried to lash the tow-rope to the tree and haul it clear, the same thing would happen. There was no real point in getting out. To back the car along the track until he reached the first place wide enough to turn would be very tedious, and the lights would have to be on while he did it, making him a sitting target. It was doubtful that he could get through the obstacle by reversing and taking a run at it; the Land-Rover was built for rugged going but not really designed to mow trees down, and the lamps would be smashed in any case, so he wouldn't be able to drive on even if he got through.

Walsh had said: "Take my tip and you'll always keep this gun handy. There's more than tiger in this bloody outpost." Duffy had said: "The next time you come here, I want to see your gun." It was very smart to ignore the advice of people who lived here and knew the ropes, but the price looked high. He switched off the lights and the engine and sat listening, opening his eyes wide to help them accommodate. After half a minute he could see the rough outline of the tree in the moonlight. There were small sounds from the jungle as life stirred there; the hunt for food that had been made in this leafy dark for a million years was not going to stop now, just because a stray biped was suddenly involved in the business of the night and was to die here and become carrion like the mouse-deer and the tree-rat and the jungle fowl.

Some of the sounds he could identify; he had grown used to them in the sleepless nights on the airstrip. He was waiting for a different one: the click of a breech. Nothing came. They were waiting for him to get out of the car. Unless they had a machine-gun they'd be taking a slight risk; if their first shot was inaccurate—and however close they were among these leaves the light was poor—he would return their fire and might make a chance hit. They weren't to know he was unarmed. He didn't think they had a machine-gun, because the tree would be quite unnecessary in that case; they would have simply raked the ca as it neared.

137

He needed to know their position; it might be behind the tree or deep in the bigger leaves alongside the road on one side or both. There wouldn't be much chance for him even if he found their position and slipped out of the car, to plunge into the jungle. They would know it better than he did and would easily catch him there. This must be what they were waiting for him to do; so he would match their patience. He mustn't get out of the car.

It took him a few minutes to do all he could in the way of defence, which was little enough; but now, slumped right down on the seat with his knees under the dashboard, he was less exposed. A saloon, with its high doors, would have afforded him better armour; on the other hand he could get out of this car very much faster if he had to.

He waited. However strong his patience, it would only delay the end, because they would move in for him before morning; but he didn't mean to walk into their fire and give them best, right at the beginning. They would wait for half an hour, perhaps, hoping that he would reconsider and decide that it wasn't an ambush after all, but only a freak tree-fall.

The small sounds went on, and he kept his wits alert by listening to them consciously and identifying those that he could. The cry came unnervingly and his scalp crept, because it was human, and not far away. It wasn't repeated; it was the kind of cry that would never again come from the same throat. Then he began doubting. With the nerves pitched, fancy was free; nothing was unimaginable, here in the night and the waiting. There was nothing he could do about it, anyway. If that had been human, it might have simply been an attempt to draw him out of the car. Whatever happened he must stay here. His nerves were good. They could shoot him down but they couldn't out-fox him.

The next interval lasted some ten or fifteen minutes. New sounds were rising now, coming closer. Something—man or animal—was moving towards the road. He waited.

Everything was logical. Nothing was without a reason. What fitted in, here? There hadn't been a wind for weeks but that tree was down. Its leaves were fresh; it was still alive. Why no shooting, yet? They wanted him in the open. All logical. But that cry: if human, whose? If a man had just died in the thick of those dark leaves, who—or what— had killed him?

Too late, he was ready to listen to others. To Arthur Duffy again: "He'll be around here for a while unless they can shift him. He's a lone male, working a pattern of his own. Yesterday he took three rubber-tappers—not mine—on the other side of the ridge."

Working a pattern. Everything was logical, and the mind of a tiger worked within the bigger mind of the living jungle, according to its laws.

It was no better for him, then. Bullet or tiger, he'd no defence. A gun was a very important thing, here along the jungle coast; Walsh had known and so had Duffy. Only the greenhorns out from England relied on their British passport to see them through.

The sounds neared. He moved his hand slowly, getting a grip on the cutaway side of the car, ready to heave himself out and fight in the open rather than be found here in the morning, cold meat in a tin box.

"Have you got a gun, Copland?"

He jerked in his breath. The voice in its suddenness had had the effect of an explosion on his nerves.

"Yes!" It was the only possible answer. Many Chinese spoke perfect English, as Chong did.

"Don't shoot, then. Put your lights on."

A shape moved along the side of the track towards the front of the car, unhurriedly, and passed within a few yards, walking across to the broken tree. Hugh tried to understand the impossible situation, and failed, giving it up and turning the light-switch.

The man was inspecting the tree, tugging at the leaves and testing the stability of the tree-trunk with his foot; now he turned and came back to the car, walking into the glaring light with the loping stride that Hugh had first seen in the Rest House the day Duffy was shot at. The cat that walked by itself.

"You'll have to drag it clear," he said. "Have you got a rope on board?"

"Yes." He levered himself up from his prone position, feeling a fool. Stratton was already fishing about in the rear of the car, looking for the towing-gear. Neither of them spoke until they had tied the rope to the tree and taken the strain on it.

"Get going," Stratton said. "I'll tell you when we're clear." There was blood caking on his neck, at the side.

"Is that a bad wound, Stratton?"

"Scratch. Jungle thorn. Back up and I'll swing the tree."

As the trunk shivered and then began dragging along the ruts, Stratton heaved at one end to bring it round. Then he signalled, and Hugh brought the Land-Rover forward again and they loosed the rope and stowed it. The end of the tree was bright yellow-white in the lamp-beams; it had been recently felled with a sharp blade.

Hugh found some cigarettes in the car and lit one; Stratton shook his head. "Where are you bound, the air-strip?"

"Yes. Just checking up."

Stratton nodded. "So-long. Take more care." He went loping across the road and out of the direct light.

"Stratton!"

"What?" He stopped and turned.

"I heard a shout, ten minutes before you came. It sounded like a man."

"Jungle dog. Bark's deceptive at night."

Hugh looked at him steadily. This had been an ambush: that tree had been hacked down very recently; but no one had come for the kill. A man had cried out with death already in his throat, ten minutes before Stratton had appeared to help him shift the tree. There was blood on his neck from a skin-wound that almost anything could have made: jungle thorn, or claws, or the finger-nails of a hand flung out too late in defence.

"This was an ambush," he said to the lean grey-eyed man. "Wasn't it?"

"That's right."

140

"Who set it up?"

Stratton was silent for seconds, staring into the swamp of light where Hugh was standing. Then he came very slowly towards him with his big hands stuck into his belt.

"You've been here a week. Time you got your eyes open. There are C.T.s in this area. Most of them are fanatics. They try anything they think they can bring off. So far you've been lucky, but don't rely on luck, Copland. The fourth time they may get you. Try and remember—"

"This is the first time they've—"

"Third. That ambush on the coast road was for you. They thought you were coming in by car, not by air. Then one of their half-blood aboriginal trackers tried the snake-trick on you—they couldn't get a krait or you wouldn't be here now. Tonight they heard you coming and sent the same man; it was meant to be very quiet, no shooting. I know you're young and fresh out from Europe, but try to get it into your head: you're marked. We all are."

He turned away and dropped silently from the edge of the raised track. A few leaves stirred as his body twisted between them and then there was silence and he was gone.

141

15

THREE days later a note came from Santha and he kept it in his hip-pocket unopened until, after only an hour, he weakened, and took it out. He could no more burn this envelope still sealed than hold his hand in a flame.

She had been told that her duty-schedules had been changed, she wrote, and would be on board the S. and P.A. transit flights breaking their Singapore-Bangkok runs at Pasang and Kota Bharu during the next two weeks. Her new schedule would begin on Friday, when she would have to make Pasang an overnight stop. She hoped that he was well, and that his appetite was now fully regained. She signed herself Santha May Swee, with no flourish.

He read the letter three times during the morning, taking it out of the rapidly-soiling envelope and finding a new meaning to each of these cold little statements. They were open to several interpretations, but the facts at least were sure: for two weeks she would be here once every day, and he would see her for a few minutes. On Friday—in two days' time—she would be in Pasang overnight.

Was the stiff little letter a warning that when she landed here on Friday it wouldn't be with any intention of spending the evening with him? Probably. She hoped his "appetite was now fully regained". In other words, that he would in future be able to eat an entire Chinese dinner in her company without emotional upsets. So there was no joy in this; he stood holding a letter written by (touched by the hand of, seen by the eyes of) Santha May Swee, the ringed faun strayed from a fable into the room where the lamp and bamboo had cast their magic; he had prepared himself never to see her again, and she was coming; his own name was on her letter, and that small gold hand had written it, so that in his mind as he read it he pronounced it Hee-yoo. But when she had sat writing to him there had been delicate green light flickering in cold sparks across the paper, thrown from the bracelet on her wrist. So there was no joy in this.

He dropped the letter into the waste-paper basket in the staff office some time during the afternoon, without considering; the cheat in the brave gesture was that he knew every word by heart, but it was better than keeping the thing in his pocket as if it were something valuable.

"Manager sahib!"

He went up the wide wooden steps into the compressed heat of the control tower. "Well, Haji Ahmad?"

"Flight 17 from Singapore has called up, sahib. Will land in ten minutes."

"Thank you, Ahmad." He went to the east windows and looked out at the thin white haze. There hadn't been a storm for three days and the air was gluey, and the horizon of coconut palms a half-seen mirage above the coast. Birds had already begun flying up from the mangrove swamps, hearing the aircraft that was still invisible above the haze; the parakeets feeding on the seed at the edge of the perimeter track were dispersing and grating out their petulant chorus; the gibbon went swinging into the higher trees to settle like an audience before the show. Below the tower, at the doorway of his restaurant, Wan Chai would be standing and watching the sky, counting on customers. He had been even more generous, lately, in his offers of hospitality; at the same time he had chased the cook and waiter about their work unmercifully and for no good reason. Wan Chai was a worried man, and Hugh was more frequently wondering why.

"Haji Ahmad."

"Sahib?"

"What was Mr Chai saying this morning, about Friday?"

"That he has ordered special delicacies from Singapore, for the celebrations, sahib."

"That's right. What celebrations, though?"

"It is the Moon Festival, sahib."

"Ah, yes. The Moon Festival."

Through the open window they could hear the first far

droning of the aircraft. "What will you do, Ahmad, on this important day?"

"I shall become drunk, sahib."

"Why?"

"It is the custom for us all."

"Will everyone become drunk, Haji Ahmad? Ricksha boys and bus-drivers too?"

"Those who have money, sahib. All those."

"It should be very exciting, then, on Friday."

The aircraft came into the circuit and he reached for the signal lamp.

"Flight 17 is about to land, sahib."

"Thank you, Haji Ahmad."

He went down a few minutes later to sign the aircraft-receipt form, and Ismail came bustling through from the customs room.

"Tuan Copland, we have two passengers who do not wish to pass through customs."

"Right, I'll go along, Ismail."

The two men were waiting patiently at the end of the long counter, sweating comfortably in their neat grey suits and black shoes.

"Can I help you, gentlemen?"

"It's only a question of procedure." They showed him their papers. "Are you the manager?"

"Yes."

"For your information, Mr Copland, we've nothing dutiable to declare." They watched his face with eyes like X-ray machines.

"You've handed in your landing-tickets?"

"We have." They put their papers away.

"That's all you need do, then. If you're going into Pasang right away there's the airport coach outside."

"Thank you."

He watched them leave the building. He should have said —as he always said to passengers who were strange here— that he would be at their service if there was anything he could help them with; but these two men didn't need any-one's help. They knew what to do. They had been told. They were here to play a brief part in the life of a small town at the edge of the South China Sea which they had never seen before and would never see again; and it didn't concern them that they would carry anguish with them into the town and stand at that one door with it in their hands like a gift from a traveller. Nothing dutiable.

He moved to a window and watched them get into the taxi that Smith had arrived in, an hour ago. He was here to meet them. The doors slammed and their pale faces became blobs at the windows. They were driven away, and at the junction in the perimeter track the car turned to the right, away from the town, taking the inland jungle route towards the palace.

"Joe, I need your help badly."

"Allah is with thee, in the form of his humble servant." Joe stood looking up at him, dignified in his clean white robe. One would take him for a mystic or a monk, except for the interest in his eyes as he looked at other people; Joe believed that you could save a soul without actually building a temple in which to shout about it.

Hugh stared into the cave-like shadows of the shop-house, undecided to the point of momentary neurosis. He had asked the towkay to go away twice; the problem was hard enough without his being persuaded to buy things he didn't want. Joe had found him here, cast up by the tide of people that flowed along the street.

"You've seen my room, Joe—the main one. I've got somebody coming tomorrow night, to dinner. What do I need?"

"Food."

"I mean for the room. To gay it up a bit."

"Well," Joe said slowly, "we better start with some rugs, huh?"

"Yes, I was thinking of rugs."

"What's her favourite colour, d'you think?"

Hugh looked at him, annoyed. "I suppose it is a bit obvious."

"Nice and obvious, sure. I like obvious things. You can

145

kind of get your mind round them without spraining the brain. Now what say we start with the big question: how much do we aim to spend on this dinner-date, furniture and all?"

He spent an hour in the shop, poking about and digging down deep among the heaps of bric-à-brac while Hugh nodded or shrugged or shook his head and finally gave up. Half the contents of the shop was now on the pavement and across the monsoon gutter, and rickshas were being diverted to the other side of the road.

"And where can I find," Hugh asked Joe as they followed the towkay's barrow to the courtyard in Jalan Burong, "a man to cook the dinner for us?"

"Tomorrow night? That's tough. You never saw the Moon Festival before, did you?"

"No. I've been told that everyone's going to be drunk, and—"

"Wouldn't say drunk. Excited, though. This whole street'll be blocked entirely." They were already having to dodge and stoop under the festoons of lanterns that were being strung across and across the street; it was almost impossible to see the Chinese shop signs and the washing-beflagged balconies and shutters. "It'll be blocked partly by all those people," Joe said, "who would ordinarily jump at the chance of cooking your dinner for you at a reasonably unreasonable figure—"

"I don't mind how much things cost—"

"That's great—"

"I mean, within reason." Joe was making him feel like a fool, a boy in calf-love.

"Oh sure. Well, I'll find you a cook. French, Indian or Chinese food?"

Damn the man, he even knew who was coming.

"I don't know, Joe. I've been trying to decide."

"Make it French, huh? You can't get French food any-place this side of Saigon. In this town it's never even been heard of. Be a kind of compliment, no? Offer the lady the impossible—"

"If it's never been heard of, who can cook it?"

146

"I know a man. I'll instruct him."

"A bit incongruous, having anything but Chinese food on the night of the Moon Festival, isn't it?"

"Sure. Make it Chinese." They followed the barrow into the courtyard, where a mass of people were struggling to untangle a skein of strung lanterns; one man was right up inside the cassia tree, fishing with a long bamboo pole as his friends tried to pass him the strings. "Also," Joe said, "you will need moon cakes. I'll send them along with the cook."

They helped the towkay ease the barrow through the mêlée; there was already a pair of lanterns round his neck and he had barely escaped being throttled. Within half an hour they had moved the things from the barrow up the narrow staircase and into the main room, and paid the man and sent him away; and it was at this moment, as he looked at the small beautiful Persian rug and the Chinese screen with its willow leaves and the pile of black-and-gold silk cushions, that Hugh felt a sudden sagging of spirits. Safeguarding herself against a repetition of that last evening together, she would almost certainly excuse herself tomorrow and remain in the Rest House or eat somewhere else alone or with some of the passengers or crew. This extravagant preparation was pointless. The chances were that he would spend tomorrow evening in this room alone, in the cold comfort of silk cushions and the beautiful rug that he'd have to sell the next day at half the price in any case, because he couldn't possibly afford to keep them.

"I'd say," Joe murmured gravely, watching his face, "this will turn out a truly wonderful evening. You really know how to organize a date."

"She might not come." Joe seemed to make you say whatever was in your mind; it was infuriating.

"Sure she'll come. She'd be crazy not to. Now where're we goin' to have these beautiful things?"

"The rug and the screen as far away from each other as possible. They don't go together—I should have seen that before."

"They go just great." Joe began wandering about the

room, solemnly preoccupied with the problem of its re-arrangement; and after a while Hugh found the heart to help.

It was nearly midnight when Joe went home. They had gone next-door and had a meal and come back and spent another hour rearranging the room for the third time, and still weren't satisfied—which Joe said was as it should be—"Setting out to try making life more beautiful, you shouldn't ever get to be satisfied, Hugh-boy."

The Chinese lanterns were strung high across the little courtyard outside, not lit yet. The street was still crowded and people had forgotten their uneasiness about the ambush and the work of the lone male tiger; or they believed that the moon, whose goddess had granted them the harvest and seen it home, would also take care of these other matters when she found the time.

Children were running everywhere, the light of the unlit lanterns already in their eyes. In almost every shop there were moon cakes and lanterns for sale, and barrows of them plied between loaded stalls along every street.

Hugh went some of the way with Joe, letting himself drift among the lights and along the mood of the evening, trying not to think about tomorrow, not to care. Even if there were no plans possible for the evening he would walk here anyway along this street and look at the lanterns and have a good time.

People milled around them and the noise filled the street; many of the children had small gongs which they beat in time with their chanting while their mothers leaned from the open shutters and called to one another across the chasm of the street and their fathers stood at the coffee-stalls or sat in the kedais round the mah-jongg boards. Nobody wanted to go to bed.

Two faces among all the others were strange to the town, and Hugh wondered if Joe had seen them. They had looked down from the verandah of the Rest House, watching the street.

A paper lantern came adrift from the festoons and fell upon a Malay boy's head, and he grabbed it and began fighting off the horde of his friends; within seconds it was a rugger scrum.

"Those two guys," Joe said. "Just who are they?"

The paper lantern was flattened and torn but they still tussled for it; the game was the thing, not the prize.

"Extradition officers."

"Is that so? When did they get in?"

"Yesterday."

"Flew in, I guess."

"That's right."

Joe stood at the cross-roads where the ancient fortune-teller sat, her thin voice pitched against the din. Joe seemed, suddenly, lost; he looked up at Hugh with a blank face. "What're they here for, Hugh?"

"I don't know. Pick someone up, I expect."

"It's official, and all?"

"I expect so, Joe. They drove straight to the *istana* when they arrived. There'll be a delay, though, because the Sultan's in Singapore until the week-end." There had been quite a panic two days ago when Sir Rahman had taken a seat on one of the ordinary Straits Airways planes, because his own private aircraft was still undergoing the sabotage inspection he had ordered. Ismail had excelled himself. The crash- and fire-tenders had stationed themselves on each side of the plane at fifty yards distance when it began its take-off run, and if Ismail could have managed it they would have taken off with it, Federation flags flying.

"They out from London, Hugh?"

"Yes. Direct flight London-Cairo, then Karachi-Bangkok to Singapore."

"Not just a vacation."

"No."

"Be nice when they go, huh?"

"Be nice if they go alone."

Joe moved on again and because of the way that frail paper lantern had fallen from all the others Hugh didn't want to talk any more. "I'll be getting back now, Joe. Thanks for all your help."

"You're welcome." The warmth had gone out of the night for Joe too; his face still looked lost when Hugh left him, and walked back alone among the crowd past the stalls of piled moon cakes and the coffee-shops and the corner where the old woman sat with her stool and table, crying that she would lift the veil on the morrow and reveal its fortunes, one had only to bid her, one had but to ask.

16

THERE were a dozen or more streets in Pasang but this
evening it seemed that the whole population had flowed into
Jalan Burong, where the lanterns were hung from the Rest
House right down to the shore a mile away.

He was already late, because the waste land was aswarm
with children weaving with their lanterns in the pattern of
a maze, and he had had to leave the Land-Rover parked
outside the police-station, where it would be safest from the
fireworks. By the time he had reached the house in the
courtyard and changed, the hired cook had arrived, and
he had to talk to him and make sure that everything was
prepared.

Yun Fu reassured him impatiently. He had cooked for
Mister Joe many times, and always there was satisfaction.
Tonight there were not enough dishes and there was trouble
with the stove, but he would manage, and Mister Coplan'
would be very satisfied. Had he brought the moon cakes?
His impatience waxed. There were moon cakes in every shop
and on every stall and even the ricksha-boys were selling
them. It was not possible for Mister Coplan' to step
outside this house without receiving a bombardment of
moon cakes, so perhaps he would be kind enough to bring
some back with him while Yun Fu struggled with the
stove.

Hugh left him to it, not daring to ask whether Yun Fu
knew the working and the ways of stoves; doubtless he would
have retorted that he had invented them himself.

He pressed into the thronged street—

"Taksi, tuan! Taksi!"

"Moon cakes! Moon cakes fresh from oven!"

"Lanterns! Cheap now! Only few left, velly cheap
lanterns!"

The voices were mostly Chinese but the native Malay

population had adopted the festival years before, since it established another official holiday and was therefore to be supported nobly. Everyone was dressed in their best sarong or samfoo or Palm Beach suit and the youth of the town strutted Singapore-style in narrow striped cotton trousers with white shirts hanging loose at the waist. One Malay had found from somewhere, unbelievably, a silk top hat, once sported, perhaps, by Mr Comyns-Edge, the Resident now departed.

"Tuan take taksi! No good walk—must have taksi!"

He dodged the thing and forced his way across the pavement and into the Rest House, whose large ground-floor rooms were as crowded as the street outside and hung with as many lanterns as the ceilings would take. Most of the passengers from the S. and P.A. plane were in the main lounge and three or four house-boys with loaded trays were consoling them in their sorrow at being so far from home on this festive night. There was no white drill uniform to be seen.

He was nearly fifteen minutes late. Had she gone out to a restaurant, on principle? Gone up to her room again, hurt at the slight? He made his way to the house-telephone but it wasn't working. Mr Sahgal, the manager, said he had not seen Miss Swee. He had not seen anybody, any more than he would be able—he explained in the Malay equivalent—to see one tree in a forest of trees. Thirty people had booked tables in the Rest House restaurant, and there were exactly nineteen tables. Also, two of the S. and P.A. passengers had become drunk and were singing, and his Asian guests did not like it.

Hugh left him and went back to the main lounge. The present was in his trouser pocket but he wasn't sure when to give it to her, here in the crowd or alone in his own room. He had been an hour in the shop before deciding on this small exquisite moonstone set in gold, its filigree work forming a chaplet of lotus leaves; he had seen a brooch like this in a shop in Singapore but then there had been nobody to buy it for. It would be months before he could finish paying for it (Mr Loo had fixed things up on his behalf), yet the emerald bracelet must have cost fifty times as much. He thought the brooch more beautiful.

The piano in the bar sounded through the babble of voices and he pushed his way to the door and looked in, but it was Chong's navigator playing, and it was not the Piaf song. He came back and saw her immediately but not for the first time this evening. Often he had seen the turquoise sari edged with gold, moving through the people; but her back had been turned to him and he had been looking for a white drill uniform. Now he saw her face, and her smile; and he thought: "She's too beautiful for me."

"Good evening," she said. He loved her shy formality and her cool small hand, the trembling smile and the way her hair was done—drawn back and caught with a thin gold band—and the way she looked at him, her dark eyes on the brink of glancing away out of modesty.

There was nothing about her that he didn't love, he wanted to say.

"Good evening, Miss Santha May Swee."

But the present must stay in his pocket, because the brooch she wore at the cleft of her breasts was exactly the same.

"I thought you were not coming," she said.

"Did you?"

He made way for her through the crowd. At the airstrip when the S. and P.A. Dakota had landed, he had simply asked her: "Would you spend the evening with me?" Still formal of speech—perhaps thinking her grasp of English was still too weak and an attempt at idiom might appear as slang—she had said: "I would be delighted." She had been surprised at his sudden laugh, and later Ismail had been surprised by the friendly slap on the back the manager had given him when the last plane of the day had taken off.

On the steps of the Rest House he said: "You look so lovely, Santha."

"I should be wearing my cham-song, because it is a Chinese festival."

He took her hand without thinking as they went down to the street, and she looked round to see if anyone were watching. Tonight, despite the cold little letter she had sent to the airport, she was warm and tremulous and didn't try to take her hand away; the impossible had happened, and she was here with him as magically as a bird flown into his room.

They took a jinrikisha because he wanted the privacy the raised hood gave, but the street's ceiling of lanterns was so wonderful that he asked for the hood to be lowered, and they sat without saying anything, all the way down Jalan Burong to the sea, and all the way back.

"Now I will tell you," she said.

They sat by the window looking down; the courtyard was a cloud of colours below them where the lanterns glowed. Beyond the lanterns the street had lost identity; it was a slow movement of people, their many voices lifting and falling in a kind of music.

"Not yet," he said.

Yun Fu had gone. He had cooked the meal well and they had eaten some of it; sitting at the table with her in his own room, host to her in private, his servant for the night attending them, he knew it was impossible that there could ever be this scene again; and she had been pleased and had pleased him with every glance and word, confirming what he knew already: that this was to be the last time for them.

He had thought of asking Yun Fu, secretly, to take away the moonstone with him and change it for something else, so that there should be a present for her after all, a keepsake; but there hadn't been the opportunity, and perhaps it was better to leave things as they were; she would only have to thank him and pretend she would cherish it as something valuable because he loved her.

Through the street and through the moving people, children were running and darting and dancing, each with a lantern in the shape of a fish or a bird or a crescent moon.

He had sat at a window like this before, overlooking a small green lawn and Southampton Water; that had been over for what seemed a long time now, and by morning this would be over, too. So he took her gold-skinned hand and kissed it and said: "Tell me, then."

She spoke slowly at first, afraid of hurting him more than she must; while she was telling him, it occurred to him that it was a mistake—he didn't need to hear these things, and hadn't asked; but she wanted him to know, for her own reasons, so he helped her as much as he could. Whatever happened, he resolved, he mustn't let himself be involved; there was no need to torment himself when the morning of the long tomorrow was so close. But before she was halfway through he was committed, and appalled.

"It was not only that they were kind to me," she said, her hands lying together as if in penance. "They spent all they possessed, trying to give me some of the things I had been used to. They denied their own daughters, even, because their station was held to be lower than mine. They lost their daughters in the war—the Nipponese soldiers took them away and they were never heard of again. But they have never let me see that they would have wished their own children back, in my place."

Her voice was low, its sweet tone hardly changing; some of the words he missed because of the noise in the street below; but he could picture her childhood now and the Swee family in Singapore, scraping the means of life among the stony streets, giving her all they were able and denying themselves, because she was the daughter of the house they had served and these things were her due.

"I was too young, in the war. I was seven when the city fell, and the soldiers had no use for me, as they had for the Swee girls, so I was spared. All my life in their house I was given beautiful things and shielded from ugliness as much as possible. As I grew up I began to see how poor they were and how mean their house was. When I had learned English I went to work in a shop and they were in despair about it, although I brought money home to them. Then I went to live in a room away from them, so that I could work in my spare time without them knowing. In this way I saved more money for them, but it was very little. For my work I have to buy clothes and try to look smart. When one of them becomes ill I take work in one of the Worlds, at a dance-hall or cinema when I am on leave. It is difficult. I used to lie awake trying to think what to do for them. They are among the poorest of the city when they are ill and can't work. Have you seen the poor people there, Hugh?"

"Yes. I've walked down those streets."

"I considered becoming a prostitute." One hand had moved, on her lap, and he put his own over it. "I have never told anyone."

"Thank you for telling me."

"I worked it out, and found I would earn much less than on the airline. I was glad, because it would have been annoying."

It was a Santha word, "annoying".

"Mr Swee has been ill now for a long time. He has tuberculosis—most of the poor have it. Soon he will have to go to the dying-house. Have you seen them?"

"No, I haven't."

"There are many of them, because the hospitals are crowded, and if everyone dying of old age or tuberculosis or cancer were to apply for treatment and comfort at the hospitals, the city would have to be rebuilt to take them all. Six months ago, Mr Swee applied to go into a dying-house. Mrs Swee would no longer have to look after him and see his pain. He is not old, but he is dying. I did not let him go there but—"

Her voice broke and she stood up from the wicker chair, standing with her back to the window, so that he couldn't see her face but only the fall of the sari and the gleam in the dark of her hair where the gold band caught it. They had turned out the lamp after the meal and had sat in the glow from the courtyard.

He stood up but didn't touch her; he looked not at her but down at the street; she wanted to be alone, suddenly, and this was as much as he could do, not to look, not to touch.

Her life had been full of wonderful people, she had told him; and these were the two most loved, one an applicant for a dying-house, the other a candidate for solitude.

"It is all I think about, Hugh. To repay, while there is a little time left."

"Yes." When would she let him touch her, comfort her?

"Not long ago there was a Chinese industrialist going from Hong Kong to Singapore on one of my flights. His name is Mr Fei Moi Toi. He has honoured me with an offer of marriage, and I have accepted."

She wasn't wearing the emerald bracelet tonight, only the other moonstone, the first one.

"It often happens," he said dully, "on the airlines. They choose such—such pretty stewardesses." It would be dishonest to congratulate her. She had said at the restaurant: "There is something I have to do."

"Now they will be safe," she said.

"Yes. And you can stop worrying. I'm very glad for them." He badly wanted a cigarette but knew she didn't smoke. He wanted her to go, because there was nothing he could do to help her. She had decided on this, and would be happier for it; he mustn't persuade her otherwise for his own selfish reasons. Nor could he make the effort of pretending she was right, of giving her the solace of feeling that someone else in the world agreed with her. He couldn't speak the truth and couldn't lie, so there was nothing to be said, not even a single word, at this of all moments when he'd give so much to help her.

A sound stirred and he looked away from the window into the room; she had turned and was staring at him, the few tears gone, her deep eyes shining.

"I wanted you to know, Hugh."

Just as he had wanted her to know about his marriage in England; but he had told her that so that she should know he wasn't simply wanting an affair. What was her reason, now?

"Why did you tell me, Santha?"

"Because I love you." She didn't look away. "Because I needed someone to—to hear these things and keep them secret with me. It will help me, sometimes, to remember you."

She came to him as he moved and he held her slight body for a long time while the sound from the street flowed in at the window, so that her harsh sobbing was covered a little

by the voices and the laughter of the children outside. After
minutes, when the shuddering of her body stilled and she
could raise her face, he kissed her brow and she closed her
eyes; he was at a loss for what to say, because he had never
imagined this, and it was so very complicated. A heart,
already breaking, was in his hands.

"It was when you stepped on the little old man's foot,"
she whispered, her eyes still closed.

In a dream, one had to accept the irrational.

"What did you say then?"

"In Raffles Square." He said nothing, trying to fathom it.
"That was when I first liked you—when you started being
not ordinary to me."

"I don't remember."

"He was a Chinese. He was rather like Mr Swee."

"I honestly don't see—"

"No. I think odd things."

Then he kissed her as he had kissed her on the beach,
when the lightning had flashed and they hadn't seen it; this
time she pressed herself against him with a sudden movement of her thighs, and feeling the heat of her body through
the thin sari he remembered that her manner (the shyness,
the formality, the gentle self-effacement) was Chinese only
because she had been brought up by the Swee's, and that
she was half French, half Indian, with the sexuality of both
cultures in her.

Her bare arms lifted across his shoulders and the kiss went
on, and the last clear thought in his mind was that when he
had chosen the six black-and-gold silk cushions that were on
the floor it hadn't been with any idea of this, the undreamed-
of. He felt for the moonstone brooch at the cleft of her
breasts and unpinned it, out of courtesy to the giver.

★ 17 ★

THE surge of voices was even louder now along the street, though it had gone midnight. When he had lain beside her in the coloured gloom of the room they had heard the distant crackle of fireworks; and once a small rocket had gone soaring across the indigo sky.

He stood by the window finishing the cigarette, thoughts coming fast because everything had changed, not because of their love-making but because of what she had said, and must have meant, before it. That she loved him.

When she came back from the other room, he crushed out the cigarette on the window-sill. Whatever he said to her, he mustn't let the anger show; it had started when with gentle insistence she had denied him entry, and though he had accepted it and the climax of mere love-play, he had thought about the implication more and more clearly and bitterly since. It hadn't meant anything, to unpin the moonstone and put it aside out of sight.

"I will make some coffee for us, Hugh." Her tone was questioning; she was diffident again, perhaps knowing that any man would feel a little angry now, after denial.

"Would you like some?" he asked.

"Not really. It is late."

"If you love me, Santha, we can't just end it, now everything's begun."

She stood looking down across the cloud of lanterns.

"Because you don't love him," he said.

"I should have told you that whatever happened tonight wouldn't change anything . . . It was wrong of me, not to——"

"He's not a young man." All the things he'd been unable to say before must now be said.

"No."

159

"What would Mr and Mrs Swee say, if they knew why **you** were doing this?"

"Please don't ask me things now——"

"I couldn't ask you before."

Turning half aside she murmured: "You must have made love to many women, without it meaning anything."

"It's not because of that, Santha; it's because you said you loved me. Or was that just kindness?"

She swung her head. "No!"

"Then everything's different. I'm not a stranger any more——"

"I have to do this thing——"

"So that they'll be given money and made well again?"

"Yes!"

"For how long? A few years. But you'll have to go on with your life, go on paying for what——"

She was shocked by his vehemence. "For what I am being paid?"

"You're not wronging anyone, only yourself."

She moved away from him and spoke into the shadows of the room. "I have accepted the offer, and given my word."

Here, he thought in despair, was the greater part of her life as a beautiful woman summed up. An old man had bought a concubine. Standing in the doorway in Singapore with her, only a little time ago, he had heard the piping of the birds in the shop and had thought: with her beauty and her voice that chimed, shouldn't she too be in a wicker cage?

"Don't listen to me," he said. "Listen to the two people you trust—ask them what they think——"

"They must never know!"

"Because they wouldn't let you do this and you know it." He went nearer her, expecting her to draw back, but she stood dreadfully still. "I can't bargain on his terms, Santha— I can't help them, except a little, in that way; and even if I could, and you chose me instead of him, I'd feel that——" It seemed impossible to reason without hurting.

"That I'd changed hands in a market-place." She came towards him, her eyes shining with an anger of her own. "This is so strange to you, isn't it?"

"The ways of the East——"

"Isn't there prostitution in England, Hugh?"

"Don't hurt yourself——"

"We accept it here, sometimes even as an honourable thing——"

"Half the marriages in the West wouldn't have happened if the man didn't have a decent job——"

"But still you don't understand."

"I understand you're doing this for them, not for yourself."

"For my own peace of mind."

He said, "But you hate yourself——"

"Yes. That's why it will be easier for me, because I shall love you, or the memory of you——"

"Santha——"

"No." She turned away, clasping her arms as if they might escape her and fly to him. "This one night was for me to keep, to remember. It is for you to forget as soon as you can. So I have made use of you just as I shall be making use of him. I need his help, and I needed yours and you gave it to me."

Some of the voices were louder in the street below the window and he moved farther away from it but not towards her, because if he held her she would cry again and their bitterness would seek relief and when it was over, nothing would be different.

"You love them too much, Santha."

"They gave me all they had!"

"They didn't mean to make a cage for you——"

The voices were louder still and strong light flickered on the ceiling, so he went to the window. People were running about in the courtyard and now he saw that two of the paper lanterns had caught fire and that the small flames were spreading to the third. The festoon-strings reached to the wall of the house, and the people were anxious; with a word to Santha he went down the narrow stairs and into the courtyard, helping to drag at the strings and reach the burning lanterns. They fell to the ground and were stamped to ashes; the smell of candle-grease was in the air.

"Often happen, tuan—must put out at once!"

"Very dangerous, yes." A Malay house was so much tinder in the dry intervals between the rainstorms.

He went up the stairs again, but she had gone.

Joe had said: "I haven't seen her." He asked him if he would like to come up and drink some wine but Hugh excused himself.

"I missed her, in the crowd, that's all."

"You try the Rest House?"

"Yes. It's not urgent."

"Sure, I understand."

That was three hours ago and now the town was quiet and all the lanterns were out. The full moon touched colours along the littered streets where paper flowers had fallen and the little streamers lay, blotched and ragged under the passing of many feet.

A bearded Sikh lay on his back across a flight of steps, the bottle still in his loosened hand; on his face was the peace of Christ; he would sleep until morning, for these few oblivious hours a child again. Pariah dogs were poking at the debris outside the darkened restaurants; the smell of *chandu* crept from the doorway of Yat Kee's house. Two ricksha-boys were sitting hunched on the wicker seats, their eyes not open, not quite closed, their lips blued with smoking. He thought of Thomas Thorne. What was Thorne doing on this festive night?

Along the monsoon-gutters everywhere was the glint of broken glass.

The Land-Rover was still outside the police-station, and a Malay constable leaned against it, smoking a cheroot.

"The night is over, Tuan Coplan'."

"Yes, constable. It was very noisy."

"And there were many drunk."

"It is to forget."

"A man swam in the sea. There were friends with him, but they could not save him." He closed his palms together.

"What happened?"

"They say it was a sea-snake. It is the fourth this year."

The moon was touching the tallest palms at the edge of the

162

jungle and the first thin shadows began seeping over the ground.

"I will go home, constable."

"Allah watch over thy sleep."

But he had no wish to turn into the courtyard where the ashes of the lanterns lay; even the scent of the loved cassia tree meant nothing to him, because home is where the heart is and she wasn't there.

There was no one along the length of Jalan Burong, except for the sleeping Sikh and the drugged ricksha-boys, and the old woman at the cross-roads. She was always there, even now, so this must be where she lived, and slept, with her stool and table and tins of mystic cards and her shapeless canvas bag that must hold all she had.

She was not sleeping, though she didn't call to him as he passed her; perhaps even she had moments of being off-duty, and was tired by the confusion of the long evening.

"Goodnight, mother," he said quietly in Malay.

The moonlight fell on her face, etching more deeply the web of wrinkles; her ivory skin was shrivelled against the bone.

"Do not pass," she said. Her voice was low and hoarse; she had talked so much this evening, answering so many questions. "I can give you courage."

He stopped because he might as well be here as anywhere until he could face the return to those empty rooms.

"Choose, my son." Her hand, bloodless as a chicken's claw, held up one of the rusting tin boxes; he took a card; it was dark with handling. One couldn't simply ask her: what should I do? It was written in the cards among the jig-saw hieroglyphs. She began reading the little soiled book, finding the place indicated by the card he had chosen; and already he was bored, and felt for a half-dollar piece. She seemed to sense his lack of interest, for she closed the book suddenly and looked up at him with eyes incongruously clear in this ancient face.

"I will tell you, though you already know." He gathered the sense from the few words he understood; she wasn't a Straits-born Chinese and her Malay was uncertain. "You

163

have youth on your side, my son. Use it as a sword." She was trying to straighten the half-burned joss-stick that was stuck into a piece of wax on the table, but when she rummaged for matches in the canvas bag she could find none, so he got out his box and struck a match; before he could light the joss-stick she blew out the flame with a sudden hiss of breath— "No, no, it is for me to do." She took the box and lit the stick; as the match flared it threw her shadow on the wall for an instant. She held the box to him.

"Keep them, mother."

"They are blessed by your charity." They went into her canvas bag with the speed of a conjuring-trick. "So I shall give you courage. The woman has great love for you. She does not love the other. He is old."

Doubting his understanding of the language, he asked her to repeat what she had said; and she obliged him, choosing different words—even using an English one when she could —so that he shouldn't mistake her. She seemed insistent that he understood what she was saying.

"He has no need of her, as you have need. She will be to him a thing of his household, and not its heart as she would be in your house. Do not let her go that way, but keep her with you."

The white tendril of smoke climbed from the joss-stick in the unmoving air. In the silence of the street he was ready to believe anything, even that she could know these things about him.

"You see much, wise mother."

"I see all, all. Go back now. Think upon what I have said. You will not need me again."

Touching a finger to her lips she pinched out the red tip of the joss-stick, and he straightened up, but didn't take out the half-dollar piece.

Earlier tonight he had been moved to do an odd thing. After he had lain with Santha and she was washing in the other room, he had taken her moonstone brooch and examined it; like the one he had bought for her, it was new, and couldn't have belonged to her family. The hall-marks in the gold were the same and the stones were identical. So he

164

had put her brooch into the pocket of his slacks and had left in its place the one he had bought for her, so that for this one night, at least, she would wear his present, unknowing. In the morning he would tell her.

But now, as if these clear eyes in the shrivelled ivory face were directing his thoughts, he put his hand into the other pocket and gave her in payment the moonstone.

18

AN hour after noon when the town lay blinded by the sun's heat and the shutters were closed against it and the pariah dogs were spread limp in the shadows, Stratton walked into the jungle. He had passed through deserted streets, walking with his effortless lope as if the heat were not enough to stun a man and bake him alive on the stones.

Five minutes into the jungle and he was in a changed world where the trees dripped and the earth was moist and there was no dust. Only in the clearings and in the chance gaps left by the leaves was there sunshine, and these he avoided, aware that any sunlit target could bring a bullet.

He had told Copland: "You're marked. We all are." He hadn't thought fit to add: "And no one more than I."

Half an hour and he was skirting the opium plantation of Loy Lin Chai, just as he was careful to do on every mission through this area north of the town. Loy Lin Chai would be dismayed if he knew that a stranger's eyes were here where he tended his slender crop and farmed the dreams for the men who found life without them insupportable, and who would give their last coin to buy them. Loy Lin Chai was not of the town, and not a man of law; it could well be that a word from him to the hidden enemy would ensure that the loping Englishman would never come this way again. Stratton lived in risk and counted it carefully, and knew that one hundredth part excess could tip the scales and sell him to the dead.

Two hours and he neared the camp, and picked his way cautiously through the low scrub that ringed the clearing, already within earshot of their grating voices.

He sat for an hour, listening to nothing that was important to him. They had eaten and were not active; two or three lay asleep in the shade, the cunning and fear gone from their eyes, their faces defenceless.

On two occasions one of them came over to the edge of the clearing to urinate, within yards of where Stratton lay in camouflage; and he watched their lean yellow faces, their eyes, ready for their eyes to wander and perhaps note that the prone leaf-covered log had not lain here an hour ago. On each occasion he fingered his knife and not his gun. If they came to investigate the log and he were forced to shoot at them he could drop them with one bullet but the sound would bring the others. They were fanatics, difficult to kill even with a gun; he had seen men like these running fifty yards with a bullet in their guts and their own gun firing; he had heard them curse on their last breath in an effort to wound the enemy.

It had been the knife—this knife he was fingering now—that had done for the man who had heard the Land-Rover coming and who had felled the sapling to lie in wait for Copland five nights ago. But that man had been alone and it was not difficult. Here there were more than thirty.

Two others joined them from a path that led west to the ridge; he judged they had come from the town through secondary jungle; they were dressed as rubber-tappers. Excitement was stirring among the others, and the leader—one of the petty thieves that Stratton himself had released from the Singapore gaol to save them from the invading Japanese—came out of his cave among the rocks. He was now much older and no longer a thief, but a killer in uniform; few men failed to make some progress in their lives.

They set up the radio transmitter and gathered in a group, jabbering in their excitement until the leader brought his hand down with a stroke that seemed to cut off their tongues. He spoke to them with an absurd solemnity for a full minute and then gave way suddenly to his own elation; and they began shrilling again like vultures sighting prey.

Stratton began sliding, inch after inch, crawling over the moist humus of the earth, backwards on his stomach with his wrists and the toes of his jungle-boots digging as silently as moles at the ground until he could turn his body and go forward, and then stand in a crouch and move with great stealth through the first of the taller trees, avoiding a shaft of sunlight but in doing so breaking a twig and raising a crack of sound that carried clearly on the stagnant air.

On the first shout he doubled forward and began running, knowing that it mattered more to him now to gain distance even at the expense of silence—they knew the jungle but so did he and on these terms the chances were equal. They were breaking into the low dense scrub and shouting again as he found the path and increased his stride, and the first shots went into the leaves with a wicked pattering because as he ran he dived where he could be between thickness of under-growth; but it was dangerous; he might take a gap and find himself running headlong into a dead end and be trapped there.

A creeper tripped him and he staggered, pitching at a tangent and righting his feet and running on through a patch of sunlight, enabling them to take better aim—three or four bullets snicked among the leaves and there was a slight impact on his shoulder and he knew that the question was not whether he could out-run them but whether he could keep on running while the blood flowed from the wound; the harder he ran, the faster it would be pumped out; but he couldn't stop. He must reach the airstrip.

There was no more shooting, because he had now reached a path they knew nothing of; he had hacked it with his own jungle-hatchet over the last few months, making it in places like a maze whose secrets only he could know. They wouldn't waste bullets, for they were hard to get now that the gun-boat was off the coast on the watch for arms-smuggling. But they would follow him as far as there were tracks of him; so he must gain all the ground he could before the first drops fell away to leave their red signals on the ground.

There was also the question of how long he could live; it wasn't just the shoulder, but the lung; and it was an hour to the airstrip, even running.

The aircraft had taken off ten minutes before, but there would remain signs of its going for a while: in the gold drift-ing of the dust and in the jibbering of the monkeys, and in

Haji Ahmad's patient beautiful face as he tried and tried again to contact Kota Bharu, to tell them the machine was airborne.

"Coplan' sahib!"

"Coming, Ahmad."

He went up the wide steps to the tower; it was as hot up there as in the staff office or anywhere else, but there'd be no stench of betel-juice.

"I have informed Kota Bharu of take-off, sahib."

"Good, Haji Ahmad."

There had already been complaints from the telephone company about Haji Armad's persistence in making so many calls. The telephone company was reminded that the calls were made by order of the airport manager and therefore in the name of Sultan Sir Rahman Hamid Alam Sha ibni Al-Marhum Alaiddin of Tamarah, who was a director of the airport. If they wished the airport manager to pass on their complaint to his director, he would be glad if they would let him know, and he would see to it at once.

Probably, Hugh thought, he was being officious; but once an aircraft was airborne from this strip it must stay airborne until it could reach a landing-place where there was ground control: there wasn't a square fifty yards of flat land anywhere else, and a forced landing on the sea was the only alternative to coming down in the jungle. Engine trouble was not rare in this climate and storms were common.

"I am awaiting the report from Singapore," Haji Ahmad told him, "that Flight Twelve is taking off."

"Good, Haji Ahmad."

He stood by the south windows, drawing a thumb beneath his eyebrows to clear the sweat. In the last two days he had thought too much, remembered too much. On the morning after the Moon Festival he had said to her:

"I would like to meet him." He'd forgotten the name, perhaps subconsciously hating it; it was, now he remembered it, an absurd name anyway: Fei Moi Toi. And besides, there was no need to speak it; she knew whom he meant.

"He is flying Singapore-Bangkok via Pasang tomorrow," she said, "so you may see him. But please remember it is not

169

for you to dissuade him. It is for me, if I wish to. And I do not wish to."

He had watched her plane away, that morning, knowing she was right. Even if he were quite certain by some kind of clairvoyance (*You see much, wise mother. I see all, all*) that she would be happier in the long run if she gave up Fei Moi Toi, he hadn't the right to do anything about it, just because he loved her. And Mr Toi was an elderly industrialist, no doubt with two wives already and a pot belly; why should he be dissuaded from taking over his new purchase, since he had offered to pay for it?

When his thoughts over the last two days had turned as bitter as this he had pretended to console himself by remembering that she was wearing the moonstone, his moonstone; but he'd had no right to do that, either; he was stealing comfort by deception on the pretext of desire. What had the old fortune-teller done with the other moonstone? Was it worth more to her than to Santha May Swee?

He listened to Ismail berating one of the Tamils below the building. As soon as the Sultan came back he would keep his promise and ask that Ismail should be made Assistant Manager, Pasang Airport. What would happen then to the little Malay? The seeds of ambition were already sprouting, for good or bad.

"You should not have been there!" Ismail was shouting to the man below. "Why were you not cleaning the fire-tender as I ordered?"

"But I heard him calling, Tuan Assistant-Manager!"

"The monkeys call all day long—"

"It is not a monkey this time—they are bringing him now, and you will see!"

Hugh turned from the south windows, his temples throbbing with the heat and with the ache of thought.

If only he were able still to say of her no more than that she didn't mind storms, and couldn't manage high heels awfully well . . . There was so much more to remember, now, her tawny skin against the cushions in the glow of the paper lanterns, the sweetness and the leap of her and afterwards the denial; so much more to forget.

170

His own fault. He had never been very resolute in the face of false hopes.

He heard men running below the tower, bare feet thudding over the concrete path; and voices raised. He must tell Ismail to stop shouting at the Tamils; they were fair game for any insult.

"Sahib, there is trouble."

"Yes, Ahmad? Probably a storm over Singapore—the wires are crossed."

"Trouble here, sahib. Below us."

"You think so?"

He went to the south windows but couldn't see anything; the three Shell engineers were trotting briskly across to the building from their bowsers. He went down through the staff office; the clerks weren't there. He found them with the little crowd of men at the end of the building.

"What's going on?"

"Tuan wounded! Much blood—"

They let him pass and he was suddenly looking down at Stratton. His face was swollen with the whip and scratch of the jungle; he had run through creeper and thorn.

"Stratton!" He bent over the man. The bush-shirt was soaked in blood. "Was it tiger?"

The head lolled. Hugh pulled away the loose ribbons of the shirt but there was too much blood to see what kind of wound it was. "Ismail! Bring the Land-Rover here and tell Haji Ahmad to telephone the hospital. They must send the ambulance at once and we will meet it on the road into the town. Tell them very urgent, Ismail."

"Understand, tuan."

Stratton could lie flat in the back of the car and they would drive slowly.

"Jangitta! Bring cold water and linen—ask Mr Chai for them—hurry. And get back, the lot of you—he needs air."

He moved the torn shirt carefully; there was no mark of a claw. A trickle of blood was forming at the corner of the mouth as the head lolled. Stratton was trying to open his eyes.

"Stratton—What sort of wound?" Tiger couldn't reach a

lung without leaving the flesh ripped, but there was blood in the mouth. "Bullet?"

A sound came from the mouth and Hugh put his ear close. The words bubbled and there was no strength in the breath. "They . . . put bomb . . . Flight Twelve . . ."

"You say 'bomb'?"

Stratton's tongue moved and he tried to suck the blood away; for a moment his eyes came wide open and looked at the face near his. "They put bomb—on board Flight Twelve —all I heard. Terrorists. Do something . . . Do something . . ."

Hugh straightened up and said: "Look after him and don't move him."

He lurched up the steps into the oven-heat of the control tower. "Get Singapore, Ahmad. Priority."

19

HE forced himself not to look up at the wall-clock again; he studied instead the saintlike patience of the Pathan at the switchboard where the green light went on winking.

"It is not good, sahib."

"Keep on trying."

"There is no result, sahib."

"There must be results, Haji Ahmad."

The heat stuck to their faces. A mosquito settled on his hand and he smashed its small life out against the wall.

"Tuan Coplan'!"

The voice came from the steps. Ismail.

"What do you want?"

Ten minutes had passed since Haji Ahmad had switched his leads to the Pasang exchange. It usually took as long as this even to get the exchange to answer, but now he thought: are the wires down? Have those bastards cut them?

"Ahmad," he said. "Stay on that line and also call up the *istana* direct."

"Sahib."

"Tuan Coplan'—"

"One minute, Ismail."

The beautiful hands of the Pathan moved at the switch-board, linking lines.

"Ask them at the *istana*, Ahmed, to telephone the airport at Singapore and say—"

The green light stopped winking.

"Sahib!"

"Yes—tell them it's urgent and that an aircraft is in grave danger."

While the Indian spoke into the mouthpiece Hugh turned and looked at Ismail. "Well?"

"I have the car ready, tuan, but we are afraid to move Tuan Stratton because you left orders——"

173

"I'll come down, Ismail. Bathe away the blood and see what kind of wound it is, but keep the dust out and tell the others to get back to their work." Ismail went down the wide wooden steps. "And, Ismail—make some kind of shade for him!"

"It is already done, tuan."

The clock on the wall was electric and made no sound, so the waiting was worse; it was like being watched from behind without being spoken to.

"The airport, sahib!"

Hugh took the head-set. "This is Pasang Airport. Can you hear me clearly?"

"Loud and clear, Pasang."

"I have a report that a terrorist bomb has been put on board S. and P.A. Flight Twelve, due to leave you at 16.00 hours. You must stop take-off and make a search."

There was silence, a deadness on the line.

"Ahmad get the *istana* direct.'

—"Speaking?" the English voice cut in.

"What? Copland, manager. Did you get my full message?"

"Yes. Hang on a minute."

Ahmad was speaking to the *istana*, repeating word for word what Hugh had told Singapore.

"Hello, Copland?"

"Yes?"

"How reliable is this report you say you have?"

"It's pukka enough for you to keep that flight grounded and make a search. My responsibility. Listen, I—"

"Flight Twelve took off fifteen minutes ago."

He closed his eyes against the yellow glare of the windows and stood listening to the thud of his heart.

"This is quite a facer," the unsurprisable English voice said on the line.

"Call them up. Call them up and tell them to turn back."

"It's about all we can do—"

"Then do it now. I don't know how much time they've got. Just get them down and out of that aircraft. Your responsibility now."

"Hang on, will you?"

"They will save them, sahib."

He blinked to clear the sweat away from his eyelids. The air of the whole room was throbbing. "I wish I had your patience, Ahmad. What do they say at the *istana*?"

"They will telephone Singapore, sahib."

"Well, it'll confirm my alarm." He gave the head-set to the Pathan. "Keep this line open no matter what happens and shout for me if you want me. Tell them I'm trying to find out more details."

"Understand, sahib."

He went down through the staff office; the clerks had come back but were staring from the windows. When he went outside the crowd was still surrounding the man on the ground, and his anger came up in a shout—

"Get back to your work! Didn't Assistant Manager Ismail tell you?"

They moved back a little, their faces turned to him.

"The tuan is dead," one of them told him passively.

He stood looking down at Stratton. More blood had come from the mouth than from the chest-wound; the once-white linen from Mr Chai's restaurant lay bloodied and water-soaked around the body.

The eyes had closed and there was no pulse in the wrist. He looked at their quiet faces. "Did he say anything to you?"

One of them nodded quickly. "He say *ah-liz-best*, tuan. Many times he say it."

" 'All is best'—is what he said?"

"No—no—" They began competing for the credit of passing on the message, but Wan Chai tugged at his arm and said:

"*Er-liz-bert*, Mistah Coplan'. *Er-liz-bert*."

"I see."

"Velly important message."

"Yes, thank you, Mr Chai." Flies had already begun circling above the body and he took two of the clean table-cloths and covered it. "Please go back to your work now. There is nothing more to be done."

Going up the steps to the tower he wondered who she was,

and where she was, Elizabeth. The cat who had walked alone had died in the company of her name.

"Haji Ahmad, did Ismail ask you to call the hospital?"

The man was looking calmly at a list he had been making out and didn't even turn his head. "It is very bad, sahib. The passenger with name 'K. Ramasamy'——"

"Have they given you the passenger-list?"

"Yes, sahib. This one, 'K. Ramasamy', is the Sultan himself, travelling unknown. Is this not grievous?"

"The Sultan is on board Flight Twelve? Incognito?"

"They informed me, sahib."

Hugh looked at the list of some fifteen names in alphabetical order. Below the name of Ramasamy was that of Toi, and at the bottom were the names of the crew: Chong, Sen-Yi, Swee. Captain, navigator, stewardess.

.   .   .   .

S. and P.A. Flight Twelve had left Singapore precisely on time at 16.00 hours and had been airborne more than fifteen minutes before receiving the message. At this time the storm that had built up from the south sea now smothered half the sky and the speed of the approaching rain-area was estimated at some five or ten miles per hour; direction was due north.

The aircraft had been permitted to take off on schedule, since its own northward path would take it ahead of the storm, and even if the wind rose higher and the storm reached Latitude 5 to encompass Pasang, there would be time for the aircraft to fuel-up, leave freight and mails, and take off for Bangkok in clear weather. Even if the weather were not clear enough for the plane to leave the transit airport, that would be Pasang's concern, not Singapore's. In other words no blame could be attached to the Singapore controller for having permitted take-off, bearing in mind the met. report. Nor could he be blamed for not having foreseen that at 16.17 hours Singapore would have to call up the S. and P.A. flight and advise the captain to turn back: that is, to head into the storm that was now reaching the island.

Already there were questions being asked, and within

minutes they led to the classic: "Why didn't So-and-so do so-and-so?" But there was an answer to every one of them. As happens ninety-nine times out of a hundred when an aircraft takes off in any part of the world, all was in order. Flight Twelve became airborne with every paper correctly signed by competent authorities and every requirement of efficiency and safety fulfilled. But it was already in grave peril.

No scapegoat could be suggested even among the ground-staff who had attended the aircraft before take-off. There was no regulation calling for a constant guard on every aircraft while it was on the ground, nor did the customs officers have any instructions to search every single item of baggage before passing it. There was no blame to anyone except an unknown group of men somewhere in the jungle who had sent their agent either to stow the bomb on board where it wouldn't be seen, or to take it on board with him in a suitcase and sit there with it unrecognized.

To the question of why there was a bomb on board at all, the answer was immediate: "Mr K. Ramasamy" was on the passenger-list.

To the question of what was to be done to protect his life and the lives of all those on board the answer was less easy, and only one man—Captain Chong—could make any decision.

By 16.20 hours the whole of Singapore was blotted out by heavy rain, with visibility on the airport runways a matter of yards: all flying was stopped. The Met. Office estimated that the storm area was some thirty or forty miles across, so that with a ground wind-velocity of ten miles per hour the rain would not clear Singapore for at least three hours. If the aircraft were to turn back, it would arrive over Singapore within twenty minutes from its present position at 16.20 hours and would have to circle the storm area for two hours and forty minutes before attempting to land on a runway that would be under several inches of standing water. If the aircraft were to fly on, it would reach Pasang within eighty minutes and could land in clear weather.

By 16.23 hours Captain Chong had received reports on

177

these factors by radio from Singapore and at once made his decision to remain on course and at the same time have a search made for the bomb.

At 16.50 hours the aircraft reached its point of no return and came under radio-assistance from Pasang. Its last message to Singapore gave its position and added that a search for the bomb was in progress.

The light along the south horizon had turned to bronze and the fringe of coastal palms, seen from Pasang tower, had lost its greenness under a lowering yellow haze. On the runway visibility was still perfect but the sun, its outline rapidly losing sharpness, was nearing the great peak of Gunong Tahan in the west. The temperature in the sun was lowering from 140 degrees but the glare persisted and the haze was more blinding than a clear sky. There was an hour of daylight remaining. Twilight would last perhaps five minutes in this latitude; then it would be night. There would be very little light from the moon, although it was only a quarter waning, because of the thickening haze.

The first call from S. and P.A. Flight Twelve to Pasang came soon after 17.00 hours and Hugh recognized the meticulous accents of Captain Chong even over the radio speaker. He gave his position, course and speed, adding:

We are still trying to locate the bomb. My navigator is helping the stewardess. They think it must be among the mails, but Miss Swee is asking passengers to open their personal baggage in case we have someone on board with a suicide-mission. We have told the passengers we are searching for a small consignment of very dangerous drugs, so they are not alarmed. Without arousing suspicion we have persuaded Mr K. Ramasamy to occupy one of the most forward seats because the bomb is almost certainly somewhere aft, and as it must certainly be a small one there might be a chance of landing the aircraft even after an explosion. Unless we have anything special to report we will come in at five-minute intervals.

In the control tower the heat was getting worse as the humidity rose. The sun, now pale behind the haze, was sickly and cast indistinct shadows. It hung a few degrees above the peak of Gunong Tahan.

"There will not be much daylight, sahib, when the machine is here."

"No, Haji Ahmad. Five minutes. We will make arrangements for a night-landing in any case."

He had sent Ismail to see to it already. There were enough electric and oil lanterns in the store to provide runway marker lights, and the ground staff were detailed. A man had been told to take the Land-Rover into the town and fetch oil for emergency-flares, but to tell no one of the situation. Probably he would shout it from the market-place but it had to be risked. He couldn't, at least, tell anyone who was on board the aircraft; only he and Haji Ahmad knew about Mr K. Ramasamy.

Singapore telephoned, asking again for details of the report, and he told them:

"A man whom I believe to be an unofficial agent working against C.T. activities in this area was shot at on his way to warn us here at the airport. He has since died of his wounds. I place the highest possible value on what he could tell us before he died. That's all I know."

"I see. We want to investigate, of course. It might be some kind of scare, for its nuisance-value."

"I hope so."

"We're extremely concerned here, because of the passenger list."

"From my knowledge of Captain Chong's reputation I don't think he'd take less trouble if that list were one name short. Even commoners have a certain value."

"Oh, quite, but you know what I mean——"

"No. But never mind. I'd be glad if you don't phone again unless you've something urgent for us. We'll be pretty occupied from now on."

He cut the switch on his last word and looked down at the quiet philosophical face of Haji Ahmad. The Pathan was Malayan-born, a loyal subject of Tamarah, quietly at this moment grieving the probable death of an earthly god, the father-figure of his country. But that bleating voice on the telephone was utterly dissociated from any such personal identification.

He watched Ismail from the south windows; he and two Malays were slinging the lamps on board the crash-tender and in a moment it swerved away to the far end of the oval perimeter road. Half a dozen other men had clambered on board with wick-drums to be dropped off at their stations and wait for the signal to light the boundary-flares.

There was nothing for the rest of the staff to do until the aircraft, if it ever reached here, was sighted. The ambulance had come some time ago to take Stratton's body into the town.

Three more times Flight Twelve reported position, now through worsening static. There was no message added other than: *We are still trying to locate it.*

If it were really there, and was a powerful one however small, only three people in the aircraft would die knowing why they had died; only those three knew now, as the sun touched Gunong Tahan, that the dark might fall upon them sooner than for others.

"One must use great patience, sahib."

"Yes, Haji Ahmad." He realized he had been hitting the palm of his hand rhythmically and stupidly on the ledge of the window, staring up into the diminishing glare. The clock on the wall showed 17.30 hours. By theoretical calculation they should hear the aircraft's engines in ten minutes. In this haze they wouldn't see it until it came down below two or three thousand feet; the ceiling was thickening, the cloudless sky congealing as the glass fell and the air grew heavy.

"Five minutes, Ahmad. They should be calling up again."

"I am waiting, sahib."

"Tell them that if—that when they reach here we have all in readiness for them. Also tell them——"

Calling Pasang——

"Sahib!"

"Yes——"

Calling Pasang. We have found the bomb and will try to jettison . . . Static crackled and in the south sky the first lightning traced out the towering flanks of the thunderheads.

In the special consignment compartment . . . can manage to . . . for our report . . .

The rest was unintelligible. When Hugh looked down from the speaker he saw that the Pathan had closed his eyes; probably he was praying.

Below the tower the crash-tender came bouncing to a halt from the perimeter road and Ismail jumped down and when he was halfway to the building he stopped and stood facing the south, cupping his ears.

"Tuan Coplan'!" His face was a pale smudge against the dark ground.

Leaning from the window Hugh stared upwards but could see nothing, hear nothing. Hurrying up the steel ladder to the roof he stood as Ismail did, cupping his ears, stilling his breath.

"Tuan Coplan'!"

"Yes, Ismail—I hear it!"

The far thin drone was intermittent, the sound-waves shifting as they met heat-pockets near the ground; but as the seconds passed the drone loudened. In the fading light the aircraft would appear as a dark line across the yellow. But there was no dark line yet visible; there was only the sudden orange-white flash, and after nearly half a minute the sound of the explosion.

181

★ 20 ★

"HE is on the roof."

"Did you hear it, Haji?"

"Yes. I heard it."

"I will go up."

"Go up."

Since his promotion Ismail had worn canvas shoes with
rubber soles. They squealed like mice on the metal rungs of
the ladder. On the roof it was very quiet; even from the
forest there was no sound because the explosion had shocked
man, animal and bird. It hadn't been very loud but it had
been strange and not at all like the crackle of the thunder.

In the dying light the man stood like a pillar, like the
shrine they had built for the Tuan Doktor up on the ridge.

"Tuan Coplan'."

The manager did not move.

The day had a few minutes yet, but the north-running
storm hurried it.

"Tuan . . ."

"Yes, Ismail." His face was perfectly blank and his eyes
looked blind, and Ismail was for a moment frightened to see
what the noise up there had done to this man.

"Now we can do nothing, tuan."

"No."

"Tell me what I shall do."

"Nothing."

The shadow poured softly across the roof, dulling the big
white letters and darkening the blank blind face.

"You can't do anything!" His voice was raw and Ismail
was shocked by it. "No one can do anything—not even God
—Allah—anyone! So why ask?"

"Wanted to do something, tuan."

The Englishman's hand hooked round Ismail's arm, so
hard as to bring pain. "So did I."

182

The thunder came tumbling through the still air and the roof shivered under their feet. Following the long-drawn rumble of it there rose the lighter sound of engines in the sky, and they listened to it. The sound rose steadily.

"Tuan—"

"Quiet."

The sound pulsed, the difference in the speed of the two engines setting up periodicity; gradually the revolutions became equalized and the pulsing became a single steady note. Below the building men had begun shouting.

Hugh moved suddenly to the roof-trap and Ismail ran to follow him down the ladder. In the control room the Pathan was standing at the switchboard, the chair knocked over behind him. Ismail began chattering to him and Hugh cut him short—

"Ahmad, is their radio dead?"

"Yes, sahib—"

"Telephone the shop of the oil-seller and ask him to give our man as many rockets as he keeps there, as well as the oil he has gone there for—hurry and we might be in time." There might be a few rockets unsold after the Moon Festival; there weren't enough signal flares on the airstrip for this situation.

"It is perhaps another machine, tuan—"

"I think it's Flight Twelve, Ismail. The explosion sent it suddenly off course and the sound was taken away from us for a time. We may have to—" but the plane was down low and its noise drummed in the control room; they ran to the windows and saw the black shape of it go slipping through the haze a few hundred feet above the runway. There was no light anywhere on the machine. "Ismail! Get out there and turn on the lamps—light every flare—hurry!"

Calling Pasang . . . K-2-O calling Pasang . . .

The after-sound of the aircraft faded but a long peal of thunder overwhelmed the speaker; it was some seconds before the message could be heard again through the violent static.

. . . And other damage . . . Must decide if—or take the risk . . . Repeating . . .

The distant sound of the engines settled to a low constant volume; it had gone into a wide circuit.

... But exploded as the navigator threw it clear ... Badly hurt but all others safe. Have rigged trailing aerial and hope ... Can see your tower but ...

Hugh went to the main building lights and switched them on. "Take down all messages, Ahmad."

"Sahib."

He went down the wooden steps in leaps and told the clerks: "Every man stays here till ordered to leave—tell any others who come in here."

They wanted to know what was happening but he was through into the customs room and nearly pitching Wan Chai over, interrupting his lamentations.

"It is doom—it is doom come now! It is the—"

"It isn't—it's a bloody miracle! Put all your lights on, Chai!"

"It is reward of transgressor who—"

"Get those lights on!" He ran out of the building. Dark had come down like a black shutter, blotting out the airstrip and the trees, but at each end of the runway the flares had come to life and their yellow flickering showed men running about. The lamp on the crash-tender sketched an uneven path as the vehicle dipped and swerved along the perimeter road, going its rounds of the flare-crews.

The whole scene went blue-white as lightning split the clouds and for an instant showed up the dark shape of the aircraft. Hugh judged its height at less than a thousand feet but its angle was level.

With four wick-drums he outlined the landing-T and when Ismail came back in the tender he told him to rig some kind of covers for the main directional flares before the rain reached the area and doused them; then he went up to the tower again.

"Are they still calling, Ahmad?"

"Two minutes ago, sahib."

Hugh took the written message and worked out the sense of it. They had found the bomb and the navigator had thrown it from the aft cabin door, but it had exploded before clearing the aircraft and had damaged the tail-section. It was still possible to control the machine crudely in the air but the chances of making a safe landing were doubtful. It would have to be attempted, so they would circle the airstrip to use up the fuel; the time necessary was estimated to be one hour thirty-five minutes. If the tail-section broke up they would try to ditch on the sea. The radio was working and they were receiving Pasang clearly apart from static caused by the storm. The navigator was losing blood and without expert medical attention was not expected to live. It was requested that Pasang should provide what lights were available and stand by for a crash-landing in an hour and a half.

"Ahmad, did you telephone the shop of the oil-seller?"

"It is arranged, sahib. The man will bring rockets."

Hugh set up the signal mortar on the window-shelf and dragged the box of flares over. There were three red, a green and two white. "I am going below. Shout from the window if you need me. Tell them we are doing everything possible and wish them good fortune."

He found Ismail directing the group of Tamil labourers; they were to take the bamboo and canvas from the stores and make covers for each wick-drum and oil-flare.

"They must make them as tall as possible, Ismail, so that the light can still be seen from the air."

Wan Chai was hobbling about in the glow of the building lights; he had already fetched half his kitchen equipment out and the cook and waiter were loading it on to a barrow.

"What are you doing, Mr Chai?"

"Must lemove all things velly quick. When machine come down will bleak evelything and all lost."

"Well, don't move across any of these lights, that's very important—and leave the lamps burning in your restaurant."

"Am sad. Am glieving for poor Lee Kwei—"

"Wait till he's dead before you grieve. Haven't you ever heard of hope, man?"

The cook and the waiter were dragging the refrigerator through the doorway, two ants with a sugar-lump.

"Saleh is coming, tuan."

"What?"

The Land-Rover's headlamps brought their beams swinging off the perimeter road and Saleh pulled up outside the crash-vehicle shed. He had brought three drums of oil and a bundle of fifteen or twenty rockets from the shop in the town.

"Who are these people, Saleh?" Half a dozen Malays were dropping from the back of the car.

"They come to help." Two of them were rolling the drums into the mouth of the shed. "Others are coming, many others."

"There's nothing they can do. Tell them to keep out of the way." Obviously Saleh had spread his news and soon half the town would be trekking their way along the airstrip road, drawn here by the drama. Anger with them was no answer. Reminded of a point he had missed he called up to the windows of the control tower and Haji Ahmad's turban appeared. "Ahmad! Telephone to the hospital in the town. Tell them we shall need both ambulances, two doctors and as many nurses as they can send. Tell them the aircraft is likely to crash here. Understand?"

The drums were clear of the Land-Rover. "Ismail!"

"He is with crash-tender, tuan."

"Saleh! Take the car to the beginning of the runway and stay there with it. Leave it pointing directly down the runway, understand? Then—"

"Not go alone, tuan—"

"What?"

"It is night. Not go—"

"Take one of these men with you. Only one. Listen very carefully. When the car is pointing down the runway, put the lights—the big ones—on and off three times, so that I can see them. Then wait. Every five minutes—as long as it takes a pan to boil—switch the lights on and off three times. Tell me if you do not understand."

"I am signal for aircraft, tuan—"

"That's right, Saleh. You are as good as Assistant Manager Ismail. I will depend upon you. Go now."

"I take friend—"

"Yes, take friend. Hurry."

When the Land-Rover had gone he stood listening to the sky. The sound was still there, the constant note of a cello-string. He took the bundle of rockets and went up to the roof beside the tower, stowing them beneath a tarpaulin. As soon as he had seen the three headlamp flashes from the beginning of the runway he went down to the control room.

"Did you telephone to the hospital, Haji Ahmad?"

"I await the reply, sahib."

"Keep trying them. Say it is very urgent."

From the windows he watched the boundary flares and the four electric lanterns marking the runway limits. It looked more like an aboriginal camp in the jungle than an airport prepared for a night landing, but there was nothing more to be done. Ismail had orders to take his men and find every tin can, beaker and empty drum in the place, to fill them with oil and make wicks from canvas. From the air it would look a little better than from the tower; here it wasn't easy to define the pattern made by the lamps.

"Contact the aircraft, Haji Ahmad."

Waiting, he saw the triple flash of the headlights come again from the runway. Saleh was among the most intelligent of the staff and one of the only three men allowed to drive the car; also he would do his best. Even as Hugh thought of this he realized he had missed another point. He would instruct Ismail about it.

Can hear you, Pasang. Waiting. Over.

He went across to the panel.

"Chong. Tell me what you think of our lights. There will be others very soon. They are taking extension-beacons out and will light them. There is a car positioned at the west end of the runway. It will flash its lights three times every five minutes so that you can get to know the bearings. When you signal us that you're going to land, the headlights will be left on for you to mark the beginning of the runway. We have rockets ready to signal you when the rain closes in. We have sent for a medical team and ambulance for your navigator—he will be in safe hands the moment you land. Will repeat."

Within ten minutes he had repeated, received acknow-ledgment and had added two messages detailing the dis-position of emergency lights in the landing area. Ismail was in the control room by the time he had finished.

Somewhere in the darkness the Malay had lost his cap; there was a long gash on his right forearm and his feet were bare, his eyes bloodshot, his face smudged with the smoke of the oil flares. He didn't look like a man ambition would destroy.

"All is done, tuan."

"I can't see the extension marker beacons yet, Ismail. We need—"

"The men are on their way. They are running, but it is difficult for them across the rough land and the swamps, with the heavy drums. But it will be done."

Haji Ahmad's voice spoke quietly behind them; he had got through to the hospital.

Hugh told Ismail. "Please give instructions to the two men in the Land-Rover, Saleh and his friend. When we flash them a white light from here, on-off, on-off, they must switch their headlamps full on and leave them on. They must then run away from the car to safety, for the machine will then be landing." He asked Ismail to repeat this in slow Malay, and added: "Before they leave the car they must start the engine and set it running at a quarter-throttle, so that the dynamo will keep the big lights bright."

Ismail repeated, nodding many times, impatient with this precaution. "I will hurry, tuan."

"Yes. And Ismail, we have a message for every single man out there. Make sure it is understood. They must work at their best, because the Sultan is on board this aircraft."

Ismail's eyes widened and his head jerked forward an inch as if a hand had struck it from behind.

"Sultan Sir Rahman? Up there?"

"Yes, Ismail. So we must do all we can."

He turned back to the window nearest the control panel, watching for the two beacons that would extend the runway direction a mile on either side. Within five minutes they were lit. Soon afterwards the rain came, blotting out all but the nearest flares and drumming on the roof so that the sound of the aircraft was lost.

Flight Twelve had long since overtaken its point of no return, Singapore-Pasang; it had flown from sunlight into the dark; now crippled, it flew in the thick of storm.

"Haji Ahmad." He had to shout against the beat of the rain. "Call them up and request we maintain constant radio contact from now on."

21

IN the deluge the airport building with its lighted windows
stood out of the night like an ocean liner hove-to in a storm;
around it some of the flares still burned and the few electric
lamps shone steadily with a whiter light. People in the town,
seeing one of the ambulances taking to the airstrip road,
had chartered the only three motor taxis and had followed.
A score of others had got on to the Straits Airways coach and
were now gathered in the crash-vehicle shed. Fifty or sixty
people had come in from the town, in rickshas, on bicycles
and on foot; they had started out before the storm reached
the area but were now standing drenched, caught by the
rain along the Burong road.

A minute ago, lightning had ripped down from the
swollen cloud-base and struck an ipoh tree on the far side of
the swamp, and some of the Straits-born Indians were
huddled together chanting a prayer.

The last call from the aircraft had been brief and urgent:
*Estimate we have thirty minutes to go before fuel low
enough to attempt landing. Cannot see the east beacon. Am
flying blind most of the time. Weight of rain on mainplanes
affecting lift. Height now 500 feet. Urgent: please move
headlamp-car to other end—east end of runway. If I over-
shoot and can't get up height again we'll ditch on the
swamp instead of jungle and stand a chance. Please get
east beacon burning, need it badly.*

The Land-Rover had been moved down the runway and
turned round, its twin lamps now flashing at minute-
intervals. Two men had been sent out to the east beacon and
it was flaring wildly, spilled oil having caught fire. Most of
the flares doused by the first deluge were now burning again
and men could be seen milling around them as they fed
more oil and struggled with the rain-covers against the
weight of the downpour.

The word had been passed that the Sultan of Tamarah was on board the crippled aircraft, and there was a fervour rising among the men working at the flares.

Coming through the customs room Hugh had found Joe and Arthur Duffy. "I heard the plane in trouble and came along." Duffy's arm was still in a sling. "Just tell me what I can do, laddie." He summed up the extent of the crisis with his first look at Hugh's strained hollowed face.

"Nothing, yet. Half an hour before anything happens, providing they stay airborne." His shirt was blackened and singed; he had made two circuits of the flares to check up and had gone out to the east beacon when the drum had caught fire from the spilled oil. His voice was hoarse from shouting orders in the rain's roar. Here under the roof it was worse. "Got a cigarette, Duffy?"

Duffy had none but Joe passed a packet round. He had walked the three miles from the town, starting out soon after the storm broke; he stood soaked in his white robe like a sculpting in wet clay. "You hear about Stratton?"

"What?" The rain's sound beat at the ears.

"The bastards got him," Duffy said. "He's dead."

"Yes." Hugh thought of saying: if it weren't for Stratton there wouldn't be a last chance left, because they wouldn't have looked for the bomb. But his throat was raw and he didn't want to have to shout under this roaring roof, didn't want to talk to anyone or explain anything to them; he wished they would all go away so that he and the men could devote themselves to bringing that invisible and now in-audible machine down from the dreadful sky. He wanted to see her face again, alive, unmarked, smiling; let her stop loving him, let her sell herself on the market, but let her live through this night and see the morning. The need of this was like a thirst in him.

"Duffy," he said, "there's something you can do. Keep this mob clear of the landing-T and the boundary flares—those that aren't helping. And if they start chanting their prayers again tell 'em to shut up. If the aircraft comes any closer we want to be able to hear it."

The planter nodded and walked through the doorway into the deluge.

"Joe, where is Thorne tonight, d'you know?"

"Home, I guess."

"Drunk? Doped?"

"I wouldn't know about that."

"I wish he were here. He's probably the best emergency surgeon in the State."

Joe stood thinking and then asked: "You want me to go get him?"

"Would it be easy, Joe?"

"Nope. I think he knows now he's being watched. He hasn't been outside of his place since those two extradition men moved into town. But I'll try."

A Malay was tugging Hugh's arm—"Ahmad says come quick, tuan! He says——"

"Right." He told Joe: "Forget Thorne. Prob'ly drunk anyway and we've got a doctor here."

When he reached the control tower the speaker was carrying Chong's voice against the drumming of rain.

. . . And very loose now. Tanks only a quarter full, so I'm going to try a practice run. Don't think I can control rudder much longer. Have no visibility except east beacon, head-lamp-car and building lights but may pick up the others on the run-in. This will be practice run only. Please give all possible assistance. Over.

Haji Ahmad threw the switch and Hugh said:

"Chong, we are ready for you. But wait till you see steady continuous light from headlamp-car. Drop flare as you begin run-in. We will send green rocket. Will repeat . . ."

Lightning flashed in the south windows. The thunder crashed almost simultaneously and the tower trembled.

"Take over and keep contact, Ahmad." He grabbed the white signal lamp and flashed it from the window towards the east runway limit until he saw the headlights glowing steadily through the rain. Beyond them to the left the yellow flame of the east beacon burned, steady but smudged by distance. On the metal ladder he grazed a shin and had to wrap his arms round the top rung and cling there sweating while the pain sickened him; then he was on the roof, ready with a green rocket and a fusee match below the edge of the tarpaulin, crouched and watching the black west sky, the rain beating upon him and streaming over his face. The pain in his shin and the strain of staring brought nerve-lights across his vision so he shut his eyes and counted one . . . two . . . three—and stared again at the void, enraged by the rain that half-blinded and deafened him as he tried to pick up the first sound of the engines. In the sky there was no sign of light, no sound.

Lightning flickered and he closed his eyes again, counting, waiting for the thunder to die away and leave only the rain's tattoo. He thought of praying; if he did, it took the form of reasoning: Chong was a wise, fit, experienced flyer and his voice on the radio had been calmly articulate. The tanks were down to a quarter and if he failed to gain height after the practice run he would hit the swamp and the risk of fire would be minimised and this rain would beat at the flames if friction sparked them off.

He said her name once in his mind, for an instant seeing her face; then he opened his eyes and stared again through the storm-haze and saw nothing, but heard the sudden rising drone of the engines in the west and without waiting for the aircraft's promised flare he thrust the rocket-stick into the tube and struck the fusee, crouching over the small red glow to keep the rain from it. On the periphery of his vision-range he could see the flare blossoming in the dark; another few seconds and the rocket was away and he was smothered in its smoke; red sparks drifted across the roof.

The drone loudened and he could see the dark smudge of the machine coming in very low across the jungle tree-tops, the white flare floating and casting a pale light for another moment before dying. Below the roof, voices were calling: they believed Chong was attempting to land, and were anxious for him. The next time . . . the next time . . .

Flight Twelve was suddenly with them out of the night, a huge darkened shape adrift above the airstrip with its aluminium panels gleaming in the light of the ground-flares, the trailing aerial whipping in the water-haze as the great mass of the machine drove at the deluge a hundred feet above the runway and the line of flares.

The wings lifted above the east beacon and the dark wastes of the swamp beyond; now only the sound came back for another half-minute before that too was gone.

Hugh dropped through the roof-trap and down the metal rungs.

"It was good, sahib! It was well done!" The beautiful bearded head was thrown back to look up at him and the black eyes shone.

"Did they call up, Ahmad?"

"Not yet, sahib. Shall I——"

"No! Wait for them. Keep open."

Duffy had come up the steps to the tower. "Was he trying to land?"

"No. Practice shoot-up. Next time round."

"Think he can do it?"

"Yes. Yes. Yes . . ."

A new sound came: it was the lack of sound, of the rain's percussion on the roof; the fringe of the storm was passing across the area, going its way northwards.

"Rain's easing, laddie."

"Yes. It's all we need." Another fifteen seconds broke his patience and he knocked the switch down—"Pasang to K-20. Chong! How is it with you? Call us!"

The loudspeaker was dead.

There were feet on the steps, and voices.

"Duffy, get them out of here!"

Static whispered and then: *Pasang. I can't get height. Controls won't anwer . . .* Bad static broke into the message and he went to stand immediately below the loudspeaker. The rest of the words made a broken chain. *Can't reach the sea . . . trying to bring . . . only keep what height I can . . . luck, wasn't it, Copland? It's no . . .*

He hit the switch. "Bearing, Chong—give us your bearing! Over."

Haji Ahmad sat with his lips moving silently. There was no static from the speaker in the ceiling. The rain was hushed to a long-held sighing above their heads.

194

The clock swept away one minute, two, three.

Hugh heard his own voice saying very calmly: "We can't fail now. Not now."

Faint rumbling came from the north and a panel of the switchboard vibrated. Thunder. Only thunder. The storm moving north.

Static was on the loudspeaker and someone was talking in Chinese; perhaps it was Chong; a voice sounded different when it spoke another language; it was very faint, as if it spoke to someone in the cabin with the set switched on. Then it changed to English and was a little clearer.

Am losing height rapidly and all control gone. May be a chance. Hope you will find us. About five miles inland over jungle . . . Unless there's . . . in tanks and I am switching off engines now. Tail-unit broken away and . . . much chance . . .

The voice broke into rapid Chinese and the speaker went dead.

Haji Ahmad was praying aloud as Hugh wrenched himself into movement and climbed the ladder, to stand on the roof in the last softness of the rain. Thin light flowed from the clearing moon and the jungle was touched with silver.

The deep orange glow came minutes later, spreading in the west and staining the low-flung cloud, brightening slowly until its light touched his hands that were for some reason held out in front of him, palm-upward to the empty sky.

22

WITH the going of the storm the night recovered its calm. The moon, three-quarters full, lighted the flooded airstrip; and in the lakes of standing water the flares were reflected, sending the giant shadows of the men about them flitting across the buildings and the jungle's edge. Someone turned off the engine of the Land-Rover and for a little while there was a kind of silence.

They stood in groups near the main building, drawn together instinctively so that their shock might be shared. From the orange glow in the west the light tinged their faces; and somewhere a cockerel, deceived by the false sunrise, began crowing.

Then some of the Indians sought relief in prayer and their chanting covered the smaller sounds from the jungle. In the taller trees the gibbon were restless, eyeing the west; more intelligent than cockerels, they knew the orange light to be that of a fire, and were afraid of it.

From very far away there reached a single sound, more distant but deeper than any of the others; it was the voice of the tiger, and the gibbon began squealing among the leaves in the sky, their fear sharpened.

At the edge of the runway Ismail stood weeping, no more the assistant manager of anything, only a child born of this land and weeping because in the stories his father had told him over and over again in the cool of evening, the king had never died.

Men had begun moving about near the building, and in a moment he turned in that direction.

Hugh had come down from the control tower and found Duffy among the others, standing with Major Yassim and Joe and the little Malay doctor from the hospital.

"I've told Armad to phone the *istana*. They'll send out

jungle troops. Duffy, how long will it take from here on foot?"

"What hope is there, laddie?"

"How long?"

"Two days, three." He looked into the wet haunted face and was surprised at the strength of its voice.

"Major Yassim!" He spoke in English. "Can you take off within one hour in the Sultan's aircraft?"

Yassim jerked his squat strong body round and looked across the airstrip; from where they stood it looked like a lake.

"I don't think so."

"Would you try?"

The broad head nodded. "Yes, I would try."

"Good. I want you to drop me and another man by parachute over the wreckage. We've got to pick up supplies and gear and you've an hour to get ready—"

"It would be too dangerous—"

"To fly there? Your plane's equipped for night-flying—"

"To drop you and the other man—"

"Not your concern. We report to you in one hour."

Yassim beckoned his two mechanics and they followed him across to the main hangar. Joe said:

"Just why?" He spoke quietly so that no one else heard.

"If there are any survivors, I want to help them."

"Them?"

Hugh turned away. "Duffy, I'm going into the town. Can you get together what gear I'll need out there? You know the jungle, I don't."

"Have you got guns here?"

"Yes. Ask Ismail—that one there. And will you tell the doctor to let you have everything we'd need for emergency surgery in those conditions? There must be some stuff on the ambulance."

Duffy didn't answer for a moment but stood looking at Hugh with his head on one side as if he'd never seen him before; then he said: "I'll do all I can in the time. If you've gone mad, I'm game. There'll be a search-party going out on foot. There's no hope for those poor souls—you can see

197

the blaze. But someone'll have to go and pick you up, what
there is left. The trouble with you is you're too young for
this place, and too bloody ignorant."

Ismail was at Hugh's side and spoke as if his mouth had
been hit, because his father had lied and the king was dead.

"What is to be done?" he said.

"Help Tuan Duffy—you're under his orders." He took
Joe's arm and walked him away from the others. "Now we'll
go and get Thorne."

The power-station had been hit by lightning and most of the
lights in the town had gone out. People were on the rooftops
watching the glow in the west sky; others tried to halt the
Land-Rover as it ploughed through the flooded streets: they
wanted to know what had happened and why the aeroplane
had come down. Joe pressed them away and shouted at
them to keep clear; the front wheels threw a bow-wave across
their legs and they scattered, leaping the monsoon gutters
that were choked with debris. Rats ran everywhere, desperate
for dry land, and children beat at them with bamboo sticks.

One of the extradition men was standing in the doorway of Thorne's house, but said nothing as they went in.

"Have those two guys any authority?" Joe asked.

"I doubt it, or they'd take him."

They lurched through the dark passage until suddenly the
door at the end opened and Kamala stood there in a flood of
light; she cried out in Malay: "Who is it?"

"Only Joe, baby. Joe and friend. Tom in there?"

She let them pass; the fright had left her eyes very wide.
Thorne was sitting with a gun on his lap; it was levelled at
them and there was surprise on his white wedge-shaped face.
The air smelt of *chandu* but his eyes were alert.

"I thought it was my friends from the homeland," he said
forgetting to lower the gun.

"Just friends, Tom." Joe was glad to find him sober and
free of the drug; he must be disciplining himself so that the
two men shouldn't take him while he was helpless.

"What do you want?" Thorne asked, looking at Hugh's
singed shirt and blackened face. Joe said:

"A plane's come down. We need you, pal."

"Everyone does. Would you mind getting out of here? I don't like being needed."

"See here, Tom—"

"Get out. I'm sorry to put it like that but you came crashing into my house without much formality. I thought it was the other two—you're lucky I didn't just fire without looking."

Joe tucked his arms under his wet robe. It was going to be a long business.

"You wouldn't have fired," Hugh said. He stood close to the man in the chair, right over him, looking down, feet apart, arms folded, voice quiet. "If they'd come for you you'd have turned that gun on yourself. You've nothing to lose."

Thorne raised his eyes to stare up at the boy's bright smudged face.

"There may be survivors, Thorne. I'm going out there by air with a parachute and I want you with me because there's no one better than you in the country."

Thorne blinked slowly, amused.

"Is that the fire Kamala told me about?"

"Yes."

"Then take a priest, not a doctor."

Hugh kept his eyes cold; Thorne musn't see the leap of triumph in them. "There won't be anything left of the plane, but I heard the pilot on the radio when it crashed and it was minutes before we saw the fire break out. There's a chance, you see."

"I wish you luck."

"You too. The actual drop's going to be tricky but you can brief me on the way out—you were doing this kind of job when I was so-high—"

"You're one of the brats who complain they missed the war—"

"That's right. We get bored having to admire men like you with your bloody D.S.O.s—a hero soon sticks in our throat like a fishbone. Now I've got a chance to do some good too—why should you have it all your own way?"

199

He paused, because another word either side could tip the balance. Thorne was persuadable; what a man did once he would do again for the same reason. There'd been the day when this man had saved the life of the girl here in the room, because there hadn't been any choice for him; and there was no choice now. It didn't matter that they were strangers out there in the jungle night. A doctor was used to strangers. It must have been a long time since Thorne had given himself that title, but the word had come straight up from the buried memories: *Then take a priest, not a doctor*.

"Why the hell should I go, boy?" His face with its clown's hurt mouth was changing, suffering. God only knew what memories Hugh had tapped by mentioning the decoration, by showing the admiration that could still be felt for a wreck of a man like Thorne.

"Because you've nothing to lose. Given half a chance you'll finish yourself off—you've tried it twice and you're ready to try again." He looked down at the gun. "This isn't for them."

Thorne said in his throat: "Damn your impudence!"

"You don't like the truth when you hear it, do you? But it works, you know. It works like a bloody charm. And I'm not talking about your feeble leaning towards suicide—you know that. Ever since your trial in England you've hidden up to lick your wounds, but you can't go on doing that, doing nothing." He felt himself getting weak on his feet; he had swayed a little, with the strain of the uncertainty of what would happen here in this room, and what was happening out there where the flames were dying.

Then he saw the tears and he looked away, as one is able, having won. "You got a cigarette, Joe?"

"Guess I haven't, no. The pack's soaked.

"I find cigarette," Kamala whispered.

"Good kid."

Hugh turned away from Thorne and when the girl came back he and Joe lit up; they weren't cigarettes, but thin cheroots heavily spiced with chicory, raw in the mouth. After a minute Thorne stood up; the gun hung from his hand and he looked like an overgrown urchin with a toy he was bored with.

"All your reasoning's wrong," he said bitterly, "wrong as hell."

"But you'll come, won't you?"

"Yes."

Some of the monsoon gutters were clearing themselves of the blockage that the debris caused, the force of the water tossing aside the broken palm-fronds and rattan waste; some of the streets were no longer under flood, and people came out of their houses to join the others along Jalan Burong, so that Joe had to bang the metal side of the car with the flat of his hand and shout for gangway. Once they saw Duffy, who must have followed them into the town for supplies or help; he was waving his one good arm to a uniformed Malay policeman, urging him to do something for him, perhaps to clear the road for his commandeered taxi.

Water shot up from the front wheels as Hugh ploughed through the streets and reached the airport road where the crowds were thinning and he could pick up speed. There were four of them in the car, for the extradition officer had begged a lift to the airstrip as they had left Thorne's house and Hugh hadn't even thought to refuse him. Joe was in the back with Thorne; it was impossible to hear if they were talking for the noise of the makeshift roof as the car took the bumps; for half a mile the track was ribbed and the wheels span free half the time, snatching at the transmission.

"It's very difficult for me, Mr Copland," the extradition man said, pitching his voice. It was the first time he had spoken since begging the lift. "I've my job to do, just like you."

"Of course." He didn't know what the man was trying to say, didn't care. Thorne was on board, sober and in fit condition to work; if there were anything of this dread night to be saved, they had a chance of doing it.

"Can I ask where you're taking him?"

"What? The airstrip."

"I've got to keep—" but a wicked rut sent them slewing

wildly and the rear clouted a bamboo-clump before Hugh
got control again. They were near the airstrip; a steady
drone persisted and loudened: the Bee-76 was out of her
hangar and running-up. The man tried again. "I've got to
keep him in sight, you see. Those are my orders."

"You've had it." The Bee-76 was a four-seater and Yassim
would want a navigator on board.

"I can't allow this man to leave here by air unless I go with
him, Mr Copland. You must see my position—"

He broke off again as they curved in a four-wheel drift
round the oval perimeter road. Men scattered as they slid
to a halt outside the main building, and Ismail ran to the car
—"All is ready, tuan! All good!"

Major Yassim came through the doorway with his flying-
helmet on, the strap hanging loose; and suddenly Smith was
between them, saying: "You can't take that man with you—
I expect you realize that?" His eyes were feverish and his
mouth jerking, his arm raised against the sky as if to keep
Thorne from reaching it. "I'll tell you the situation, and
you'll realize—"

"Joe!" Hugh spun round to the car. "Keep this bloody
fool out of the way, can you? Major Yassim, are you ready
for take-off?"

"Ready—but I cannot promise. There is an inch of water
on the runway—"

"Do your best, it's all I ask. Ismail, where is the equipment?"

"Inside the machine, tuan! Only you now!"

"Thorne!"

"That man can't be allowed—"

"Joe!"

Smith's face, the extradition man's face, bobbed in an
absurd dance as he grabbed Thorne's arm and joined
Yassim, their feet trudging through the deep pools where
water was still trying to drain from the runway.

"—Authority!" someone was shouting behind them and
Joe's voice came, more quietly, reasoning with them.

Three or four Tamils were waiting at the wingtips and
the mechanic in the cabin eased the throttles; they moved

into the low slipstream and Yassim helped Hugh and Thorne into their parachute-harness while Thorne talked rapidly:

"Only four things to remember—jump well clear to miss the tail. Count ten before you pull this ring. You can steer yourself in the air by dragging on the cords, one side or the other, if you look like hitting anything dangerous. Relax when you fall and then hit this release. I'll go through it again when we're airborne. Christ, it's been a long time . . . a long time."

His tone was strong and his movements sure; this wasn't the dead sack of a man who had sat in the chair an hour ago with tears on his broken face.

Ismail was demanding attention: "Tuan Duffy say he will take search-party along below ridge—come there two days! Must hold on, he say!"

"Good, Ismail. You are in charge here until I come back—understand? My orders."

Thorne stood by the open door of the cabin, zipping the front of his flying-suit. Yassim was instructing the ground-crew, his voice pitched against the flat beat of the exhausts, gesturing carefully until he was satisfied they understood the procedure; then he turned to the others. "I am ready, gentle-men."

"In you go, Thorne!"

The man Smith was with them again, dodging someone—Joe or one of the ground-staff—as he came at a tilting run towards the aircraft, hands flying up in front of him—"You're forbidden to take off with that man on board, Major Yassim! You understand that? I have authority—"

"Mr Smith!" The extradition officer caught up with him but Smith was trying to get at Thorne, shouting in his thin angry tones:

"This man is wanted! He can't be allowed—"

"What authority have you?" Yassim spoke not to Smith but the officer.

"None, in writing. But the fact—"

"Please remove this man before I am obliged to shoot him." Thorne climbed to the cabin and as Smith tried to

grab at his legs the Malay Major drew his gun, again address-
ing the extradition man, who seemed to have more sense.
"I am embarking on a mission affecting the security of the
State, and am permitted to shoot this man dead if he
obstructs me—"

"Smith, I've no written authority—"

Hugh didn't wait but dropped a blow across the man's
neck in case he tried damaging the aircraft to stop take-off;
then he climbed on board.

"What happened?" Thorne asked.

"He's fainted."

Yassim's navigator was in one of the forward seats watching the instruments as the twin engined idled; and now the
Major climbed in, calling a final word to his ground-crew
and slamming the door. Hugh was still checking the two
Straits Airways zip-bags and the Red Cross box as the aircraft began taxi-ing.

Gunning up at the beginning of the runway they were
surprised to see a green signal beamed to them from the
tower. Even in these conditions, Haji Ahmad was obeying
the few regulations still extant. Just before releasing the
brakes Yassim said to them: "Will have to be first time
because there's water in the brake-drums!"

They put up their thumbs and heard the kick of the
hydraulics as he triggered the brakes off. Beneath them the
wheels rolled.

Hugh wondered how hard Yassim meant to try. As the
pilot—the human factor—he could only judge the timing
and try to pull the machine off the ground before the runway ended and the swamps began. The real problem was
mechanical: given a certain depth of standing water on the
runway, the plane could take off; given a centimetre more,
it could not. But Yassim wouldn't know the result of his
efforts until he had made them.

Hugh didn't envy him. It was easier to sit here and just
think: whatever happens, we've got to get up. He wasn't the
pilot, the human factor involved. The sole question for
Major Yassim was: with one chance in fifty of the Sultan's
being alive, how much was it worth risking these four lives

in a take-off-or-crash attempt? Because there was a definite point, towards the other end of this narrow strip, beyond which was nothing but that choice; it was an invisible, imaginary point on the runway that governed their four lives, now they were committed to its laws; it was composed of simple factors: the power of the engines, the lift of the main-planes, the depth of the water and the degree of its drag on the wheels.

When the brakes had come off the revolutions had dropped as the propellers bit at the air; now they neared peak and the water began flaring up from the wheels with the sound of a fast bob-sled over snow. The cabin trembled and was still again and then started up a steady vibration while the revolution-counter needles marked off one more degree and the boost-gauges steadied at full.

The sound of the straining engines beat at the nerves because for another few seconds there was nothing for Yassim to do: then they saw the end of the runway coming, and the twin marker flares and the far beacon looming fast in their path; and he began trying to get them up before they hit the swamp.

23

THE actual bearing was seven miles east by north-east from Pasang, an area of scrub and rock a couple of hundred feet higher than the surrounding jungle. There was no ground-mist at this altitude.

They looked down as Yassim circled. There was nothing identifiable as an aeroplane below; there was just the glow of ash, of no special shape; from this height, a cigarette-end thrown down among grass. The moonlight turned the jungle to a waste of milky cloud where the mist lay; its light was too feeble to make any detail of the wreckage in the scrub. There came no gleam of any lamp, no movement that could be a signal.

"I would not advise it," Major Yassim shook his head. Thorne didn't look at him but went on checking the rounds in his revolver.

Hugh asked: "Are we about right for height?" Thorne nodded, snapping the safety-catch on. There'd be nothing to shoot at down there but he was damned if he was going to fetch a tree-spike through his guts and just hang there waiting for it. He had always demanded quick comfort when hurt, all his life.

"In the morning there will be helicopters," Yassim said. This was stupidity, typical of the British who had never learned that the reed that bends in the wind survives. There could be no one alive down there among that funeral ash, and they were as liable to smash a limb and die of burns, gangrene or loss of blood before help arrived for them. "We will turn back now," Yassim said.

Hugh saw what Thorne was doing and followed suit, running his waist-belt through the loops of the zip-bag; then he got the long metal Red Cross box balanced under his left arm.

"Give me that," Thorne said, and stood up, head bent to

clear the cabin room. "Remember what I told you. You go first so I can see where you are." He leaned over Yassim. "Left circuit, if you will—have to jettison the door."

"It is very foolish to do this!" He looked into the hard bright face and did not understand the light in the eyes.

"Be a sport." The old phrase came back, and the gap of eighteen years suddenly closed. "And thanks for the ride." It was what they had always said to the pilot.

Yassim looked away from him and moved the controls; the two men braced themselves to the tilt and half a minute passed; then the navigator pulled the hinge-release pins and Thorne kicked the door out.

"Get well clear and count ten. See you down there."

Hugh jumped and in fifteen seconds Thorne followed.

The ridge north-west of Pasang was high enough to thrust upwards through the mist. It was a dark spine of rock ten miles long and apart from the lizards and rock-snakes it had remained as barren as the surface of the moon since the earth was formed.

Low down, along a natural path of lichen and loose shale making a ledge for foothold, the tiger moved.

For an hour it had been moving westwards towards the dying glow of the fire, curious about it, as it was curious about everything, being a cat. Many times it had stopped, diverted by a sound or tempted by the scent of prey crossing its path. Now, within a few miles of the glow, it stopped again, hearing the sound of the machine in the sky.

Near the shoulder the bright hide was marked by a long bullet scar, and this scar marked also the deaths of the woman of the fishing-kampong and the two rubber-tappers and others, for it had been the wounding that had turned the tiger's mind to killing men. The tiger is not an instinctive enemy of man; it dislikes the taste of his flesh and unless it has grown too old and slow for quicker prey, or is sick and must find whatever meat it can, or is for some reason deprived of its natural prey and cannot choose, it will not kill a man. Or unless it has been wounded, by men. The tiger learns quickly to know its enemies; and man is the natural enemy of all living things, even of his own species.

The beast was not hungry. Two days ago it had taken a half-grown buffalo and broken the neck, carrying the carcass a mile in its jaws to the privacy of the jungle, there to eat. It was curiosity alone that moved it towards the glow of the dying fire.

Now it paused to watch the machine in the sky and the two strange shapes that were floating from it to the ground, unlike any bird. After a long time, when the sound of the machine had faded to silence and all was still, the tiger moved again on its way, its curiosity increased.

A party of six men, two of them dressed as plantation workers and the others in makeshift uniform, had been sent from the concealed encampment north of the town two hours ago. Their orders were to reach the wreckage as soon as possible and finish off any survivors. If by remote chance the Sultan was still alive and able to be moved, he was to be brought to the camp. Such a hostage would be of immense value to their cause. If his wounds were such that he would die of them en route, he was to be killed off by methods that would make it appear he had died as a result of the fire. All care must be taken to ensure that he could be identified by the first search-party, providing he was still identifiable; this would establish without any doubt the high success of the original operation: the placing of the explosive on board the aircraft at Singapore.

The six men moved with difficulty through the matted undergrowth, their lamps of little use in the mist save to light the compass and reveal the next obstacle for their jungle-knives.

From the *istana* a platoon of jungle-troops drawn from contingents of the royal guard had been despatched along the seven-mile airport road in three military trucks in response to the telephoned message that the crashed aircraft had had the Sultan on board. Three miles along the road there was a clearing where a track to the Duffy Estate joined it, and here the troops were disembussed to strike on foot through the area of secondary jungle that lay between the estate and the site of the crash, nine or ten miles west.

The men had been going forward for two hours, pressed on by their commander. It was the first time since the Sultan had come to the throne that these troops had been ordered to mount an operation in direct accordance with their sole and special duty: the personal protection of the Head of State.

Above them, out of sight beyond the blanketing mist, the royal aircraft was returning from its mission. For minutes they could detect the sound of its engines as they hacked their way through the trip-ropes of fallen creeper and the murderous barbed-wire thickets of jungle thorn.

The sound of the aircraft died away and they were alone again.

Duffy had taken his party by road, packed with their kit and provisions in the airport bus, east from the airport to the town and then south-west by the track that led through his rubber-estate and the rice-fields to the isolated scattering of one-family farms beyond. They had stuck out on foot through scrub and rock and crossed the derelict pontoons that were thrown over the swamp areas twenty years before by the Nipponese invaders.

Now they met the secondary jungle and made almost due west through the mist, their pace a yard a minute with their long knives hacking at the stems.

Duffy had kept the number of his party small. They were ten, including the Englishman Smith and the extradition officer. These two he had allowed to join him on two conditions:

"You'll carry your own food, water and drugs. And if any one of us has to drop out, one of you two will stay with him to look to him. A man can lose himself in this terrain more easily than in the desert. Is that understood?"

"I have to reach the wreck," Smith said. "I shan't stop for anyone who—"

"Then you don't come with me. Without me you won't get a mile into that terrain. Your choice."

Smith was no longer hysterical but there was some kind of fever in his soul. "I've reasons for wanting to go, Mr Duffy—"

"So've I. To save life if I can. I'm not taking passengers." He had dismissed them, but they were on the coach with him when it left, and they joined him on his terms. He took them because he couldn't stop them coming anyway: anyone could tag along behind, anyone. But they carried their own stuff, and by God they were going to obey him once they were in the jungle, because there there'd have no choice.

Smith and Tewson, the extradition officer, brought up the rear, carrying their own packs and two other men's besides. They walked heavily-burdened, not complaining, waiting patiently while the path was hacked from the living barrier, coming on again like pack-mules, never saying a word even to each other. For all the passivity of their task they seemed more dogged and more determined than anyone else, and Duffy had the uneasy impression that if all the others dropped down dead of fatigue these two quiet ones would stumble on against the wall of jungle with a kind of dreadful robot insistence, until it caught them and held them like two flies on a web and they died too.

For Duffy and his team they at least provided a bit of amusement: Smith's thin stretched-looking body was draped in a borrowed suit of jungle-green too loose for it, and Tewson had stepped straight out of a cheap London tailors into the Malayan jungle, except for his ankle-boots. He'd look an odd thing, Duffy thought, if he got lost and wasn't found in time: the king-vultures in Tamarah would find it hard picking, with cuff-links and braces and all.

In the rear of the hacking-party and ahead of the two Englishmen was Mr Chai, loaded with two packs and the medical kit; and he too was silent as he waited, and hobbled forward, and waited. Wan Chai had reached his decision while he and his cook and server had laboured to put back into the restaurant all those things they had so urgently taken out, even the big refrigerator.

He had joined the search-party in order to motivate the mechanism of his decision, the component parts of which were very simple. On board the aeroplane was a man who resembled Fate. He was the merchant who was coming to reveal to them how they might refine the crop of beautiful flowers and so increase their fortune from it. But the aeroplane had been smashed, and that was very bad joss, an omen from on high. There was to be no fortune for the transgressor. There was instead to be awful punishment.

Watching the aeroplane when it had circled the airstrip, Wan Chai had suffered the bewilderment of deep uncertainty: would the aeroplane crash? If it crashed, would poor Lee Kwei Chong be killed? If he were killed, would there be found among the wreckage the bundle of dollar notes that was payment for the last consignment? He did not dare to know. Would the merchant be killed? If he were not killed, would he prove powerful enough to persuade them to refine their beautiful crop and so lead them into disaster? Chai could not guess. It would be better if the aeroplane were to crash, and Chong were to live, and the merchant to die, and the bundle of dollar notes to be saved from any flames.

It might well be that this precise pattern of circumstances had already been followed; but he did not think so, because of the bad joss. He must hurry to see what had come about.

If Lee Kwei Chong was alive he would tell him of his big decision, so that Chong would not find another merchant to lead them all into disaster. If the merchant was alive too, he must tell Chong that the merchant must be told that their plans were no longer to be furthered; and the merchant must be told not *at once* but later, in the town, with Wan Chai absent, as if Chong had received the news of the decision from another source. Or the merchant would know that Wan Chai was one of the transgressors. No man's tongue could be trusted never to speak the truth in this untruthful world.

Mr Chai waited, and hobbled forward under his burden that sat upon his shoulders and upon his mind, and waited, and went forward again, his sole consolation the penance of his unworthy journey through the mist of this grievously uncertain night.

With the party were two half-blood trackers, small men whose fathers still hunted monkey with the blow-pipe in the aboriginal village fifty miles west of the coast. Every half an hour they stopped to make obeisance to the spirits of the forest, and mark one of the trees with their knife, making a sign that no one except Duffy understood. Oriental mysticism and the placation of gods was after all no different from the Western idea of not walking under a ladder, and touching wood.

After another hour Tewson came up among the vanguard. "I'll take a spell at the weeds."

Duffy looked at him in the eerie glow of the lamp; the party was marooned in the mist. "All right." He gave orders and a Malay shouldered the Englishman's load. Tewson took the long heavy knife and began swinging it. "Will there be any survivors, Mr Duffy?" He seemed to think him omniscient.

"May be. Mr Copland thinks so."

"They won't have any arms with them." He was finding the rhythm with the blade and swung it together with the other two men.

"There'll be the pilot's gun. Copland and Thorne have one each. Not that it'll profit them if we get there late."

Tewson had his jacket off and worked in his braces.

"What would attack them?" he asked.

Duffy raised his arm and brought up the party as the knives cleared their path on to a stretch of rock fifty yards across. Tewson walked by his side.

"In the Malayan jungle," Duffy said, "about the only beast that'll attack a man without provocation is a man. We'll be moving into the terrorist area before dawn and they'll be on their way there by now to look for loot."

He swung his left arm as much as he could; he'd got fussed with the sling at last and had taken it off, and high time. Of course, Elspeth wouldn't have let him; but here he was safe from her.

They met scrub jungle again and the two Malays and Tewson worked for another hour, until their shirts were ribboned and their forearms bleeding. Tewson worked as strongly as the Malays and Duffy watched him closely for a moment in the glow of the lamp. The man was absorbed in his task, oblivious as a dog at a rabbit-hole.

"Where do you live, Mr Tewson?"

"Putney."

"That's a pleasant spot, I remember."

The long blade swung up, swung down, hit the creeper and bit deep and severed it clean.

"The wife and I like it. The evenings are nice."

They dragged the creeper away; it was thick as a man's arm.

By dawn they had made two miles, and stopped to rest. Not long after, they heard the far lifted voice from the higher ground.

"What was that?" asked Tewson. He was inspecting his boots for leeches.

"It was the tiger."

"Where would he be?"

"He'll be on his way there, to take a look."

Tewson was putting his boots on again.

"Hadn't we best get on?"

"In a bit. The boys need to rest. They're not so determined with the weeds as you are, Mr Tewson."

24

AFTER the headlong plunge into the night his stomach had soured and now he swung beneath the spread silk pod fighting off sickness, disbelieving his safety here between earth and sky. The sound of the plane continued; but if anything happened now, Yassim couldn't help them.

When he opened his eyes he saw the glow on the ground; it still didn't look like the wreckage of anything man-made; it looked like one of the jungle worms he had seen that went on glowing after they were dead.

The ground swung in the moonlight and the drone of the plane ebbed and flowed in his ears. He caught the glint of liquid near the glow; perhaps it was the glycerine coolant still seeping from the burst tanks.

There were small trees—bamboo or saplings with a channel gouged through their midst where the aircraft had struck and run; as he floated lower he saw its shape grow more distinct. He was falling through smoke now, and fumes began stinging his eyes. He felt the heat, and the ground came up at him suddenly faster.

The heat became intense and he panicked, tugging at the cords to spill air as Thorn had said; but the silk seemed taut above him and he couldn't tell if he were changing direction or not; there was just the sickening swing of it and the black wave rushing up, and the dreadful heat. Above him the silk was tinged with orange light and he dragged again at the cords, gasping for cool air and finding none—and then black leaves loomed and something whipped at his legs: the cloud of coloured silk spun and caught, cleared and spun again, and his feet hit ground ... *Relax and go limp* ...

The heat flowed over his body and then the silk caught and began flaring as he lay bruised and trying to find the release-punch, blinded by the flames, his untrained fingers darting and searching until they found the metal clasp and felt the spring flex and free the buckles. The straps went loose and he threw them off, crawling away to where the world was dark and not flaring red, crawling and then with an effort rising to his feet and lurching, pitching down on hot ash and struggling up again, sobbing for air, choking in the fumes with pain searing along his legs and into his stomach, trying to swamp him and bring him down again. But he kept his feet and ran on and hit something that spun him round and he tripped, and fell sideways, cursing, sickened, enraged at his feeble efforts. Hands gripped him and lugged him to his feet—

"All right, you're clear." They stumbled together across rough soft ground and Thorne lowered him gently and let him lie prone. Cool water gushed over his face and his brain came into full consciousness. Thorne was twisting the cork back into his water-bottle, his face looking very fresh and alert.

"You—you look very fresh, damn you . . ."

"I didn't come straight down the chimney like a bloody fool."

Hugh leaned on one elbow and was sick, and felt angry about it. He'd always done it, whenever his nerves were tested; even as a child he had been sick on the doorstep of every new school.

When he was on his feet again he found Thorne with a torch, stooping over and swinging the beam, going forward and stopping to look again at the ground. "They didn't all stay trapped," he said. The beam glinted on fresh bloodspots. Hugh went as close to the burnt-out plane as he could, sweeping aside ash and debris with a branch he had stripped, making a path for his feet. Over an area of a hundred yards the ground was blackened; the fuel-tanks had burst on igniting and the area had been a lake of flame.

It was impossible to see details in the moonlight; the plane was a carcass, blackened and with a few errant flames still licking along timber.

Here was S. and P.A. Flight Twelve, airborne on schedule from Singapore, every document duly signed by competent authorities and with a passenger-crew complement of seventeen people. But it was useless to hate the unknown men who had done this; one might as well hate mad dogs or ignorant children.

He turned away when he could no longer stand the heat of the embers on his face. He felt numbed. Now that he was here he didn't want to do anything, because whatever he did it could only lead to the final certainty. He shouldn't have come.

The heat pressed at his back and sweat was running from the nape of his neck. He walked back along the path through the cooling ash. Thorne called to him, from farther away, and the sound of the other human voice dispelled some of the numbness. Thorne was offering his services again, as he had done a long time ago: let him see the sick and he would try to heal them. And even if there were only one survivor, even if he were dying, the man with the clown's face would ease his pain and let him die in peace. Even for that it had been worth coming.

He looked up but couldn't see Thorne any more, so he went forward towards the knoll of trees from which his call had come. He must help Thorne, and others. There was nothing strange about his numb feeling: it had happened in the first few days following the scream, when he had lived in total disbelief of what had happened.

The comb-thin saplings were riven where the plane had struck across them; their plant stems had eased the impact, and that was why its carcass lay still in one piece and was not scattered in sections across the earth beyond. A light flashed and he made his way over and around the white wounds of the trees where the sap gleamed and scented the air.

Thorne was in a hollow where the taller trees fell back and made a clearing.

"Copland! Lend a hand!"

He began running.

This was where they had come, to get away from the heat of the flames; here they had dropped to the cool earth. Some were moaning, as children will moan in their dreams. Two were standing up and moving across to where Thorne was crouched with his lamp.

Lee Kwei Chong lay on his back. The light shone harshly on his burned left arm and Thorne was working as he listened to the slow but still articulate accents:

"I heard your plane and asked someone to make a signal, but we are all rather groggy."

Hugh held the lamp for Thorne, who was busy with the Red Cross box. The sulphanilamide powder rose as yellow as pollen through the gleam of light.

"My navigator was dead before we crashed. He saved those of us who got out. Chen Sen-Yi."

"Yes," Thorne murmured, his voice gentle. "I don't want you to talk, though." The needle flashed as he held the syringe vertical, watching the gradations.

"Chong . . ."

"Hello, Copland. I didn't expect—"

"I don't want him to talk," Thorne said.

"Chong, what happened to the stewardess?"

He couldn't believe he had asked, in such casual words. He hoped Chong would never answer. Perhaps if Thorne put the morphine in very quickly, Chong would lose consciousness before he could remember, and answer.

"Keep that lamp steady," Thorne said.

Someone in the hollow of trees was moaning monotonously, the sound driven out upon every breath.

Chong said: "She's here, somewhere—"

"Here? Did you say here?"

"She was helping the Thai woman—"

"Copland, find whatever you can that we can use as blankets—leave the lamp on the lid of the box."

Hugh straightened up without saying anything, and moved away, and stood looking into total darkness until his eyes lost their reaction to the lamp and he could see details in the moonlight. There were ten or twelve people here, some of them in white saris or coatees, so that it was a few minutes before he could pick out the white drill uniform of the stewardess.

She was kneeling beside one of the passengers, a small Chinese in a European suit. In the pale light he couldn't see whether it was Mr Fei Moi Toi. Before she looked up, he stood watching her, his eyes stinging and his breath held while he looked down at the miracle of her living body here among the trees; then she heard the sound he made—something that escaped him suddenly on a breath, perhaps her name—and looked up at him, not recognizing him because the moon was behind him and reflected in her eyes.

"I'm glad you're all right," he said.

After a moment she asked: "Who is it?"

"Me. I brought Dr Thorne here to help. Or he brought me." He kept having to swallow and the words sounded odd. She stood up and stared into his face.

"Hugh?" She reached for him and he took her hand. "Hugh?"

"Yes."

"Here?" Her hand trembled.

"They dropped us by parachute, to help."

Her eyes were very large and glistening, so that as she closed them, clinging to his hand, it was like a shadow passing across her face.

"I didn't think I would see you again," she said.

"I know."

She pulled his hand towards her and held it against her like a present someone had given her; the shadow went, and she was looking at his face again, now smiling.

"It would have been annoying," she said.

25

AT dawn they began moving away from the site of the wreckage. The decision had been made by Thorne and Captain Chong after a talk with the Sultan; they had sat round the lamp and spoke quietly so as not to wake those who were sleeping.

"I must leave the final word with Dr Thorne," Sir Rahman said, "for the sake of the injured." He was unharmed but for bruises and the loss of hair on one side of his head where the flames had brushed him. He had brought three people out of the plane before the tanks had gone up, Hugh had been told; the Thai woman, still distraught because her husband had not escaped, had been one of them. "But I must warn you that the terrorists in this area will be coming here. I know them and feel quite certain of it. If they find us it will mean a massacre."

"We must move, then," said Chong.

Thorne squatted with his palms pressed to his brow. He had worked for three hours without pause. "Try to rest, Captain. I gave you enough dope to drop an ox."

"My wits are used to opiates, Doctor. It's like giving a Scotsman whisky."

"Thorne, can they be moved? The worst ones?" Hugh was gazing beyond the glow of the lamp; he had seen them, the worst ones. Santha was with them now, trying to comfort them.

"Look here," Thorne said with weary impatience, "it's like this, surely. Sir Rahman says it's on the cards they'll send helicopters in, by daylight, but there's no guarantee. By daylight, anyway, the C.T.s will be either here or damn' nearly—so we've got to pull out. If I say there are cases here who can't be moved, it won't make any difference. Two are going to die, as it is. The others will be all right unless infection sets in or we run out of water. Need stretchers, of course."

"We can make stretchers," Hugh said. "What about Mr Toi?"

"Who's he?"

"The Chinese. Internal injuries, you said——"

"Haemorrhage. Move him too. I can't do a major abdominal here." He squinted at Hugh with bloodshot eyes. "A burst appendix is rather simpler."

"We don't expect miracles, Thorne." Even the man's presence here had healed, easing their shock. The murmured words had given them hope, a few hours ago when he had gone round with his lamp: "It's all right, I'm a doctor."

He spoke again, into his hands. "When we were flown in, Copland, I noticed a clearing about four or five miles from here—I thought it was where the plane had come down. It's pretty well due east and there's only tall-tree jungle to get through. Start at dawn and we can reach there by noon, and if there's the smell of a helicopter we can signal with smoke."

After a silence the Sultan said: "There seems to be no question of what we should do. I'll be obliged if you'll give me something useful as a task."

"I should rest," Thorne said. "We didn't hit the ground so hard as you people."

"How many stretchers do we need?"

"Five."

"If you'll excuse me, I'll start work." He left them.

Hugh stood up. "Do me a favour, Thorne. Take a rest yourself. We may need you later, more than ever."

Thorne lit a cigarette and put it between Chong's lips. "Get it into your head—I don't like being needed."

Hugh smiled at the absurdity. "Then all I can say is you're in the wrong job." He went to help Sir Rahman cut bamboo.

When dawn came the party moved off through the thinning mist. The dry rasping of the cicadas greeted the day; a few minutes later they heard the deep voice of the tiger. Chong, on the stretcher, asked the Sultan:

"How far away?"

"A mile."

"Has it heard us?"

"It's been listening to us for hours."

"Is it coming for us?"

"Oh no. It took a buffalo, two days ago. If we don't provoke it, it won't attack. There are too many of us."

"Just now," Chong said, "I don't feel up to provoking tigers."

"You have instructions not to talk."

"How do you know it took the buffalo?"

"I am always in touch with the *Istana*. There are hunters out, because we have to kill the beast. It has turned against men. We know every move it makes, and it knows about the hunters. It's like a game of chess. We shall be sorry when they kill it, but people will be safe again."

Chong closed his eyes; staring up at the cathedral roof of the trees made him dizzy.

"And the terrorists?"

"We have to kill them too."

An hour later they heard a spotter-plane circling, west of them above the wreckage; but it was impossible to signal; the sun, even the sky was shut out by the great trees here.

The party halted many times. Of the eleven survivors, five were stretcher-cases; the shock of the crash and of burns had left some of them feverish; two were still unconscious and badly injured; Fei Moi Toi was alert but in pain and had refused to be drugged; his male secretary and another passenger carried him gingerly over the network of roots. Much of the time he spoke to his secretary in Chinese, his voice monotonous in the quiet of the trees.

"What's troubling him?" Thorne asked once, and Chong said:

"He is preparing to die. It's rather amusing. In the last half an hour he's proposed a merger between two of his chemical laboratories and put a tin-mine on the Hong Kong market. I'm thinking of making a bid for the Cadillac."

"Then hurry."

Hugh and a Malay walked past them from front of the file. There were only eight able-bodied people for the stretcher work and these two were exchanging shifts with Sir Rahman and a huge Sikh textile-merchant, taking a stretcher well forward and leaving it, to walk back for the fifth and bring it on. Santha May Swee was helping to carry the Thai woman, whose weeping broke softly out whenever she woke, her grief worse than the pain of her burns.

At mid-morning one of the worst cases died and they stopped for an hour to bury him among stones not far south of the ridge. He was a Chinese, and great care was taken to choose a burial-site with good *foong-sui,* where there was a pleasing view of a towering ipoh tree and where the elements could not beat at the grave when the monsoons came. Wild flowers were replanted to half-encircle the mound, and a sketch was made of it and of its approximate disposition so that the family could make pilgrimage here and commune with the departed.

To the inscription carved on the tree above the grave were added the words: *In the presence of H.H. the Sultan of Tamarah.* It would look very well, Chong told Thorne, when repeated in the *Straits Times.*

They moved on through the green jungle gloom, their mood lightened rather than depressed by the hurried funeral; the Chinese had been unconscious since he had been dragged from the wreckage, and his burns had been hideous to see.

Towards noon the stretcher-bearers were lurching as they walked, some of them still suffering from shock, all of them stifled by the humid heat. Santha trudged in boots too big for her, borrowed as protection against leeches. When they halted for brief rests she knelt by Toi's lowered stretcher, talking to him quietly in his own tongue, the delicate cadences suiting the timbre of her voice. Nearby, listening but not understanding, listening as one does to music, Hugh thought there could be no language in the world that this voice wouldn't make beautiful.

Passing him once, she looked into his eyes without smiling. "Don't despise me."

"I admire you." Their hands brushed together, perhaps by chance.

By midday the soft song of the insects had faded a little; it was the beginning of their siesta. In the tree-tops the monkeys ran and leapt but made no sound, except here and there where there was a squabble in progress. The tiger had not called since dawn. The clearing Thorne had noticed from the air was in front of them, but before they reached it the Sultan halted them with an urgent signal.

"There's movement somewhere ahead," he told Hugh and Thorne.

"What kind?"

"Men."

Hugh loosened his gun and moved the safety-catch. Of the whole party he and Thorne were the only ones not suffering from delayed shock, but Thorne was haggard with fatigue. He went forward from tree to tree, pausing to listen. Voices were audible, calling in Malay dialect. Movement came among the lower leaves on the far edge of the clearing and a man—two men, three—came into the haze of sunlight and stood looking around them. The tallest was a European.

Hugh went back and called: "It's all right—it's Duffy and his party." Then he turned to meet them.

The stretchers had been lowered beneath the shade of leaves at the edge of the clearing. Santha was holding the hand of the Thai woman, giving her the comfort of the light false phrases that can never assuage grief, that are never listened to, but that must be said because silence would be worse. Thorne was examining Mr. Toi again while the thin young secretary stood with his hands clasped and hanging in front of him, perhaps not yet ready to believe that so powerful a man was going to die.

The others were gathered at a little distance from where the stretcher-cases were lying. Of Duffy's party no one had dropped out, but one of the Malays had twisted an ankle and was in pain; their hands were shedding the skin of burst blisters, for their journey—its route hacked yard by yard with the heavy knives—had taken them twice as long as the other party, though it was half as far.

Smith was complaining, during the last hours of their trek, of the heat and loss of blood from leech-bites; but now that he was here he fell silent, sitting by himself with his arms across his knees and his eyes on Thorne.

Duffy shared a cigarette with Hugh after they had eaten. "What makes that man look at Thorne with such gloating in his eyes?"

They watched the weedy figure in its too-loose jungle green. Smith was oblivious to everything else. Thorne seemed to fill his world.

"I don't know, Duffy. I don't know anything of Smith, except that he's out here to fetch Thorne and get him shipped to England."

"I heard them say he's wanted. What for, laddie?"

"Murder."

Duffy looked away from the crouched figure and watched Thorne, who was moving wearily among the injured.

"But the man stood trial—it must be three or four years ago—Elspeth read me the case when it was in the news." He dropped his cigarette-end. "He was acquitted."

"They've dug up evidence about another death. That's all I know."

Duffy wiped the sweat from his moustache with the back of his freckled hand. "Would you say that man would murder anyone?"

"Only himself."

In the shade of the trees Thorne passed the stewardess. Her white tunic had been added to the motley of garments that served for blankets; her shirt was torn and dark with sweat between the shoulder-blades, and the blue-black hair was matted.

"We're going to make more stretchers," he said. "One for you." Her fatigue wasn't serious but the shock was in her like a fever.

"I would rather walk." Her large eyes were over-bright and her hands unsure. "Can you do anything for Mr Toi, over there? Anything?"

"He won't let me dope him."

"He is in great pain."

"Not really. He's too busy to feel it."

"He thinks he will die."

"If he does, it'll be with all his affairs in order. Not many men can do that for themselves." When he had finished his

224

examination a little while ago he had left Toi signing papers with his secretary, his speech clear and his eyes absorbed, the blood still oozing into the mattress of leaves on the stretcher. It was odd to see blood so red from a man so like a ticker-tape machine.

The girl whispered, because the Thai woman was sleeping now: "Will you operate on him when we reach the hospital in Pasang?"

"If he can spare us the time."

Sitting alone below a tree, Wan Chai savoured the news of his salvation. Chong had told him that the bundle of dollar notes had been burned in the flames, but Chai was not sad, because the merchant had also perished. The secret of the beautiful flowers was forever safe. With the bad joss there had come good. Nor could he be sad for the merchant, whose resting-place had been chosen for its good *foong-sui*, even in the presence of H.H. the Sultan of Tamarah, as Lee Kwei Chong had described. Such honours were not given to many.

Tomorrow he would carry the tidings to his brother, Loy Lin, and they would celebrate their decision to turn away their thoughts from greediness and pursue the tenor of their way as slowly as before, placing their feet with care along the winding path.

A shadow passed and he looked up. The English doctor was joining his friends, weary from his merciful toil. How good it must be, thought Wan Chai wistfully, to walk through the world like that man, devoted to his fellow-beings and free of all conscience!

The Sultan had been talking earnestly to Duffy, seated with his back to a tree to rest his lame leg. Hugh had asked him if he could think why the explosive had been stowed on board Flight Twelve, when it might seem less risky an operation at Pasang.

"At Pasang there was less opportunity, Mr Copland, thanks to your efficient management and the vigilance of the present guards at night. A big airport is like a big city: the very activity of the place can conceal trespass. Obviously the group in this area has organised first-class liaison with its agents in Singapore. They had the bomb ready and they knew which plane I was taking, even though my seat was booked under an assumed name." With the sudden under-tone of rage that Hugh had noticed in their first meeting at the *istana* he said more quietly—"My presence on board that plane was responsible for all this suffering. The first attempt on my life should have made us think more seriously. From the minute I return there'll be martial law proclaimed in the State."

Duffy picked at the ginger hairs on his hands, and in a moment asked: "There's not much question now, sir. There's an army forming, not just a nuisance-campaign in action. I had it from Stratton, six months ago——"

"There are two hundred armed men split into three main groups and a dozen scattered units in this State alone, Mr Duffy. We've had more than one report that they're planning a full-scale attack on Pasang and the airport within the month. Two days ago I was in Kuala Lumpur for an audience with the King, and later I was with the chiefs of the Army and Air Force for several hours. Of course it's in the interests of the whole of the Federation for the Government to give my own troops full support in an effort to wipe out the terrorists. Certain plans have been agreed upon. I must ask you to treat these few remarks as highly confidential, naturally."

He was silent for minutes, perhaps having regretted say-ing even this much even to these men. Conversation between the most trusted friends must always carry the risk of being overheard.

"I owe my life to Colonel Stratton, to the navigator of the aircraft, and to you. But Stratton didn't give his life just to save mine—the idea would have amused him; but for his own brave reasons he died fighting my enemies—that is to say the enemies of my people. I mean to finish what he began." He eased his leg and the pain of the strained muscle flickered across his eyes. "I mustn't keep you talking. Doctor Thorne, when do we move?"

"Straight away, sir."

Hugh looked at the sky and listened. Twice during the morning they had heard helicopter engines soon after the spotter-plane had gone over, but now the sky was blank.

Duffy got up. "We've four men available for stretcher-bearers and we can double our speed back along the track we've cut."

They had assembled around the stretchers before the sound came from north of the clearing: the single crack of a rifle.

"Hold hard," Duffy said. His mild eyes took on the look of an alerted animal's and his head was turned so that his ear could trail the diminishing echoes. For the second time they heard the voice of the tiger.

"How far, Duffy?"

"Mile." He stood like a tensioned spring. The echoes of the beast's roar died north against the rock-face of the ridge.

It was the sudden fusillade that surprised them. It sent a volley of sound ringing the great stems of the trees, closer than the rifle-shot.

"I don't understand," Sir Rahman said.

Duffy's hand was on his gun, moved by instinct.

"Tiger's hit. Wounded. Tell by the roar." He added something but the second fusillade covered the words. When the echoes died he said: "A good dozen guns—attack and reply. Can you beat it?"

Hugh said: "There's troops out from the *istana*, making for the crash-site. I telephoned from the airport—"

"So that's it! They've been closing on each other—the Tamarah troops and the C.T.s—without knowing it. Both making for the wreckage. One party sighted the tiger and fired, and the others thought they'd come under attack." A straying shot hummed into the leaves and stirred them like rain.

"Better get down."

A man screamed somewhere in the distance and Hugh remembered the night of the fallen tree. The rattle of hap-hazard firing took over from the second fusillade and they dropped to the ground as a bullet went spanging through the tree-trunks.

Duffy was trying to follow the pattern of battle by ear alone, but couldn't. It was always like this in the interior.

227

The Malayan jungle was the densest in the world and covered four-fifths of the country; otherwise the terrorist armies couldn't have survived against the grinding fifteen-year campaign of the British, now handed on to the Federation command. Most of the fighting was blind, the scattered terrorist units as hard to see as the animals and birds concealed in a children's puzzle-picture. These combatants now shooting it out had come within range of each other before realizing it, and even then it had taken the rifle-shot to alert them.

Amid the crackle of the guns there came another sound, repeated and getting louder. Lying beside the planter, Hugh asked:

"What the hell . . . ?"

Duffy had his long chin propped on his arms as he stared through the columns of the trees. "The tiger. I told you, it's hit. Running down-wind to bring its scent with it."

"Coming this way?"

"Aye. Hasn't twigged us yet—we're down-wind too." He was signalling one of his trackers and when the man came flitting over the ground with animal speed Duffy said: "Bring rifle, Sak-abu, quick."

The other half-blood was on his feet, excited, fearful. "Tiger, tuan! Tiger come!"

"Get down. Don't move."

Sir Rahman had shifted nearer Duffy on his elbows and one knee. "Must you shoot?"

"Have to, if we see it." He checked the breech and put the catch off.

"If my troops are outnumbered there, we'll give away our position to the Chinese. It happened before."

Duffy was rising to his knees. The voice of the tiger came again, nearer—a strange sound deep from the great throat and broken by shrill whimpers of pain as if the animal were still waging a lone struggle with the bullet lodged in its flesh. Duffy said:

"If it comes within sight of us, it'll smell us. You know tiger, sir, better than I do. That beast's in a rage of pain and God help us if it runs this way." He was crouched on his feet

228

now and the glow from the sunlit clearing sent amber light along the barrel of the gun. "Give me permission, Sir Rahman."

"We're in your hands."

"Copland," Duffy said quietly. "Thorne. Ready with the revolvers. Listen. Follow me at ten paces. If—" He turned his head a fraction, hearing the deep snarl and the patter of dead leaves, noting its direction. "If my first shot doesn't kill and it goes for me, do what you can—but get close first."

"Why not make a concerted—"

"Do as I say." Duffy was upright and moving like a cat towards the edge of the open ground, staring right into the flood of sunshine to get his eyes used to it, for the tiger would break from the far side.

The shooting had stopped, northwards of the clearing. One side or the other had lost, and died; the other was left. Friend or enemy would hear the rifle and make in its direction, believing that a second force was in the trees. There was no telling who would come. The risk had to be taken.

Hugh walked beside Thorne and paused as Duffy paused, following up, stopping halfway between the stretchers and the edge of the clearing. The others watched, wanting to speak to one another, not daring. The silence held them in a spell.

Duffy looked back once to make sure he was covered, took a pace and stopped and brought the rifle into his shoulder as the voice of rage came again and the leaves burst black and gold. The tiger was in the clearing, running awkwardly with crimson spread shining across the hind-quarter and bannering out like a wet red flag as the wound poured. Then it stopped and stood with its head low and ears flattened.

It had scented man. The man stood in the shadow of a tree with the long gun gleaming, as still as the animal, as quiet, as engaged.

One of the stretcher-cases moaned in drugged sleep and the tiger's haunches sank and stiffened, the wound ignored, the muscles tensioned. It waited. Duffy waited. When the beast was sure of their direction it would come for them even

229

though it could now see the gleam of the gun and knew what it was and what it could do, and what it had done before in other men's hands. Just as it understood the shape of the cobra's hood and the eagle's beak, the tiger knew a gun.

Duffy's voice came softly but they were startled by it. He spoke slowly. "Are you ready?"

"Yes," Hugh said, pitching the answer low.

"Good. I'm going to provoke a charge. If you have to help me, fire close at the head. Don't move until I go down. I want him to concentrate on me, so he'll come straight into the aim."

Hugh's scalp crept and in another second his sweat was chill on him. It was the first full-grown male he had seen and its great size awed him. The beast stood full in the sun, dominating the clearing, beautiful in its rage. There was no sound until Duffy stamped his boot and uttered a wordless shout that brought the tiger running with its body low between shoulders and flanks, swinging to one side and coming on fast halfway between the sun and shade, instinct moving it into the play of light and shadow where its colours merged, so that it seemed as if the beast had vanished by some magic of its own.

Duffy swung his body from the legs and called a second time in case the tiger saw the others and attacked them. Ten yards—less—from Duffy it halted, ears flat, jaws gleaming, a fury of hate rising from the throat before it bounded half the distance with a slight twist towards the side of the wounded leg, and leapt with the forepaws spread and claws shining, jaws wide and fangs white. Duffy fired for the ribbed roof of the mouth, but the wounded leg of the beast had altered the angle of its leap and though the man had allowed for it the bullet went into the side of the jaw and as he sprang clear to roll like a dropped bundle the spread claws ripped the boot from his foot and the animal was turning even as it struck the ground as Duffy shouted—"*Get him! Get him!*"

The revolver-shots came in unison as the two men closed in and aimed for the black and gold head. Duffy was scrambling up when the beast hit him with its body, knocking him down and falling half across his legs; the roar diminished to a sigh as the breath was forced out of the chest and the great heart stopped beating.

"*Duffy*—"

"All right." He levered himself to a sitting-position and gathered breath. "Winded, that's all. He's quite a weight." He spat saliva away and looked at the tiger's face, into the closing eyes; the heat of its foreleg was across his stomach; the claws were slowly sheathing. The blood ran red over the black and the gold and fell away, soaking into the earth. "Poor beauty . . ." he said, "poor beauty . . ."

"Thorne—lend a hand."

"Move him gently, lads. Gently now."

For an instant Hugh had looked at his face, and saw tears in the narrowed eyes. Duffy caught his glance of surprise and dragged his legs clear of the beast's weight impatiently, calling: "Sak-abu! Fetch that bloody—Sak-abu!"

The tracker dropped at his side and tried to help him up but he pushed him away. "Take N'amba and go up there north. See what men there. Come and tell. Quick now!"

He got to his feet and slipped a new shell into the breech of the rifle. Not looking at Hugh or Thorne he said: "I forgot. Thanks."

26

IN the foray below the ridge the Sultan's troops had out-numbered the terrorist group by five times yet lost eleven of their thirty men. The half-dozen Chinese had fought till they died, with suicidal fanaticism that for a time seemed to shield their bodies with bullet-proof mail. A sergeant of the Malay troops swore that one terrorist had fired at him minutes after he was dead, and would listen to no talk of rigor mortis having contracted the trigger-finger.

It was the reputation the Communist Chinese had in the area: they would go on fighting even after death. It was to discredit these rumours of immortality that their bodies were dragged through the streets of the nearest town for the people to see and remember. Thus, when the air-crash survivors reached the airport road and were put on board the waiting ambulances at noon next day, the six corpses were roped behind military trucks to make their tour of Pasang, their heads bare and their guns gone, their uniforms dark with blood.

From the jungle, forty came back alive: nineteen of the Tamarah troops, the ten of Duffy's rescue-party, nine survivors from the burned-out plane and the two parachutists. With them they brought eighteen dead: eleven Tamarah soldiers, the six terrorists, and the Hong Kong industrialist Fei Moi Toi.

He had lived for three hours after the troops had gained the clearing and taken over the stretcher-work. He had died with the pen in his hand, its ink obliterating half an unfinished signature and drying more quickly than the blood on the mattress of leaves.

Watching the thin young secretary they saw that he couldn't believe it. After minutes he had moved the pen, staring at it as if it were a broken finger.

Watching Santha's melancholy but unweeping face, Hugh

had thought: "Even now she's failed them. What will she do?"

They were carried smoothly in the big Humber staff-car with two motor-cycle outriders ahead of them on the road to the *istana*. Thorne sat with an odd expression on his pale face that Hugh found puzzling: a hint of a smile was on the set mouth but it had more irony than humour.

They both, anyway, looked strange to each other, Hugh sweating in a dark-blue Straits Airways uniform and cap, Thorne in a badly-fitting suit hired from a Chinese tailor in the town. Noon temperature had been 106 in the shade.

"It's quite absurd, of course." Thorne's voice was a drawl, relaxed, resigned, edged with bitterness. "You went out there for love, and I went out there to find something I always thought I'd lost. Both perfectly selfish reasons. This is a farce."

"Quite. You needn't imagine I've got any illusion. It would have been bad form to decline the honour, though."

"Frightfully bad form." There was a grunt of genuine amusement. "Noblesse oblige, and all that."

"The thing is, it might save you." It was the first time Hugh had broached the subject.

"It might. But from what? And for what?"

"From being taken back. For the future you found out there."

Thorne looked through the window at the jungle trees; a huge creeper hung against the massed foliage, aflame with bright orange blooms. "Now that I've got something to lose, I suppose I'm afraid of having to."

"What are your chances, if you go back?"

"Depends on simple definitions. I suppose you can call euthanasia murder if you're looking for a scapegoat. They didn't, the last time. This time I think they will. In this world, mercy's suspect."

Suddenly Hugh heard himself asking: "Would they be right, Thorne? Was it murder?"

For nearly a minute the man was silent. "Yes. I killed for

gain. My own peace. Too soft, of course. Anyone who doesn't like to watch suffering makes a bad doctor."

"How much are you excusing yourself?"

"No excuses. Motive, not right. I didn't have the right—"

"What I mean is," Hugh broke in, wanting to be sure about this, "would they have become curable?"

"Not in the present light of medical knowledge." Real humour touched the ends of his mouth again. "Wonderful phrase, isn't it? Such a pompous way of admitting ignorance."

They sat without speaking again for minutes and then Hugh asked: "Smith. Who is he?"

"I'd think of him as a conscience-figure of my own imagination if he weren't so bloody active. He was an assistant anaesthetist with a natural tendency to make mistakes. I was obliged to censure him twice when he was working in my hospital and he bore me a grudge. When he tried to get his own back at my trial he perjured himself to do it—and they tripped him. He was struck off soon after my acquittal and hated my guts more than ever—he's a man who can't stand moral punishment."

"Did he follow you out here?"

"I'm not sure. He might have seen me in Singapore on a visit—all the world goes through there. Anyway his knife's in me. Poor old Smith, I don't think he really enjoys this little chase."

The car ran serenely through the palace gates; the glare of the sun on the white walls was blinding after the jungle gloom.

"If they try to take you back, what will you do?"

Thorne had put on his sunglasses and looked suddenly disguised. "That's an interesting question. I must give it thought."

Two white-uniformed Malay Regiment corporals opened the door of the car. An aide-de-camp came down the steps to meet them. Going through the great hall, they passed three Europeans waiting in the archway of an ante-room, their hands behind their neat dark suits: Smith and the two extradition officers.

Vultures, Hugh thought instantly, had the same kind of stillness.

The ceremony was brief, simple and rather solemn. The Sultan was in the uniform of colonel and wore full decorations, but the burned-away hair on one side of his head gave him a lopsided appearance. The citation, read in Malay and repeated in perfect English by the Chief-of-Staff of the State Army, was to the effect that without thought to their own safety Thomas James Kenneth Thorne and Hugh Brian Copland had undertaken a most hazardous mission of their own wish in an attempt to save life and render aid to the injured. That their courage had in fact achieved its ends was salutary, but failure to reach their objective would not have lessened the worth of their high intentions, since they had voluntarily placed themselves at the mercy of hazards beyond their power to combat.

The medal of the Malayan Order of Honour was in the form of a gold star. With it was traditionally bestowed a short dress sword, the hilt engraved and the black leather sheath encrusted with lace-fine Kelantan goldwork. The swords were presented by the hand of the Sultan from a purple cushion borne forward by two captains of the Tamarah Regiment.

It was at this point that Hugh saw a flicker of hesitation on Thorne's face; then one end of the mouth moved to a fractional smile and he took the sword—and as he took the sword Hugh knew what had crossed his mind in the instant of the smile. How good it would be to run at Smith with this wicked and beautiful blade. . . .

Sir Rahman had arranged an informal meeting with them immediately after the ceremony; they drank tea in the alcove where there stood the two great rosewood chairs; today a third had been brought in. On the bright lawns a peacock minced, just as before. The Prince thanked them very simply for their services to him personally, as one of the crash survivors.

"I also wanted the pleasure of telling you quite unofficially that the Federation Army has agreed to certain measures against the terrorist group in my State. As a crude political move, the second attempt on my life calls for a reply in the same terms. Your position, Copland, of airport controller Pasang will oblige our commander of operations to signal you a few hours before his action is mounted, so that you'll know what is going on." He gave a charming smile. "I do hope you'll enjoy it."

Less than five minutes after they had taken their leave they were stopped on their way through the marble halls. An aide addressed Thorne.

"Your presence is required immediately by His Highness. I should like the privilege of escorting you."

"I've just been with His Highness, Captain."

"This concerns another matter."

Thorne looked at Hugh. "Look after this lovely thing for me. See you in Pasang." His mouth was dead straight and his eyes had gone cold.

"I'll wait for you here."

"It may take some time."

"I'll wait. Good luck."

Hugh stood the swords against a carved ebony chair and felt for a cigarette, ignoring the statuesque footman at their post beside the doors. With any luck, permission to smoke inside the *istana* might be among those privileges accorded a holder of the Malayan Order of Honour.

Did it also provide that you couldn't be deported?

The audience was in the presence of the Sultan's official secretary and a barrister of the court, to whom Thorne was first introduced.

"In view of your services to my people," Sir Rahman said unhappily, "this is very painful to me, but I felt that you might prefer—as I do—to have the matter done with as soon as possible."

He sat very upright behind the massive desk and faced Thorne across neatly-assembled papers.

"Had you infringed any law of this State, you would be responsible solely to me as supreme custodian of the law in Tamarah. Were it then my opinion that there were mitigating circumstances I would be able to help you. As it is, your own Government has requested your extradition and has sent its officers to accompany you. If you have in fact infringed any law, it's a law of England, and of course I've not the slightest influence. Nor have I the power to refuse this request. Only the Sultan of Negri Sembilan, who is also Supreme Head of State in Malaya, could do that. If you wished, I could ask His Majesty to consider your case; but I must tell you that even though your services have been honoured in a state of the Federation, he would see no proper grounds for giving his refusal to your Government. Mr Bajeb-Sindi here with us has advised me fully on this, and he'll give you a detailed summary of the situation if you would like him to—here and now."

Thorne hesitated only for a moment.

"I won't trouble him, sir. I don't see any cause for protest on my part."

"I wish there were. You would find a great deal of support. Probably you know something of the workings of international agreements, and you'll know in any case that the relations between the Federation of Malaya and Great Britain are very cordial. In the absence of real grounds for our refusal to deport you, such a refusal would be viewed as discourteous and unethical."

His hands touched the documents in front of him. "It remains for me to sign the papers. Before I do that, I want you to have time to think, and to consider whether you want to make an appeal. There would be no point in it, but you have the right to take your time. The law allows two weeks— as I interpret it in your case."

"I appreciate the concession, sir. But if I'm to go, I'd rather go now. Patience isn't my strong point."

Sir Rahman looked relieved. "I think you're wise. If you delayed—even for two weeks—it might seem to be in your disfavour. We'd like to think that every chance will be on your side when the time comes. Naturally I shall have a full report sent to the British Foreign Office, detailing the extent of your high services to this country and mentioning that in all respects your sojourn here has been noteworthy. You have married a woman of Tamarah, I understand?"

"Yes."

"If she wants to go with you to England, and if you would like that, we would see to it that the few formalities—her visa, and so on—are hurried through. If she stays here she'll be accorded the privileges due to the wife of a man honoured by the State, so you'll be able to feel free of any worry about her comfort while you are absent. We very much hope it won't be for long."

The gold nib glinted as it moved; for a few seconds the signature shone in the reflected sunlight and then went dull; by this small degree the processes of international law were already advanced.

"Mr Bajeb-Sindi, will you please serve this document to the officers waiting?"

Before the barrister had closed the door Sir Rahman nodded to his secretary, dismissing him. Alone with Thorne in the small ornate chamber he folded his hands and studied them for a moment.

"Mr Thorne, I was educated in England, as perhaps you know. That's why I have grown up to respect law and justice. Your country has also taught me less easily-defined modes of attitude and conduct, among which there's the readiness to give a man a sporting chance whenever the circumstances seem to justify it." He got up from the big carved chair and limped round the desk, pausing to look from the window, putting his hands into his pockets and unwittingly striking a very English attitude, turning to face Thorne, who had risen to his feet.

"When you leave the *istana* it will be in the custody of the two British officers, and you'll remain in their custody until you leave the country." His dark eyes were grave, but there was warmth in them; in his tone there was a certain note of mischief, conspiracy. "If by some chance they lost track of you—in a crowded street, for instance—there would be no specific orders for the police of this State to help in the search."

Hugh had finished his cigarette and could see nowhere to hide the butt in this expanse of shining marble. The nearest approach to an ashtray was an onyx amphora nearly six feet high, so he put the butt into his matchbox after making sure it was out.

Thorne came alone into the hall, walking briskly and without expression.

"How did it go?" Hugh had meant not to ask until the man chose to tell him.

"Very well. I rather like that young chap."

"Sir Rahman?"

"Yes. Got a heart. Listen, you'll be riding back alone in that grand motor-car. I'm off with the boys." He was feeling with quick hands in the pockets of his hired suit, and found the box with the decoration in it. "Look, give this to Kamala. The sword, too—she loves things that shine. Tell her——"

"But you'll see her before you——"

"No—make her unhappy. Joe will look after her—give him a hand, will you? She's too proud to go back to her family—bloody silly really because they're wonderful people." All the time his eyes were restless. An odd thought struck Hugh: in such a short time he had seen this man come of age. The face in the opium-house had been bedevilled by black despair and a bitterness against his fate. In the jungle this same face had been unrecognizable as Thorne's: drawn with fatigue, pained by the sight of suffering, yet all of a piece—a man's face with steady eyes and a soul at ease. Now there was this mien, different from either of the others: the face set against challenge and the eyes alert, judging the enemy that had become the name for circumstance.

"Thorne, I just hope you know what you're doing."

"Oh yes. All I don't know yet is what I'm going to do." He buttoned his jacket and tugged it straight. "I won't shake hands now. Say goodbye when I get on the plane."

He walked briskly away and the footmen drew back the doors for him.

Hugh picked up the two swords and followed more slowly.

In the distance he could see the huge archway filled with sunshine. Thorne had become smaller, though now his shadow grew long behind him as he reached the doors and the three silhouetted figures met him and closed about him on their way out to the waiting car.

27

ALTHOUGH it was quite early in the evening the street was already noisy, because in three days' time there were to be special celebrations in thanksgiving for the Sultan's safe return. The bakers and the women who made the paper lanterns were working half the night while the rest of the town paraded Jalan Burong.

The restaurateur next door to the little courtyard was on his step, and bowed over his smiles as Hugh came across the monsoon gutter.

"There is beautiful shark-fin, sin-shang! Most exquisite shark-fin tonight for you!"

"It's always exquisite, Mr Soong. The smell drives me mad when I go by."

"But long time since you entered these lowly doors!"

"If I went through those elegant doors too often I would become a poor man——"

"But price is so little!"

"So is the dross in these lean pockets—but I will be there, Mr Soong, one day."

They worked out the formula between them, ringing the changes every time Hugh passed the restaurant on his way home; and the temptation must always be resisted to tell Mr Soong that the restaurant at the other end of the street was just as good and half the price. In any case Mr Soong knew that. He owned both of them and fixed his prices according to the district.

The seductive smells drifting from the doorway of the restaurant were suddenly overwhelmed by the scent of the cassia tree as he went into the courtyard, where the neighbours were already at their mah-jongg game. The glow of the high iron lamp was dispelling the dusk and dappling the wall with the shadows of leaves.

She came between the group of mah-jongg players and

the row of little trees and he stood back to let her pass, not recognising her at once, for the sari was white, a sari of mourning.

"Hugh . . ." like a quiet chime among the street's noise and the click of the mah-jongg pieces.

She drew back among the stems of the flowering trees and he followed. "They told me you'd left the hospital," he said. It wasn't much of a greeting but he was confused. He hadn't expected to see her again, except at the airstrip when she was back on duty.

"Did you call there?" she asked. "They never——"

"I phoned, three or four times."

"They didn't tell me."

"I didn't give my name." Because nothing was any different. Her sari was white, that was all.

He must have looked down at it, because she said:

"One must respect . . ."

"Of course."

"I had to borrow something to wear until my new uniform arrives. It will be here in the morning and I shall leave at ten o'clock."

He had forgotten her stilted speech; he had tried to forget everything about her in the last three days, but couldn't quite manage not to phone the hospital where she lay in her fever.

"But that's the Bangkok flight."

"Business as usual." She had seen the words chalked on a board across the smashed window of an English shop in Singapore, after the Japanese had left, and had always remembered them. "It is an English joke," Mrs Swee had explained, though she'd never quite understood. "I shall fly Bangkok to Singapore the next day, and go to see my family. I have a present to take them."

"Your safe return."

She nodded, looking away from him, hesitating. "Yes. And they will be all right now, and not so poor. Before he died, Mr Toi signed an instruction to his secretary, placing a small monthly sum at the disposal of Mr and Mrs Swee. They can have proper things now, and good

242

doctors . . ." Her smile trembled and he touched her hand.

"How wonderful——"

"It was kind of him, because I had to tell him I had changed my mind, and couldn't be his wife. It was just before we took off from Singapore and we were alone for a few minutes——"

"I don't understand." The ivory mah-jongg pieces rattled and clicked and the din of the street worried him; he wanted to hear only her voice.

She was looking up at him, not smiling. "I had meant to wait, and tell him more gently when there was more time—but suddenly I was saying it and he was listening politely. Of course there are so many young women he could have——"

"But it was you he needed."

"Perhaps he thought so."

He shut his eyes for a few seconds, trying to think, to keep away the sounds around him. He'd been wrong. Everything *had* been different, even before the plane had crashed, even before the thin young Chinese had moved the pen in disbelief as if it were a broken finger.

"He said he knew I had met you," she said quickly. "He didn't mean you—just someone—he didn't know who it was. It didn't matter. He pretended he was very sad, and——"

"Santha, what made you do this?"

"I don't know. Not any one thing. Perhaps the old woman —the fortune-teller——"

"Here, in Pasang?"

"Yes. When I ran away from this house on the night of the Moon Festival I passed her and she called me and for some reason I stopped—for someone to talk to because I felt more alone than ever before in my life——"

"And you told her? About us?"

"Yes."

The answer was so obvious now that he knew it. The white tendril of smoke had climbed from the joss-stick like a spell, and everything had seemed unreal. *You see much, wise mother.* Had the clear eyes seen the moonstone on the turquoise sari as Santha had talked? Would she have thought, later that night, holding in her hand the moonstone given in payment, that Santha had returned it to him as if it were a ring, and that he had given it away rather than be reminded?

"She said I must go where my heart had gone."

"Yes?" he said.

"I didn't want her advice, Hugh; but she told me what I already knew, and it helped me. To you it must seem very childish to talk to soothsayers."

"Not really."

"Why are you smiling?"

"To see what it feels like. I didn't think I would, again, for quite a long time. What were you doing, here in the courtyard?"

"I had knocked at your door."

"I would have been there, if I'd known."

"Yes?"

Suddenly there seemed nothing to be said, and she was shy of him again as if this were their first meeting.

"What will you do now, Miss Santha May Swee?"

"Now?"

"Tomorrow. All the tomorrows."

"I shall be back on duty."

"Then I might have the luck to see you again, if you're still on the Pasang run?"

"Oh yes. Yes."

"Won't they give you sick-leave?" he asked.

"I don't want any, and they always like us to fly again as soon as possible, after an accident. But I shall ask for forty-eight hours, at the end of the first week."

"To see your people."

"No, I shall see them before then."

He said: "If you happen to be in Pasang, would you like to spend the evening with me? There's a Chinese restaurant at the other end of this street—cheaper than the one next door here but the food's very good and we could——"

"Yes. Please."

"You have to say 'no,' the first time. Then 'yes,' when I ask again."

244

"Not any more. Always yes, now, always."

The signal from the Colonel of the Tamarah Regiment to the Airport Controller Pasang gave no clear indication of the forthcoming action. Probably it wasn't meant to.

You are requested to arrange that on Monday next, during the hours of midnight to noon, all flying will be suspended. It will be your personal responsibility to inform all airlines concerned that Pasang will be out of service during those hours except in cases of extreme emergency.

Hugh found Ismail and advised him, then set Haji Ahmad to work cabling the airlines. The notice was short: it was Saturday. He suspected that this, too, was deliberate.

"Surely we are in Allah's favour, sahib. I shall pass the morning of Monday in my garden. I am planting tapioca."

"You will pass the morning of Monday on this very chair, Haji Ahmad. When the birds do not fly, the nest must still be guarded."

He was getting very good at Asian paraphrase.

The disappointed Pathan belaboured the Pasang Telephone Exchange with unusual force, while Hugh stood at the south windows of the control tower pondering the meaning of the signal.

Ismail came up the steps and said: "I have fixed the notice to the board, tuan. Some wish to know if it is to be holiday."

"No, Ismail. The airport will be in readiness for hard work on Monday."

"I will inform all people, tuan."

Hugh looked down from the window. Below, a machine was running-up, the propellers in a haze of motion; and he was reminded—as he would be reminded for a long time—of the awkward little scene on the tarmac.

They had stood in a group two days ago, watching the aircraft for Bangkok warming up: Thorne, Smith and the two extradition officers. Joe had been there and Hugh had asked him about Kamala, pitching his voice against the sound of the aircraft.

"She's at the house of one of her sisters," Joe said. "Only a woman can help at a time like this. I had trouble—she wanted to come here to say goodbye, but that would've been a heap worse."

There were six troopers of the Tamarah Regiment drawn up near the aircraft in parade uniform and with rifles shining. The other passengers came out of the building but had to wait until the pilot throttled down.

Hugh and Joe stood with Thorne; the other three were a little apart, willing to let it seem that Thorne was a free man taking a plane to a destination of his own choosing.

Thorne spoke only once, standing rather stiffly in the badly-cut suit he had bought from the tailor for the journey. "Copland, I've got a lot to thank you for. We'll have a party when I get back. You too, Joe."

They didn't say anything, but moved their feet. The roar of the engines made speech difficult, and difficult speech impossible. Thorne had turned his head to see where his escort was; then he looked in front again and watched the aircraft. Hugh looked at his face obliquely and was surprised by its expression. Thorne's skin had gone very white and the eyes were widening to a bright stare; and Hugh realised what was happening: the aircraft was some twenty yards away, facing the building, and Thorne's stare was focused not just on the aircraft but on one of the propellers that was whirling at peak throttle.

Hugh moved in the same instant and broke Thorne's run before he'd gone five yards and blocked him squarely, gripping his arm and shouting above the engines' sound—
"Don't try anything like that again—you hear me?"

The white face stared at him stupidly like that of a man coming out of hypnosis. His arm was slack in Hugh's grip.

Joe and the others were running up and one of them called something. The engines were throttling down and the stewardess was leading her flock across the concrete.

"Listen," Hugh said close to Thorne's ear, trying to keep the anger out of his voice, "don't chuck it in at this stage. It's too late, and now you've got too much to lose." He began walking him steadily to the plane, holding his arm as if impressing him in casual argument; the passengers had noticed nothing and the three men were following at a discreet distance now that their prisoner was no longer alone.

"Call it a relapse," Thorne said. The colour was coming back into his face.

"Just don't let it happen again, all right? You owe it to us, don't you? Kamala—Joe—me. Don't let us down."

He shook Thorne's hand and Thorne said:

"My word any good?"

"Yes."

"You've got it."

Hugh stood back as he went up the steps. The sergeant in charge of the troops called an order and Hugh heard the slap of the rifles.

"Thorne!"

He turned in the doorway of the cabin and saw Hugh's arm pointing. Very smartly, and proud of themselves for getting it right, the military escort was presenting arms. Thorne stared down in surprise, an odd look on his face; then he waved a hand and turned and was lost to sight.

Looking down from the control tower now, Hugh thought for another moment about Thorne. There was nothing wrong with Thorne except that he couldn't stand suffering: his own or anyone else's. That was why he had killed, in England; it was why he'd been found in the sea here, a bit of flotsam; it was why he had saved Kamala and why he'd been so easy to persuade when they had gone to his house to ask his help on the night of the burning plane. It was why that propeller had mesmerised him two days ago with its promise of release: a quick short run and there'd be no drawn-out agony of another trial, no prosecution, no defence, no sentence but his own.

That wasn't such a dreadful thing in a man, intolerance to suffering. A weakness, not a vice.

"I have informed Thai Airways, sahib."

"Good, Haji Ahmad."

247

Surely it could be hoped that an English jury would find worth in a man so honoured by strangers for what he had done even in his days of bitter self-exile, a man whose name was on a shrine together with the words: *Come ye who seek comfort to this sacred place.*

28

He had driven to the airstrip while it was still dark and for the last hour of the night was alone there except for the two Malay guards. He had flashed his headlights to them, coming round the perimeter road, giving the signal they had arranged between them weeks ago. It was to save any fatal misunderstanding when he approached them on foot to show his identity: with martial law proclaimed just after the plane-crash they were very trigger-happy on the airstrip at night.

Going up to the control tower he stood for a time on the roof, watching for the dawn. At one moment there was nothing to the east but the few feeble lamps of the town; a moment later there was the ghostly materialisation of the coastal palms against a pink wash of light. The edge of the sun floated suddenly on the sea's horizon and mounted so fast that the illusion of its movement was exposed: it was the planet that moved, the whole horizon swinging down across the face of the sun.

A voice called his name and he went to the top of the iron ladder. Climbing it was Major Yassim, pilot to the Sultan.

"The guards told me you were here, Mr Copland." He had a grin like a schoolboy's.

"I didn't want to miss anything, Major." They stood on the roof together, facing the south.

"How did you know? It's a military secret."

"I had a signal: no flying between midnight and noon. There's no night-flying here anyway, so I could only think there was a dawn attack planned. Is there?"

Yassim nodded, his bunched-up body squared to the south, hands on hips and head lifted. "Yes. They take-off at dawn from Kolu-Baran."

They stood without speaking for minutes, watching the south sky. It was clear of cloud and for another minute empty of any shape; then there came into it the semblance of a spawning of minnows.

"Formation excellent," said Yassim proudly. "You taught us well."

The dark finned shapes were already falling. A second swarm broke from the horizon.

"Two squadrons?"

"Three. There will be another."

The drone took on volume, filling the sky, and across the land the gibbon fell silent, giving it best.

The third squadron was still lifting from the south skyline when the leading group broke up and a single aircraft began its dive, plummeting on a course straight across the airstrip.

Yassim said a word but it was lost and Hugh couldn't even turn his head as he stood mesmerised by the aircraft's plunge. The second aircraft was starting its dive before the roof of the control tower shuddered to the shock-wave and debris blossomed from the jungle target-area.

Within five minutes the squadron of twelve dive-bombers had discharged their load and a cloud spread across the jungle north-west of the airstrip, tinged with flame.

The third of the new squadron was pulling out from its dive and the bombs were down when a gush of fire lit the dust-cloud and seconds later the airport building trembled violently to the percussion.

Major Yassim gripped Hugh's arm—"That is what they came for!" he called against the din. "The arms dump!"

"How did they know?"

"Colonel Stratton was working for months in the area, sending them information. We were all afraid they wouldn't take any action, but now—" he gave a big smile. "The Sultan forced them to it. He is a very angry man!"

The smell of the explosive was drifting down-wind and the cloud of smoke and dust lengthened. With the coming of the first planes there had been a crackle of rifle-fire from the trees but now the holocaust reigned unchallenged as the whole sky became filled with circling planes awaiting their turn and climbing, slipping one by one into the bombing-run and diving to the sprawling cloud, pattern-bombing to orders and pinning a net of destruction across an area two miles square to trap whatever terrorists had escaped the first onslaught and to catch them as they ran.

"This is murder, Yassim!"

"Of course. Their favourite game!"

The last squadron was going in, shaping its run a little from the east to cover the rest of the target-area.

Most of the planes had gone back into formation and were heading south the way they had come. The operation was completed and the bombs were home. It was twenty minutes after dawn.

"One for you," Yassim said in the new strange hush, and Hugh saw a machine coming into the circuit over the coast. Three more were following their tails, waiting for permission to land, a stray bullet lodged inside an engine-cowling or a fuel-gauge low. Hugh went down the ladder and ran to the south windows, checking the runway and snatching up the signal-lamp. Haji Ahmad came up the stairs, his face blank with surprise.

"The world falls about us, sahib!"

"Ahmad—open up the radio. Four arrivals!" He flashed the green, beaming it to the first aircraft, watching it settle for the approach through the smoke-haze that had reached the airstrip and was yellowing the orb of the sun.

Haji Ahmad began receiving at the control panel and giving verbal permission for the next plane to land, his face still shocked by the storm he had witnessed.

"What came to pass, sahib?" he called when he had finished.

"The Sultan was angry, Haji Ahmad."

"Truly he is a god among men!"

"Tuan, how is it with Captain Chong?"

"He is getting better, Ismail. I went to the hospital again today. Burns take long to heal."

"He is a brave man. They will give him honours." Ismail stood with his hands on his hips, copying the airport manager's stance. One should not be ashamed to learn, if only by imitation.

"Yes. The navigator, too."

"He is dead. One always honours the dead."

"But also he gave his life for others, Ismail."

"No man can do more than that, tuan." The idea was a slight worry to Ismail. What would happen if one day he were faced with great danger? Surely he would dishonour himself in the sight of all men. He looked sideways at the manager, hoping his thoughts were not evident in the air; but the tuan seemed not even to have been listening. He was acting strangely this morning, standing out here in the full sun with his newly-pressed trousers and clean shirt and white officer's cap, pacing up and down, looking at the sky. A devil was in him.

"It will be big day, tuan Coplan'. Tuesday."

"Certainly it will."

"We are making very big banner for across doorway that is written: 'Welcome to Sultan!' And they wish to white-wash all cement path here—"

"No, Ismail. That isn't the idea. The Sultan wants to see the airport just as it always is, with people working and everything clean and efficient."

"Oh."

"But afterwards, if he seems pleased, I shall ask him to make you assistant manager."

Ismail tried hard not to bounce up and down on his toes. One must try to be like the English manager, never excited or happy-looking. "But it is only the two names, tuan? Only 'Assistant' and 'Manager'?"

"Of course, Ismail."

"Oh."

"What is wrong with that?"

"Could I not continue to be called Temporary Acting Assistant Manager?" The names were almost as many as the Sultan's and he cherished each one of them.

"That would not be good, Ismail. The worth of a man is not counted by the number of his names. The water-buffalo has two names, but the tiger only one."

He scanned the sky again and checked his watch, and paced away with his impatience, to leave Ismail with his problem.

Lorries were grinding up the airport road, taking equipment for the men who were making the new track northwards through the scrub-jungle. Nearly a fortnight ago they had been put to work, clearing the track that was to run five miles into the trees as far as the stricken area that was once the terrorist camp. The bomber squadrons had done what it would have taken fifty men two years to do, felling the giant trees whose lack of tap-roots made them easy to topple to the fibrous earth. The Sultan had ordered rubber to be planted there, after the timber had been hauled in to build houses. A new estate would arise, almost as large as Duffy's, to give work for the poorest fishermen whose daily catch was hardly enough to earn them a bowl of rice apiece.

The unease had gone from the town, gone with the tiger and the terrorists.

The lorries crawled over the rough ground, skirting the mangrove swamps; on one of them a man was perched as if riding an elephant, singing his head off and bringing a derisive chorus from the gibbon on their grandstand high in the trees.

Outside the emergency-vehicle shed a Tamil was washing the two Malayan flags in a bucket; the smoke and dust from the cloud left by the bombing a fortnight ago had soiled their colours and they must be bright again for the Sultan's inspection. Hugh had thought of changing them anyway for the correct plain yellow ones, but it might have meant a minor revolution and he hadn't risked it.

A voice called him and he looked up to the control tower, where Haji Ahmad was leaning out.

"Call-sign, sahib!"

"Thank you!" He checked his watch. It was ten minutes before noon. Going into the building he passed the troubled Ismail.

"Tuan Coplan'—what you have said about the water-buffalo and the tiger is true, but they are both beasts, and I am a man. It is different."

"I have an idea for you, Ismail. Why not call yourself Assistant Lord High Cook and Bottle-washer?"

Ismail's bright eyes filled with enchantment. "How is it spelled?" he asked eagerly.

"That would take a little time. Come and see me about it." He went up to the control tower. Ismail stood trying to remember the string of splendid-sounding English titles. Even Tuan Copland had seemed pleased with his idea, for, although he never looked excited, his face had been happy.

In the close heat of the control room the Pathan was sitting composed and dutiful at his panel. The big fan stirred the air above his turbanned head. Hugh had brought him a glass of iced Coca-Cola from the staff-office on his way up.

"The sahib comes with gifts," he said with formal pleasure.

"When the river runs far from a man's door, its refreshing waters must be brought to him. Have you the passenger list, Haji Ahmad?"

"It is here, sahib." The beautiful beard was buried in Coca-Cola.

Hugh checked only the last three names on the paper: pilot, navigator, stewardess, S. and P.A. Flight 9, Singapore to Pasang.

Standing at the south windows he watched the clear sky; after three minutes he saw the thin black splinter appear there, poised as if motionless from head-on. In a little time it took on size and colour and was now in the circuit, settling across the coastal fringe of palms and straightening for its final approach.

He took a last look at the landing-area and picked up the signal lamp, giving it the green.